RESET

...in a dystopian utopian woke near-future...

WAYNE DARNELL

Cover design, illustrations and formatting by Wayne Darnell
Published by: Creative Zen Publishing

ISBN: 978-1-8383393-0-2

DEDICATION

This book is dedicated to:

my children

my inspirational friends Pete, Steve, Paul, Ian

&

my soulmate,

Helen

ACHTUNG!

BRITISH LIBRARY HISTORICAL CENSORING UNIT

To the best of the author's knowledge, no member of his family has been involved in the slave trade for at least four hundred years.

WARNING

GRIEVANCE-MONGERS AND MORALITY OLYMPIANS

This book has not been read, or approved, by any sensitivity readers and contains rampant cultural appropriation. If you suffer from a nervous disposition or are easily offended, please retreat to your safe space and do not proceed.

You have been warned.

RESET

The Social Justice Police,
protecting the public from offence

TABLE OF CONTENTS

"In our schools, our newsrooms, even our corporate boardrooms, there is a new far-left fascism that demands absolute allegiance. If you do not speak its language, perform its rituals, recite its mantras, and follow its commandments, then you will be censored, banished, blacklisted, persecuted, and punished.

It's not going to happen to us."

President Donald J. Trump

Mount Rushmore, 4th July 2020

PROLOGUE

"When tyranny becomes law,

Rebellion becomes duty."

Thomas Jefferson

Ministry of Globalisation, London, England

Sometimes extraordinary things happen to ordinary people. In a turbulent world, people unknowingly embark on journeys with unforeseen challenges, unimagined consequences and unknowable destinations, some never return or are forever changed. Mrs Evans and the Maasai warrior were two such people; oblivious to the known-knowns, the known-unknowns, unknown-knowns and the unknown-unknowns with which they would soon be confronted, challenged and have to navigate in a strange new world.

The low hum of the air conditioning maintaining an ambient temperature was the only noise in an otherwise silent room. Mrs 'Nain' Evans, resplendent in her Welsh National Dress, curiously observed the motionless Maasai warrior seated across from her. The

Maasai warrior observed her. Mrs Evans was always taught not to stare but in the sterile, wall-to-wall grey environment of the waiting room, she found it almost impossible to resist. The Maasai warrior had a similar problem.

The pair silently and curiously looked one another up and down, both static apart from their inquisitive eyes which occasionally met before moving on with their visual exploration. Both Mrs Evans and the Maasai had a lot to take in.

Eventually the Maasai lost interest in the white old lady in the top hat and relaxed slightly in his grey chair. He clutched his spear as the light above his head reflected brightly off his mud-red cornrows, simultaneously casting a dark shadow under his brow and the hollows below his cheekbones.

Mrs Evans took this as a cue to relax and put her knitting needles and half-finished woollen hat in the colours of the Wrexham Football Club which she was making for young Dyfed- her best friend Doreen's grandson from the village, back in her large tartan knitting bag. She fumbled about in the bag and eventually produced a small paper bag of boiled sweets. Mrs Evans reached across and offered the contents of the bag to the Maasai.

"Pineapple chunk?"

The Maasai studied the bag for a moment before removing a sweet and popping it into his mouth. He nodded, his eyes widening for a brief moment before he sat back as before, motionless except for his slowly masticating jaw.

Mrs Evans relaxed, assured that she had made a friend. She liked making friends. It had become a guilty pastime as she had become very lonely since her Gwilym had begun his descent into dementia.

RESET

Meeting new people and chatting was her escape from an otherwise very mundane life in Pwllheli.

"Very good, aren't they?" she said to the impassive figure in front of her. "My neighbour Mrs Evans makes them." Mrs Evans beamed proudly as she popped a boiled sweet in her mouth. The two figures sat sucking on the sweets in the silence of the small grey sterile room.

Mrs Evans took a moment during this pause in the conversation to examine the room more closely. She looked down at the carpet: it was utilitarian and grey. She studied the four grey walls, one with a plain door attached: it was grey. She looked up at the ceiling with four small inset lights: it was white. The room contained four functional office chairs, constructed of chrome tubing bent to form the legs, arms and back, onto which a grey seat was fixed.

"Very modern, isn't it?" she said, as she stored the pineapple chunk in her cheek like a hamster. Mrs Evans was really starting to relax as she began a one-sided conversation with the Maasai warrior, during which time he had been informed all about her neighbour Doreen (or Dot for short) and her tabby cat Tinkle. The Maasai had no choice but to listen but found the lilt of her accent quite soothing.

Neither the Maasai nor Mrs Evans would be quite so relaxed, however, had they known what had happened to them. They had been 'disappeared,' and were currently in a waiting room deep in the bowels of the Ministry of Globalisation, Denationalisation and Ethnic Preservation, sub-level 3, Department 2B: Evaluation, Interrogation and Resettlement.

RESET

The Maasai Warrior

PART ONE

"We are going to emancipate ourselves from mental slavery

Because whilst others might free the body,

None but ourselves can free our minds.

Mind is your only ruler,

Sovereign"

Marcus Garvey

CHAPTER ONE

Somewhere near Alice Springs, Australia

The chill of early morning had long since evaporated, giving way to the blazing heat of the midday sun as it radiated down upon the arid landscape. The golden orb forced the shadows into retreat and caused the miraging air on the surface of the single-track dirt road to ripple like water as it led to the homestead. The timbers of the small collection of outbuildings were cracked and warped. The only sign of life for miles around were the wedge-tailed eagles as they circled gracefully high above, effortlessly catching thermals, expounding as little energy as possible, patiently scrutinising the world beneath from their lofty panorama with sharp emotionless vison. Far below and much further down the food chain, a lone creature with a significantly restricted world view and a precarious existence hung finely in the balance, scurried through the dry brush. Its sparkling black eyes cautiously surveyed its surroundings, whiskers twitching as it scampered through the undergrowth on an endless search for nourishment. The mouse stopped momentarily, intuitively aware of the many dangers from tooth, fang or claw. Breaking cover and darting towards a small collection of stones, it began to dig furiously in the dry ground, eventually extracting a huge white grub squirming with life. The rodent gnawed ravenously into its victim, replenishing the fluid and nutrients essential in this hostile environment, momentarily unaware of the fatal shadow that swooped down upon it. The mouse squeaked pathetically as it was elevated into the sky, the powerful talons constricting and piercing its skin. The animal was pitifully ill-equipped to fight back against irrepressible forces greater than itself, its world perspective changing inconceivably as it rose unwillingly into the heavens in a dystopian rodent version of the Rapture.

Down below, on a patch of ground centred amidst an assortment of poorly-maintained wooden structures, Bob Murphy worked furiously under the hood of his ute. Bob was the fifty-eight-year-old product of a liaison between an Aboriginal artist mother and an Irish opal-prospecting father. Taken from his people as a child and raised in an alien society, Bob had a foot in both worlds but chose to adopt neither. Always the outsider with an independent spirit, he had opted for a life of solitude and isolation in the environment he felt at one with. As Bob laboured, his temper increased with the heat, cursing every time his skin came into contact with the ferociously hot metal, acutely aware that had he repaired the roof of his lean-to, which had blown away during the last sandstorm, he wouldn't be in this situation. As he finished and began to remove his tools, Bob caught his index finger in the hood of the blue and rust-coloured Holden.

"BLOODY BASTARD!" he yelled, retrieving his throbbing finger. "Bugger bugger bugger bugger bastard BUGGER!!" Bob jumped around the yard in his dirty blue boiler suit- three sizes too big- like a cat in a sack. He ran cursing through the screen door of his rickety wooden shack that he called home. Bob went into the kitchen, yanked open the door of the antique freezer and thrust his finger into a bag of ice.

"Bugger, that's good," Bob said to himself. He looked up at the yellow plastic nicotine-coated clock, nailed half-heartedly above the dirty, crockery-filled sink.

"Bugger," he said again, noticing the time. Removing his hand from the freezer, Bob kicked off his thongs and unbuttoned his boiler suit, letting it fall to the floor to revealing a wiry, sinewy body reminiscent of a skinned rabbit. Bob ran naked to the room he occasionally slept in and sat in a rickety wooden chair in front of a mirror attached to a vanity unit. He pulled open a drawer and brought out a well-used box of 'party-time' face paints. Selecting yellow ochre, he began to apply dots to his face. Bob carried out this procedure with a number of colours including burnt umber, red and white until the craggy face was covered in an elaborate pattern of coloured dots. When he was satisfied, he replaced the paints and pulled out a red headband and stretched it over his thinning, grey hair which he then ruffled up vigorously as the flies buzzed around his head. He stood up, opened another drawer and retrieved a grubby tan loincloth with which he dressed. Bob turned to admire himself in the cracked full-length mirror on the wall above a pile of dirty washing. The sun shone brightly through the blinds, casting horizontal shadows across his thin body. He regarded his reflection seriously with dark beady eyes for a long moment before shouting "Showtime!" with a big grin devoid of a number of teeth. Bob padded back into the kitchen, retrieved his thongs and sunglasses and ran 'flip flopping' through the screen door to the pickup. He jumped in, started it on the third attempt and headed off to work in a cloud of red dust.

A kangaroo looked up momentarily to witness a streak of red dust in the hazy far distance, making its way at speed against a red backdrop towards a large outcrop of rounded red rock. The kangaroo lost interest.

Tina Arena was playing loudly as the pickup slid to a halt and was immediately swallowed in a cloud of dust. The driver's door swung open and Bob, wearing his mirrored aviator sunglasses, came out coughing, a small rolled up cigarette sticking to the corner of his mouth like fly paper. He wasted no time as he retrieved a spear, a bottle of water and a large boomerang from the back of the pickup and scurried into the maze of boulders, some as big as a house. Eventually, he came to a small sandy clearing, put down his things and from between two large boulders, pulled out a brown rolled-up blanket and unfurled it on the dusty ground. He scampered to another pair of rocks and retrieved a large box of boomerangs which he diligently arranged on the blanket. He then began retrieving paintings of turtles, kangaroos and abstracts of a similar style to his face makeup, from behind more rocks and started arranging them around the clearing up against the boulders until he was surrounded by art. When he was done, he clapped his hands together, smiled and said to himself, "Gift shop is open, ha-ha." Bob picked up the spear and boomerang and made his way out of the rock formation through a tunnel of rock until he was out in the open again. He looked down to see a number of Victoria Brew tinnies strewn about, a hazy memory of his last sleepover. Bob hurried himself, picking up the cans and depositing them behind the nearest boulder.

"Bugger! Drum!" he exclaimed to himself before scratching his arse and dashing into the rock formation, returning moments later with a small round drum. The drum had formerly been one half of a pair of bongos which Bob had customised and made more ethnic.

Bob looked up and saw a distant streak of dust drawing closer. As the black minibus neared, Bob went into his routine, dancing around in a tight circle, hopping from one foot to another and uttering a chant. Part of the dance and chant had been taught to him by his grandfather. Bob used to know the whole dance and chant but a period of alcoholism in his life had erased these parts from his memory bank. The bits he had forgotten he made up for by freestyling chants and dance moves he had picked up from watching movies featuring Native American Indians. Bob was certain that the drum wasn't authentic either but it added drama to his act. Bob remembered to take off his shades at the last minute and threw them behind a rock. "Bugger!" he said. Bob danced furiously round in smaller and smaller circles. As he danced, he noticed that the van seemed shinier than usual and when did Bruce get the windows tinted? "That must have cost a packet," he mused. "That's a new van, how come Bruce has enough money to buy a new van?" Bob pondered as he hopped from one foot to another, banging the drum with the end of his boomerang. "Maybe he's doing better out of this deal than me," he thought as he raised his outstretched arms to the sun. He stood motionless, chanting. After a long while, Bob ran out of chant and he just stood there, arms elevated as his semi-naked body sweated profusely from his exertions in the dry still air. He had his back to the van as he stood waiting for his mate Bruce to open the door and let the visitors out. Time passed awkwardly, nothing happened. Bob slowly turned around. The van door opened.

"Oh bugger," said Bob.

Bob Murphy

CHAPTER TWO

Dunedin, New Zealand

Donald MacDonald was a true, dyed-in-the-wool Scot: born thirty-five years ago in the city of Glasgow and forged on the granite streets of Aberdeen. Tall and broad with a flaming shock of long ginger hair and beard, he had a pair of distrustful ice-cold blue eyes and a bad attitude to match. Dressed in full Highland regalia, Donald was every inch the Victorian ideal of a true Scot. He had fled to this last outpost of Scottishness during the Tartan Clearances, when he had steadfastly refused to voluntarily hand over his kilt, injuring two guards with his sgian dhuh whilst making his escape from the Assessment and Denationalisation Centre set up in his home city. Fortunately, Donald had a contact in the Celtic underground (the Emerald Express) and had made his escape onboard a Japanese cargo ship bound for New Zealand, passing unnoticed posing as a ship's engineer. He had been successfully living in this last bastion of Scottish culture, Dunedin, at the very ends of the earth for the past year now. Although its remoteness had prevented the worst excesses of re-education, the backstreets of Dunedin were still places where it would be unwise to wear tartan in public. There were always those willing to make money and settle old scores by reporting neighbours to the authorities and a newcomer like Donald had to be extra wary. Donald knew nobody in Dunedin except for his second cousin Ronald whom he was off to meet tonight for an illicit practice.

The storm that had been building all day began to break as Donald made his way along the narrow cliff path towards the rendezvous. Far below, the ocean crashed against the rocks. Donald strode with purpose as the wind howled relentlessly: hair, beard, kilt dancing wildly in the gale. The rain drove into his weathered face like steel darts and Donald's jaw tightened: growing up in Scotland had hardened him against the weather and the raw elements made him feel alive. The lightening flashed and Donald's heart hammered like a heroin addict's after an adrenaline shot, with the anticipation of being able to play the pipes and express his primal Scottish nature, together with his kinsman Ronald on the drums and God on the thunder.

The Scot stopped and looked fondly at the bundle under his arm, giving it a loving pat before resolutely pushing forward against the rain, humming 'Scotland the Brave' to himself.

Donald looked up as lightning electrified the sky and illuminated the figure of his cousin standing erect with his drum at the mouth of the cave. With a grimace and a nod, he strode manfully forward. On reaching Ronald, he retrieved the set of bagpipes from under his arm and began to inflate them with deep breaths. A high-pitched whine filled the air as Donald launched into a hearty rendition of the Gay Gordons, pouring his heart and soul into his native music and so it was some time before he noticed that there was no accompaniment from Ronald.

He stopped playing, his pipes letting out a low drone as they deflated.

"What's wrong, cousin?" he asked.

"Sorry," Ronald mumbled.

"For what?" said Donald in confusion, as blinding bright lights flooded the cave. Voices came from all around. Donald held up his hand to cover his eyes as anonymous flashlights were aimed directly at his retinas.

"Put down those pipes," came an authoritarian voice.

"Och no cousin, what have ye done?" cried Donald, dumbfounded and disappointed in the betrayal of his clansman.

"I had to, Donald, I have a family," said Ronald coldly.

"But I am your family!" protested Donald.

"You're only a second cousin," Ronald spat in disdain, "I have to think of my wife and kids, and their future."

"Ye bastard!" Donald cried as he made a lunge for Ronald but before he could reach him, a blow brought him convulsing to the ground. There he lay, as rough-handlers, laughing, bound him and brought him shakily to his feet.

"Ye scum!" he bellowed as the lightning revealed the fire in his eyes. "Yer a disgrace to the clan MacDonald!"

"MacDonald, cousin?" came the calm sneering reply against the howling wind.

"Aye, MacDonald!"

"I am no MacDonald!" cried Ronald, finally shattering his calm exterior.

RESET

"Of course ye are, mon. Yer kin, ye wee wank!" Donald's passions were aroused as his thick Scottish brogue came to the fore.

"I am no kin of yours!" roared Ronald. "Why do you think my so-called kin had my mother locked up in a lunatic asylum for all those years?"

"She was criminally insane!" came a fervent reply.

"No," said Ronald bitterly, "her only crime was to be born a Campbell!"

Donald was stunned as he tried to analyse what he had just heard. "A Campbell?" he whispered finally. "Is that no the same thing?"

"No, it's NOT the same thing," seethed Ronald, in a voice trembling with rage nurtured and warmed through decades of bitter silence. "I hate the MacDonalds and everything they stand for, I spit on the MacDonalds!" He spat in Donald's face.

"Hey! Gonnae no dae that?" Donald warned indignantly.

"I turn my back on the MacDonalds!"

"Naw, you cannae mean that," Donald said in disbelief. "Surely no, cousin?"

"I don't know you, you are a stranger to me." His rage spent, Ronald turned towards Donald's captors. "Take him away."

The storm howled and the thunder roared as Donald was dragged away, struggling against his assailants. Somehow, he summoned the strength to cry the last words he would ever say to his cousin.

"Hey Ronald?"

"What?"

RESET

"Cheerio tae fuck."

Donald MacDonald

CHAPTER THREE

Waiting Room, London, England

Mrs Evans stopped mid-sentence and looked towards the door when she heard the sound of approaching footsteps and the click of the electronic lock. She had been explaining to a sleepy Maasai warrior how her hoover had been at the repair shop for three weeks now, and how she had been told by Ted the repair man during a telephone conversation that it may be another three weeks at least before the part came on account of the fact that the part needed for repair was made of rubber and there was a shortage of rubber, due to the shortage of rubber plantations.

The door slid open and a figure similar to the ones that had picked up Mrs Evans outside of her house the previous day, came in. The figure was completely dressed in black leather: boots, trousers, jacket, all topped with a glossy black helmet and mirrored visor. The only colour added to the attire was a small yellow smiley face on the helmet and a larger one attached to the left breast. Mrs Evans assumed underneath all the black was a man on account of the fact that the figure was quite large but it was hard to tell these days.

RESET

The figure was followed by a semi-naked man, who for all the world looked like an Australian Aboriginal, clutching a spear and boomerang in one hand and a can of Victoria Brew in the other. The Aborigine was followed by another black-clad figure who stopped in the doorway and folded its arms. The first figure pointed to one of the chairs and the Aboriginal sat down. The figure then pointed at Mrs Evans and then to the door. Mrs Evans smiled at the mirrored visor, stood up and picked up her bag.

"Well it's been lovely meeting you," she said to the now-alert warrior. "If you're ever in Pwllheli, you must look me up. Oh yes, and I can take you to meet Dot, she'd like that, she makes a lovely Welsh tea, double cream scones and all but she likes to keep it quiet. Loose talk and all that…but I'm sure she wouldn't mind." She gave a small wave and the figure in the doorway moved aside to let Mrs Evans out. The first figure exited and the door slid closed behind them.

Bob looked at the seated man across from him, awash in scarlet. "Nice outfit, mate," he said.

Mrs Evans mused on the grey modern interior she was escorted down.

"Wait until I tell Dot," she murmured to herself. The corridor was almost exactly the same as the waiting room except much longer, and the carpet had been substituted by a grey vinyl floor with various coloured lines running up and down the length of it, red, blue, green, yellow, orange. They passed a corridor to the left and Mrs Evans noticed that the orange line veered off down it.

"Oh, there's clever for you!" she thought, "These lines must be here to help you find your way around. Maybe I should paint some different coloured lines in the house, to help Gwilym find his way to the toilet and kitchen." Gwilym was acquiring a habit of muddling the two up, but then she remembered that Gwilym was colour-blind. "Oh, that won't do," she lamented as they came to halt outside a grey door.

"Enter," came a reply. The door slid open and Mrs Evans was escorted in. The door silently slid shut behind her.

Bob had given up trying to talk to this 'drongo' that sat silently opposite, instead he had taken to sucking air in through the gaps in his teeth, tightening the grip on his spear and tapping his boomerang in time to the tune he had playing inside his own head. It was 'Down Under' by Men at Work. He was starting to feel a little intimidated by his lack of clothes and had decided to bolster his Australianness and subdue his boredom by trying to think of the greatest Australian bands. His task had started off easily enough as he hummed the tune of 'Whole Lotta Rosie' by AC\DC but now he was beginning to struggle. His mental torment was brought to an abrupt end with the sound of the electronic lock opening. The door slid open and a large ginger man in a skirt was let in. The man sat down begrudgingly where he was directed, next to the Maasai. The Maasai was directed to the door, he stood up and was escorted out of the room. The door slid silently shut. Bob looked into the cool blue eyes across from him.

"Well, I hope you've got better chat than the last one," he said optimistically.

Donald's granite jaw tightened.

"Looks like you need a drink, mate," Bob continued, offering a beer can to the Scot.

"Thanks, but no thanks pal," Donald said as he rummaged in his sporran, eventually producing a small silver hip flask. "I bought my own, single malt!"

Bob grinned a gap-toothed smile. "Bottoms up, cobba," he said, raising his can.

"Slainte Mhath!" came the reply as Donald took a swig from the flask.

"Name's Bob," said Bob. "So what they got you in for?"

"I dinnae ken, pal," said Donald. "Being a proud Scot, I suppose. Name's Donald, by the way."

The two men shook hands.

"And your good self?" asked the Scot.

"No bleeding idea mate," said Bob. "One minute I'm minding me own bleedin' business in the outback, next I'm in bleedin' England. I just don't know what's going on."

"The Outback, ye say?" said Donald "That would probably explain it."

"Explain what?" asked Bob.

"The worlds gone mad, pal," answered the Scot. "Something to do with Social Justice and all that shite."

"Social Justice? What the bleedin' hell's that?" asked Bob.

"Och, ye really have been in the Outback," said Donald understandingly. "You see, I don't really know masel', I managed to escape just after the purges reached me in the Highlands. I'd been a wee bit cut off too, ye ken? Up to that point, I was working as a gamekeeper away from civilisation, but apparently it's been going on for years."

"What has?" asked an anxious Bob.

"The purges, man, the purges!"

"The purges?" said Bob in confusion.

Just then the door clicked.

Blodwyn 'Nain' Evans

CHAPTER FOUR

Somewhere near Huskvarna, Sweden

A slight northern breeze wafted through the tall pines, their high canopies swayed majestically to-and-fro, creating a calm hypnotic sound much like waves gently lapping on a stony beach. The atmosphere was cold and crisp as a weak sun almost imperceptibly began to melt the frosty undergrowth beneath, creating a fine gossamer mist that rose in the still air below the trees.

Jorgen 'Wulfe' Johansson had been living wild in the woods for over six months now, the sole surviving member of the Ojanvic Viking Re-enactment Society. He bit hungrily into the raw salmon he had just caught. His feet were freezing from standing barefoot in the river for so long, silently waiting for his prey but he could not afford to light a fire, for Wulfe was a wanted man. Instead, he distracted himself and assuaged his hunger by meticulously gnawing all the flesh from the fish- blood, scales and oil oozed into his blond beard. Wulfe's hearing had become acute since living in the woods and on hearing the warning call of a distant black bird, he froze, alert to the sound of nature's alarms. Another call but nearer this time, something or someone was heading in his direction. Wulfe dropped the remains of the fish immediately and reached for his custom-made fur boots with gel insoles. He hurriedly put them on and pulled on the leather cords to tighten them. He grabbed his horned helmet and battle axe and ran south along the bank of the river towards his hideout near the rapids. After ten minutes of running at full pelt, he stopped and listened again. There it was, faint on the breeze. "Wolves," he thought at first, his hands tightening on the handle of the axe. "No, something else is on the wind, yes. Dogs? Dogs! Not good, skitprat!" Wulfe froze momentarily, then he ran. He ran like he had never run before, crashing through the undergrowth like a wild animal: a hunted wild animal.

Jorgen 'Wulfe' Johansson

CHAPTER FIVE

Interrogation Room 12, London, England

Sit down," came the harsh female voice. Mrs Evans settled herself in the chair in front of a grey wood-effect table. Her inquisitor sat on the other side, a shadowy dark shape in this dim light. The interior of this window-less room was much the same everywhere else in in this place- grey- but Mrs Evans had the rare ability to see the good in everything.

"Very clean, isn't it?" she said. Her assertion was met with silence. No reply came from the occupant of the other side of the desk. Instead the shadowy shape carried on making notes.

Mrs Evans answered her own question. "Yes, very clean. Very, very clean." She smiled nervously; Mrs Evans was beginning to feel a bit apprehensive. "Have I done something wrong?" she enquired nervously.

"Wrong?" came the voice.

"Yes, I was wondering why I'm here, wherever here is. Not that I'm complaining mind, they make a lovely cup of tea," she lied, remembering her encounter with the vending machine on her initial arrival, but sometimes you had to tell a little white lie just to help initiate small talk. Small talk was what Mrs Evans did whenever she was nervous. Fumbling in her bulky bag and producing sweets, she proffered the small paper bag. "Pineapple chunk?" Mrs Evans was met with silence. She retracted her arm and waited.

Eventually the silence was broken.

"Evans, 6 Ffestiniog Way, Pwllheli, North Wales, Independent European Welsh State of Germany. Is this correct?" came the voice.

"Well yes, most of it anyway."

"Are you a Union Deny-er?" came the stern voice.

"No," replied Mrs Evans, "but everything happens so quickly nowadays."

"Yes, old people like you seem to find it hard to keep up...but that's no excuse."

"Old?" said Mrs Evans "I'm only sixty-two! Have I done something wrong?"

"Have you done something wrong?" enquired the voice.

"No, I don't think so," she replied.

The shadowy figure scribbled something on a piece of paper.

"Have I been arrested?" Mrs Evans politely inquired. "Because I really need to get back to Gwilym and my cat Tinkle- they will be wondering what's happened to me. Well Tinkle will, Gwilym gets a bit confused but I'm sure he will be a bit hungry by now."

RESET

"No, you have not been arrested but you are being assessed and investigated. Helping us with our inquiries, you might say," came the reply.

"Investigated? Whatever for? I mean, I always pay my television licence on time," asked a slightly flustered Mrs Evans.

"I will ask the questions, if you don't mind," came the voice. "And you would be wise to answer them."

"Yes, of course," said Mrs Evans.

"Good," came the voice. "So if you don't mind, we shall continue."

After a long moment of silence, the inquisitor clicked her pen and began.

"So how would you identify your gender from the following list? Are you: agender, androgyne, androgynous, bigender, cis, cisgender, CIS female, CIS male, cisman, ciswoman, cisgender-female, cisgender-male, cisgender-man, cisgender-woman, female-to-male, genderfluid, gender-non-conforming, gender-questioning, gender-variant, genderqueer, intersex, male-to-female, neither, neutrois, non-binary, pangender, trans, transfemale, transmale, transperson, transwoman, transfeminine, transgender, transgender-female, transgender-male, transgender-man, transgender-person, transgender-woman, transmasculine, transsexual, two-spirit, or other?"

Mrs Evans took a moment to think.

"Well?" pressed the voice.

"…a woman?" ventured Mrs Evans eventually.

RESET

The inquisitor slammed a hand on the desk. "No! Try harder! You have been made to think that you were a woman by a White patriarchal society. That old-think has all been swept aside and now you have the opportunity for true freedom. Try not to resist- it's for your own benefit."

Mrs Evans was puzzled.

"Now, would you like me to read the list again?" said the impatient voice.

"No, I don't think that would help," said Mrs Evans sadly.

Interrogation Room 13

The Maasai sat impassively, minus his spear, as his inquisitor threw the recyclable paper cup of ionised fresh mountain spring water at him. The inquisitor was beginning to lose it. He sat back in his grey hemp-woven chair, having used three expert translators of various African dialects, he was beginning to run out of ideas. Not a word. He was becoming impatient and angry. How could he get his report filed if the suspect wouldn't talk? He suddenly sat up straight.

The inquisitor pressed an invisible button on his desk. "Find Walker and send her to my office," he barked at the desk, then sat back and stared across at the Maasai. Long moments of silence passed in the grey windowless room before the knock came. "Come in," said the inquisitor. A stern-looking thirty-something woman came in, dressed in a grey trouser suit, her blond hair shaved short into the back of her neck. She turned her angular face to the Maasai.

"Now let's start once more, shall we?" the inquisitor said with a hint of sarcasm. The woman came in close to the Maasai and began to sign furiously, her hands a blur before the Maasai's face. "Again, which of the following would you self-identify as your ethnic group?" The woman's face contorted aggressively as her hands repeated the question.

Waiting Room

The door opened and a Viking was brought in, his frame filling the aperture of the doorway as he was pointed towards a chair. As he sat down, the chair looked like it belonged in a primary school, creaking under his weight. Bob was ordered out and the door slid shut behind him. Long moments passed in the silence of the sterile room as the Scot and the Viking sat eyeing each other warily with equally suspicious cold blue eyes.

"This guy is huge!" thought Donald uneasily, not used to being the smallest person in the room. It was an unsettling feeling and the Scot didn't like it. The giant opposite was built like a Volvo truck on steroids, long blond matted hair and beard sat upon shoulders as broad as barn doors. He was dressed in grey furs that Donald imagined had been ripped bare-handed from a wolf's back.

"The best form of defence is a good offence," thought Donald sagely to himself, always willing to err on the side of violence whenever he felt uneasy. Donald felt ill at ease now and leant forward in his chair.

"You stink, pal. Ye ken?" he said in a low menacing growl.

The Viking sniffed the air.

"Yes, you are correct," he said. "I have been living in the woods for months and eating raw meat, yes. I haven't had the chance to wash, no." The Swede leaned in towards the Scot and looked him in the eye: "I've been hunted like an animal."

Donald sat back and raised his eyebrows thoughtfully. "This guy's OK," he thought to himself.

Interrogation Room 14

The air was thick and cloying in the small interrogation room and Bob was getting irritable.

"What the fucking hell are you talking about, mate?" protested Bob.

"I will repeat the question," calmly asked a camp inquisitor. "Have you ever read 'You, me and our non-binary child makes three?'"

"No, I've never even read a book, mate," replied an irascible Bob.

"Please stop calling me mate, it's a misogynistic term and infers that you want to have sexual intercourse with me. Well, not without my consent!" The inquisitor made a note in his book, muttering the words 'sexually aggressive tendencies.' "So, you haven't read it?" he continued.

"No!" shouted Bob.

The inquisitor made another note: 'refusal to self-educate.'

"Are you a subliminal racist, Mr Murphy?" he went on.

"A what?" replied the Australian.

"Are you a subliminal fat-shamer, Mr Murphy?"

"A fat-shaver?"

"Do you exercise your unconscious bias in a discriminatory manner, Mr Murphy? How often do you exercise your unconscious bias, Mr Murphy? Is it a) Always or b) Most of the time? Are you a slut-shamer, Mr Murphy?"

"Errr..." Bob said, scratching his head. "Look cobba, I don't have a bloody clue what you're talking about."

"Ignorance is not an excuse!" pressed the inquisitor, pointing to a small brass plaque on the wall. "Your silence won't help you either, Mr Murphy. I will have to fill in this evaluation form with or without your assistance. Now, are you a feminist?"

Bob was perplexed. "How about a pair of strides and a shirt, mate?" he asked, "I've been freezing my nuts off for days."

"If you continue to use offensive and derogatory language, Mr Murphy, I am afraid I will be forced to retreat to my safe space and call security."

Bob was flummoxed.

Interrogation Room 13

The Maasai stared at the colour chart in front of him, the colours varying from a very light tan through every brown variation to black.

"Let's do it again," said the inquisitor. "Point to the colour you are most comfortable to identify your ethnicity with."

The blonde translator signed angrily.

RESET

"I take it from your silence," said the inquisitor calmly, "that you are refusing to give us the information we need for our statistics so we can make this a more empowering experience for you."

The translator drew in close to the Maasai, aggressively invading his personal space and began to sign vigorously.

"Walker!" barked the inquisitor. Walker snapped to attention. "You are taking this too far, get out and wait in my office. Maybe you can cool down a bit. Dismissed." The translator left the room with a curt nod.

The perspiring inquisitor sat on the corner of the desk. "You think you are pretty smart, don't you? Sitting there with all your gold bangles, your hunting attire, your tribal scars, every inch the warrior. Well, not to me you're not. To me, you are an archetypal male oppressive, leaving the women in the village to slave while you go off hunting innocent animals with your buddies. You sick bastard. Has the word vegan never entered your vocabulary? I'm done with you." The inquisitor reached for the paper, scribbled a few notes and pressed an invisible button on the desk. "Bon voyage," he said, nodding to the figure standing in the doorway.

As the Maasai was being hustled out, the phone rang.

"YES?" answered the inquisitor impatiently. "What is it? Oh excuse me, sorry Ma'am, I didn't know…yes…relocation…mix up…yes…yes…sorry again, right away." The flustered inquisitor put the receiver down. "Let him go," he ordered the guard, "they've made a mistake again, bloody admin. Take him to the guest facility and treat him well. Oh, and make sure he gets on the right bus."

The guard nodded as he led the Maasai gently away.

RESET

The inquisitor scrunched up the paper he had been making notes on and threw it in the recycling bin.

"It never gets any easier," he lamented to himself.

CHAPTER SIX

Los Angles, California, USA

An old flea-bitten dog padded sluggishly across the cracked blacktop of the disused car lot, seeking shade on a particularly hot day in downtown LA. It stopped by a clump of weeds and took a sniff before deciding to sit down and have a scratch. An empty soda can rolled by in the slight breeze, which prompted the mutt to take a quick sniff of the hot air before getting up to resume his journey. Crossing the lot, the dog made its way around the corner of a small collection of low-level retail units until eventually stopping in the shadow of a large green trash receptacle, where after circling around in tight spirals a number of times, he eventually laid down and curled up for a sleep. Had the dog only persevered in the same direction of travel for just a hundred yards more, he would have found himself outside the offices of Bernard Goldstein, theatrical agent.

The oscillating fan whirred gently as Bindi waited anxiously in one of the plush offices of her agent Bernie whilst he spoke to another client next door. Bernie had called her earlier in the day to ask if she would come in for a meeting, something about being the 'right' kind of ethnic minority but 'nothing to worry about'. Since leaving India, Bindi had been making a good living as a token disabled person of colour for three years now, working for the only agency in LA that specialised in Celebrity Lookalikes and Ethnic Disabled Extras. Her specialty was to be seen in the background in her wheelchair at political rallies, celebrity 'Save the World' events and Pussy Marches, as well as a number of non-speaking roles in the background of TV advertisements, most especially for fast food outlets. These involved her smiling a lot and looking like she was having 'Fun!' She also had a side-line in being an average member of the public in the background at live news broadcasts for which she was expected to be on call at short notice. She was on a handsome retainer, of course, and her local cab company had a disabled taxi set aside especially for her use. They were also on a handsome retainer and more than willing to ferry her anywhere in LA at the ring of the phone. In fact, things had never been better and she found it hard to get any time off. She had been offered work as a 'Crisis Actor', but although this kind of acting was highly paid, it was a one-shot appearance and you generally had to go into hiding for a number of years afterwards, be relocated in a safe house and completely alter your identity. Bindi had thought better of it- she wanted to stay in LA, it was Hollywood or bust. Bindi's grandmother back in India was particularly proud of her, having bought her up to be a firm believer in the merits of hard work and perseverance. Bindi's musings came to an abrupt halt, however, when she heard raised voices from the room next door.

Bernard Goldstein's former 'star' artiste and only disabled celebrity lookalike on the books, Professor Stephen Hawkin aka Brad Blanchett sat slumped in full costume, impassively listening to his agent in his customised electric wheelchair, complete with low profile tyres and chrome rims. Brad was not amused at what he was hearing- Bernie was on a major damage limitation drive.

RESET

"Look Brad," Bernard implored the young Stephen Hawkin lookalike, "times have changed and-"

"Man," Brad interrupted in his robotic 'Hawkin' voice, "I can't believe you're doing me like that, ya know what I'm sayin'?"

"But Brad," Bernie continued, "demand has fallen, fashions have changed."

"What do you mean fashions have changed, mofo?" replied an emotionless yet angry voice.

"Please," beseeched Bernie, "could we dispense with the voice box? This is serious."

Brad switched off his robotic voice. "You telling me, bitch, this is my mutherfucking livelihood. I ain't down wid dat shit, you playin' me, chukka!"

Bernie wondered if he may have been a bit premature asking his 'difficult' drug-fuelled ego maniac minor star to turn off the box.

"It's not you, Brad," he said, beginning to feel the sweat soak into his expensive Egyptian cotton shirt.

"Oh, I know it ain't me," fumed Brad, "I just got a lazy ass agent."

"It's just...science isn't sexy anymore, not unless it's based on someone's 'expert' opinion and not real fact. These are different times, Brad," implored a frustrated Bernie.

"People will always be into science!" Brad stormed. "Empirical-based data is always sexy, bitch. Come on, man, you're s'posed to be my agent! Shit, before I came along you were hustling on the street, pointing out golf sales dressed as Elvis!"

"Don't you think I know that, Brad? We've been through a lot together but you're just not attracting the work you used to." Bernie took a deep breath. "But it's worse than that," Bernie paused, "my attorney called me this morning."

"Oh, that's the way you want to play it, mutherfucker?" said Brad, in a moment of paranoid realisation.

"No, it's not like that Brad. There's a petition going about the internet: they're calling for you to be 'no platformed' and cancelled because of your public persona. It has sixty thousand signatures so far...and counting."

"A petition? What the fuck you talkin' about, foo?"

"You've been found to be a misogynist and threatening by some feminist groups- they claim that you're offensive and liable to hurt people's feelings."

"Now I know your shittin' me," said Brad. "Since when did the Professor hurt anyone's feelings? Original gangsta, dudes loved that man, God rest his mutherfucking soul."

"No, not Steven Hawkin: you...you, Brad Blanchett. All the 'bitches' and 'hoes' talk, your lack of respect for empowered sex workers. They're saying that you're sexist," replied Bernie.

"You better believe it, I'm a sexy ass bee-atch. I got that shit going on, you know what I'm sayin'?" exclaimed a cocky Brad.

"No, not sexy...sexist," Bernie tried to explain.

"Sexy sexist, what you talkin' about foo', you ain't makin' no sense," an impatient Brad said as he removed his black 'Hawkin' wig to reveal a shock of short bleached blond hair.

Bernie thought for a moment how best to explain the si.. simple terms. "OK, all that gangsta jive, bitches, hoes- that kind of talk. They say you're a crotch displayer and a man spreader, well it's just not fashionable anymore, especially with the guys that make the bookings- they think you could be a potential high-risk sexual offender. We're living in a post-misogynist society nowadays."

Brad contemplated for a moment. "Jive? Did you just say jive, grandpa? What, are you a Bee Gee all of a sudden?"

"Brad, you're missing the point. A lot of people find you offensive, especially the middle classes and they're the ones who pay our wages," reasoned Bernie. "And besides, it's the duty of every celebrity to be a good role model nowadays and you're a celebrity, albeit a minor one."

"Says who?"

"Says the United Nations for one, it's the law. It's compulsory for celebrities to be moral influencers," Bernie replied.

"But this can't be, I tick all the boxes: I'm disabled, I'm a protected characteristic! I ain't down wid dat," protested Brad.

"That cuts no sway anymore," replied Bernie. "They are also petitioning against the way you speak, your cultural appropriation."

Brad thought for a moment.

"But this is the way I always spoke, it's how everybody talks where I grew up."

"You're out of touch, Brad. Where have you been? Don't you see the internet?"

"Internet? I don't do the internet dawg, I spend all day looking at this mutherfucking screen. Why I'm gonna do that when I get home? Shit, that's the last thing I wanna do." Just then Brad had a moment of clarity. "It's cause I'm White, ain't it?" he said accusingly.

Bernie was silent.

The ringing phone broke the silence. Bernie picked up the receiver and listened, his face turned ashen. "Thanks, Bert," he said gravely as he hung up and sat down heavily. "That was my buddy from the Department. The Social Justice police have put out an APB on you-they want to send you to a non-crime incident committee and they can potentially send you to England for an official inquisition and possible Re-education."

"What am I going to do?" said a suddenly panicked Brad.

"The only thing you can do," replied a concerned Bernie. "Run!"

Bernie went through the drawers of his Art Deco white marble desk, grabbing all the cash he could.

"Take this," he said as he pushed the cash onto Brad's lap.

"I don't need no scrilla, man," said a bemused Brad, "I'm rich!"

"Only in the digital world- one push of a button and you're a bum."

Brad looked up, not missing the implication. "Thanks, bro," he said glumly.

"We have no time to waste: if you need me, use the name Malcolm King and then I'll know it's you. They listen in, you know. Now go!"

RESET

Bernie held out a hand which Brad shook before turning his chair one hundred and eighty degrees and leaving the office of his agent for the last time.

"Good luck and Godspeed!" Bernie called after him.

A despondent Brad sped slowly past Bindi as he headed for the elevator.

"Oh, hi Bindi," he heard Bernie say. "Good to see you. I wonder, have you ever considered converting to Islam?"

Bernie's office door shut as the elevator doors opened to reveal four dark figures clad all in black, except for a circular yellow smiley face on the left breast. The Social Justice Police.

Brad Blanchett

CHAPTER SEVEN

Interrogation Room 12

"Are you a naturist or textile, Mrs Evans?"

"A textile?" said Mrs Evans. "I don't know what that means."

"Do you have a problem with groups of naked men walking freely on public footpaths, as is their right?" asked the inquisitor.

"Well I don't know, I've never really thought about it," replied Mrs Evans. "But my friend Dot saw a flasher once, or so she said. Does that count?"

"Are you trying to be funny, Evans?" came the voice devoid of humour.

"No," replied the Welsh woman earnestly.

The inquisitor made some notes before starting a new line of questioning.

"Mrs Evans, would you describe yourself as one or all of the following: Transphobic, Homophobic or Femiphobic?"

Mrs Evans thought for a moment. "Well I'm not very fond of spiders," she said.

The inquisitor banged a fist on the desk.

"Are you an Islamaphobe?" the inquisitor asked aggressively. "Do you have a problem with Muslims, Mrs Evans?"

"Well, I don't know any."

"Any, any?" said the inquisitor "So, you are failing to integrate and understand a minority culture? Do you not think that sounds a little bit…racist? Mrs Evans, you do know that racial stereotyping is a crime, don't you?"

"No, I didn't," said a bemused Mrs Evans.

The inquisitor opened up another line of enquiry. "Are you a Welsh supremacist?"

"I don't think so, does growing daffodils count?" asked Mrs Evans earnestly.

The inquisitor spread her hands, palms down on the table. "Let's not play stupid, Mrs Evans," she said coldly. "You know what I'm saying. Are you a Nazi, Mrs Evans?"

"A Nazi?" came the flabbergasted reply.

"Yes, a Nazi. You may not even know you are a Nazi, that is the sad thing. You could have been a Nazi all your life without ever knowing it." The inquisitor shook her head in a pitiful way. "You could be a subliminal Nazi. Has it every occurred to you that you could be a subliminal Nazi?"

"No, I'm afraid it hasn't," came the reply.

"Well you are a Nationalist, aren't you Mrs Evans?" said the woman. "Just look at the way you're dressed, that's how it starts: Nationalist, Populist...Nazi!"

"Well I wear it as a bit of a novelty really, something of a family tradition. My mother made this shawl, her mother made the bonnet and my great-grandfather made the spinning wheel that I sit at outside my house. Well it's just off the High Street, you see, and for generations, the womenfolk of my family have always sat outside and spun, the tourists used to love it. Nowadays, I only do it when Gwilym's away on respite. The local children like it though, they call me Nain and I like to teach them the old skills. You know, the young ones are fascinated, most of them don't even know that wool comes from sheep."

"Are you saying that you don't believe in animal rights, Mrs Evans?" The inquisitor made a note. "Corrupting the youth, nothing new there," said the inquisitor in world-weary tone. "Are you a predatory paedophile, Mrs Evans?"

Interrogation Room 15

Donald sat seething with anger as the charge sheet was read out.

"Five counts of smuggling alcohol into the Independent European Scottish State of Germany, contravening the complete ban on all alcohol consumption in Scotland," said the prosecutor with a nasal intonation.

"Hey, wait a minute pal," interrupted Donald, "those jessies in the Scottish parliament may have banned alcohol in Scotland but I didnae."

"Please refrain from using the term 'jessie.' It has been deemed derogatory and sexist and is on the list of banned terms," said the prosecutor. "Now, it was ruled in Brussels by the United Independent European States of Germany that, as a race, the Scottish people were incapable of handling alcohol responsibly."

"A wee bit racist, don't ye think?" growled Donald in reply.

"On the contrary, it is a proven statistical fact. I'm sure the ban will be lifted when the people of Scotland have learned how to behave like adults," came the smug reply from the prosecutor.

Donald flew into a rage: "Listen here, sonny Jim, riddle me this: if ye cannae drink a bottle of Bucky on a summer's night, on the bonny banks of Loch Lomond as the sun sinks down behind the Ben, then what's the point of Scotland? Ya wee fanny!"

"Well you have plenty of opportunities for healthier options, outdoor pursuits such as: climbing and mountain biking," came the monotone reply.

"Och yer arse man," said Donald, "I can not and will not ever comply with such a law. Never, ye hear me? It's my right as a Scot to die of liver failure!"

The guards came forward.

"Please calm down, Mr MacDonald, or I will be forced to have you taken away for Anger Management," said the prosecutor.

Donald sat down in his chair. "'Sake..." he muttered as he folded his arms.

"One count of using grossly offensive and derogatory language resulting in a racially aggravated offence."

"I called a guy a leprechaun, big deal. Leprechauns don't exist, or did ye no know that?"

"They do under Scottish 'Hate Speech Laws', or did you no know that?" came a sarcastic reply.

"Bawbag..." mumbled the Scot.

"Two counts of assaulting Government officials with an offensive weapon," the prosecutor continued reading the charge sheet, shaking his head pitifully. "Six counts of travelling without an identity card. Three counts of impersonating an engineer. Ten counts of evading the authorities. Thirty counts of using a banned word."

"Fanny..." Donald whispered under his breath.

"What was that?" The prosecutor asked, looking over the top of his glasses.

Donald just stared back malevolently.

"One hundred and ten counts of inappropriate language," the prosecutor continued. "Over two hundred counts of failure to self-censor."

Donald sat back in his grey chair, unfolded his meaty forearms and grinned defiantly.

"Are you are being passive-aggressive, Mr MacDonald?"

"There's nothing passive about it, ya wee jessie," replied Donald.

RESET

"Well Mr MacDonald, the rap sheet goes on and on. It would appear that you are too far gone and if you insist on calling me a 'jessie,' a derogatory and controlled word I- "

"It's supposed to be!" yelled Donald.

"I will have no option other than to add your name to the Offensive Word Register," said the prosecutor.

"Oh no!" proclaimed Donald, his hands flying to his mouth in mock fear. "Not the Offensive Word Register! Oh no, I'm wetting my wee frilly girl's knickers!"

"Are you wearing frilly girl's knickers?" the prosecutor asked excitedly, missing the irony.

"Naw, ya baw bag!" snarled Donald disdainfully.

"Well Mr MacDonald, I have no option than to throw the book at you," the prosecutor said primly.

"Oh, for fuck's sake" swore Donald.

CHAPTER EIGHT

Iqaluit, Nunavut, Arctic Territory of Canada

A blizzard was blowing copious sheets of glacial snow hard through the empty streets of Iqaluit. The temperature had dropped well below zero and the town was fossilised in the grip of a billion icy crystals. Any warm-blooded creature with sense had long since sought shelter against this howling biting wind. It was late- very late- and down on main street the warm glow of the lights from the "Bottoms Up" club offered the only welcoming sanctuary against this, otherwise inhospitable, environment. Inside, a handful of the town's nocturnal residents sought warmth, shelter, intoxication and titillation from the murderous storm outside.

Jessie was working up to the finale of her act, dressed in her skimpy Native American Indian outfit- an outfit that most Native Americans would find completely impractical, as she spun athletically around the chromium pole. Jessie was a master of the pole, having spent her student days supplementing her meagre income as a pole dancer. She loved her job; it was great exercise and she didn't have to use her brain- something she was grateful for having spent seven years studying to be an architect. She was eking out a living now in this godforsaken club while she figured out what she wanted to do with the rest of her life. Jessie was in the lucky position of having a perfect body and a formidable IQ, matched only by her bra size.

Jessie found pole dancing great exercise not only for her perfectly toned body but also for her mind, for as she went gracefully through the routine that she knew by heart, muscle memory would take over, allowing her to solve complex equations if she wished or play sudoku almost absentmindedly as she spun. Sometimes she would just let her thoughts drift as the music washed over her. This particular act she performed to was a sexed-up version of 'Running Bear' by Johnny Preston. It was an old sentimental song of unrequited love between two Native American Indians who drown in a river during their first kiss. She had loved that song ever since she was a little girl and would play it over and over on her mother's record player, singing along and joining in the 'huma-huma' chant that drove the song along. Jessie was a romantic. There was a saxophone solo midway through and this Jessie took as her cue to 'sexy it up,' shaking the tassels on her skimpy suede bra as she spun around the pole, clinging on by her legs and shimmying her torso. Jessie's other act was to dress as a cowgirl and spin to the drone of Bon Jovi's 'Wanted: Dead or Alive' on weekdays, alternating with Seasick Steve's 'Green and Yeller' on the weekends when she would put more effort into it. But she preferred her Native American outfit, it made her feel more spiritual. Besides, her Daisy Dukes were still wet from the wash.

The clientele of the club had dwindled dramatically since the ban on pole dancing, lap dancing or any other form of dance involving scantily dressed women performing for the sexual gratification of men. The ban did not, however, extend to scantily clad women dancing for the sexual gratification of other women and Jessie took this grey area in the law as licence to carry on pole dancing as a form of protest for equal rights and the right to make a living. The law didn't see it that way and Jessie had found herself in the unique position of being one of the last remaining exotic dancers in Canada.

RESET

Unfortunately for Jessie, this came as a case of diminishing returns as almost all of the clubs she used to perform in had closed down. The number of regular customers had diminished to virtually nothing, unwilling to have 'sex crime' permanently lodged on their record. As Jessie clutched the pole close to her chest and splayed her legs, she started to think maybe it was time to give up the pole dancing and return to a life of mediocrity and Town Planning.

Nearing the end of her act, Jessie spun clockwise around the pole, holding on with one hand as her feather flapped against the fast-moving air. She had always considered herself more of an athlete than exotic dancer and lamented the fact that she may have to give it up and find some other way to work out. It was only when Jessie was at the very top of the pole, contemplating the works of Frank Lloyd Wright, and subtly retrieving the bow and arrow she had Velcro-ed to the ceiling ready for her big finale, that she first noticed the three shadowy figures at the back of the room. The figures moved closer as Jessie began to spin anticlockwise, drawing her bow and holding herself in place only by the strength of her inner thighs. She spun faster, letting fly the arrow once she attained maximum spin as the dying 'hoo-has' of the song faded. Jessie arched her back, spread her arms, smiled a radiant smile and waited for her applause. The room was silent, completely silent. Jessie noticed the figures came closer with every revolution she made and having poor eyesight, Jessie had to squint to make out the shapes as she slowed to a halt facing them upside down high above. The blurs slowly started to take shape as Jessie perceived a man with slicked back hair dressed all in black, shadowed either side by black leather-clad figures in mirror visored black helmets, one with a sucker-ended arrow protruding from it.

Jessie's heart froze. As her thighs began to lose grip, she started to slide inextricably down the pole, the friction between her thighs and the chrome pole producing a long low farting noise which accompanied her slow descent.

RESET

Jessie

CHAPTER NINE

Interrogation Room 12

Mrs Evans was very tired indeed but she was determined to be as helpful as she could for this officious woman, even if she didn't know what the woman was on about. She had come across types like her before; in the council office, the tax office, the police, and especially the social work office. The type of people that let a little bit of power go to their heads and whose sole purpose in life seemed to be making other people's lives as difficult as possible. Mrs Evans had learnt, like most normal people, that the best thing to do was to be as helpful and polite as she could and not allow them any opportunity to make life any harder than it already was, at least that way she may stand a chance of getting home to Gwilym and Tinkle. And she couldn't wait until she could tell Dot all about her strange adventures and her new exotic friend, hopefully she would be back by tea time, a late tea maybe as she certainly didn't want to spend another night in that tiny grey room. And so, as the humourless woman droned on, she made a mental note to rally herself and try to help the woman with her form as best she could.

"Mrs Evans! Mrs Evans, are you listening to me?" said the woman.

"Oh yes, sorry just drifted away for a moment," said Mrs Evans.

"Please try and pay attention," said the woman.

"Yes, I will," said Mrs Evans. "It's been a busy couple of days, sorry. It won't happen again."

"Please make sure that it doesn't," said the inquisitor. "Now, where were we? So it would appear, Evans, that you have no social media presence- are you not online?"

"Oh no, I don't have a computer. I prefer to take long walks and read. I do a lot of reading, non-fiction mainly."

"But how do you know what's going on?" an astounded inquisitor asked.

"Well, my neighbour Dot lets me know what's going on in the world. I'm not that interested to be honest, I've got a television but I don't use it. Gwilym has it in his room, load of rubbish on it really."

"But surely you must have a social media presence to confirm your lifestyle choices with your Friends and remember their birthdays?" a perplexed inquisitor asked. "I mean, who influences you? How do you make an informed decision? How do you show all your Friends what a fabulous life you have?"

"I'm not sure my life is fabulous but I do keep a note of everyone's birthday on my calendar," Mrs Evans offered helpfully.

"Well I am truly baffled," said the inquisitor. "your behaviour is inexplicable therefore I don't think I have any other choice than to wash my hands of you."

"Oh, thank you," said Nain, "can I go now?"

Interrogation Room 14

After four hours of intense interrogation, Bob was beginning to flag. His shoulders were slumped and his head hung low.

"Are you familiar with the works of Virginia Woolf, Sarah Waters or Sapphire?" asked Bob's inquisitor. "Have you ever read 'Stirring the Bean Curd,' or 'Doughnut Bumper?'"

"No," replied a tired Bob.

"Do you subscribe to Butch or Dyke magazine?" pressed the inquisitor.

Bob again responded in the negative, shaking his head slowly.

"What about the music of L7, KD Lang or Kae Tempest?"

Bob drew a blank.

"How mysterious," said a haughty inquisitor. "I would have thought that you would be an expert on lesbian issues, judging by the amount of times the word 'lesbian' appears in your search engine history: six thousand, four hundred and eighty-three to be exact."

An exhausted Bob looked down at his feet. He had to concede to himself that indeed for all the six thousand, four hundred and eighty-three searches on the subject he had made in the past, he knew virtually nothing of lesbian issues. Bob felt ashamed. He was cold and tired and almost broken.

"Well Mr Murphy, it would appear that we can add 'pervert' to a long litany of offences. You are sick, Mr Murphy," said the inquisitor gravely. "Living alone, remote from the power of example and the check of shame, you are a sick pervert and you need to be cured. If it's not too late, that is."

Bob covered his face with his hands.

CHAPTER TEN

The Courtroom

The in-house courtroom was on the first floor of the Ministry of Globalisation and it was much like any other courtroom, with the exception of any members of the public, the press or a jury. In fact, the large room was empty except for the Judge, the Clerk of the Court, a court-appointed defence attorney, a handful of black-clad helmet-wearing guards and the defendant.

The flags of all the United Independent European States of Germany hung behind Judge Grindhard in the state-of-the-art grey courtroom. A saccharine painting of 'Ginger and Whinger,' the Duke and Duchess of Netflix, stared down from a gilded frame as the Judge placed a rainbow-coloured square upon her wig.

"Jorgen Johansson," said the Judge gravely, "it would appear you steadfastly refuse to complete your treatment and over a number of years, have made repeated escape attempts from your treatment centre, culminating in your latest endeavour, which has seen you at liberty for over twelve months. Therefore, for your own good and for those who have your best interests at heart, it gives me no pleasure in sentencing you to nine months of hard learning at a Maximum Security Re-education Centre, from where on completion of your sentence, you will be repatriated to Sweden and returned to the medical facility from whence you escaped, in order to complete said treatment."

"I'm never going back, no, never, NEVER!" bellowed a frantic Wulfe as he pushed aside the court official tasked with leading him to the departure cell. Wulfe made a desperate bid for escape down the aisle of the courtroom towards the doors but had not made two steps before he was coshed on the back of head by his own defence attorney. Wulfe dropped like a felled oak just as the doors to the courtroom opened and Donald MacDonald was led in for sentencing.

"Take him away!" ordered the Judge.

As Donald was escorted past the motionless giant of a man, he looked down and couldn't help admiring the Swede as he lay unconscious in a small pool of his own blood.

"Aye big yin, you give 'em hell, son," he said as a small tear welled up in the corner of his eye. The Judge banged her gavel several times as Donald was led before the bench for sentencing. He looked back over his shoulder just in time to see the Swede being dragged from the courtroom. The Judge caught his attention with another round of hammering. Donald turned his head, raised his eyes to the Judge and said in the most sarcastic voice he could muster:

"Is that what ye call justice? Well, I'd just as soon ya stick it up yer arse, your honour. Ye ken?"

The Judge didn't 'ken.'

"Well Mr MacDonald" said the Judge gravely. "It would appear from your assessment notes that you are a habitual criminal with an antisocial attitude. You steadfastly refuse to lay down your tartan and join the collective and, judging from your escape from the Assessment and Denationalisation Centre in Aberdeen, you have extremely violent tendencies. It is also apparent that you pay scant regard for LGBTQFEX+ issues and treat the law prohibiting alcohol in the Independent European Scottish State of Germany as if it does not apply to you. You have been caught on more than one occasion using a controlled instrument in a public space, you are a Leprechaun-ist and your refusal to self-censor is simply mind-boggling. The list goes on and on!"

"Och yer arse!" said Donald disdainfully.

"Contempt of court!" cried the Judge. "Mr MacDonald, your arrogance in thinking you could escape justice by fleeing to New Zealand is simply breath-taking. There is no corner of this earth that the long arm of the law cannot reach and, therefore, I will have to impose a sentence on you long enough to enable this concept to sink in. You must learn to accept this free society's boundaries for your own sake and that of your fellow world citizens. Three years of hard learning in a Maximum Security Re-educational Centre."

The Judge banged her gavel.

"I can only hope that this sentence will be long enough for your complete capitulation. Do you have anything to say before you are taken away?" asked the Judge.

"Aye," said Donald, "shove it up yer arse."

"Well in that case, you leave me no option than to 'no platform' you. Take him away!" instructed the Judge.

Two burly guards grabbed Donald under the armpits and dragged him out of the courtroom backwards.

RESET

"You can take my freedom! But-" cried Donald at the top of his voice.

The door slammed behind him before he could say anything more.

Bob Murphy and Nain Evans stood together before the Judge. The Judge looked sternly at the two of them. "You two should be old enough to know better. I have before me, reports on you both that would seem to indicate that you may be beyond salvation. Racist, sexist, misogynist, homophobic, Islamophobic, Nazi, impersonating an ethnic minority. As per usual with your types, the list goes on and on."

A bewildered Bob and Nain looked at each other in confusion. The Clerk of the Court stepped over to the Judge and whispered in her ear. "Before I pass sentence, it would appear that we have a young person courageous enough to make a survivor statement."

At that moment, a particularly morose-looking young girl of about sixteen was led into the witness stand, shaking and unsteady on her feet.

"Do you feel strong enough to make your victim statement?" asked the Judge tenderly. The girl nodded in the affirmative. "Do you recognise the accused in the courtroom?" asked the Judge.

The girl answered: "Yes."

"Do you feel strong enough to address your statement directly to them or would you like to deliver it from behind a screen?" inquired the Judge.

RESET

"I feel strong enough, thank you, your Honour," said the girl in a quiet voice.

"You are very brave," said the Judge, "remember that you are in a safe space. They can't hurt you here." The girl smiled weakly in reply. "Please begin," said the Judge.

"Yes, your Honour," the girl began, "I recognise the accused because they are old people, the same old people who are responsible for killing our planet, raping her of her natural resources, recklessly polluting the air for profit, leaving a legacy for my generation of death and destruction." The young girl's voice became louder and more powerful. "Oh yes, I recognise them all right. The people responsible for melting the polar ice caps, cutting down the rainforests, driving rare and beautiful creatures into extinction!" Her voice began to tremble with faux emotion as tears welled up in her eyes. "Yes, I know these people, your Honour. For behold, they are the harbingers of death. The killers of any hope for my generation." The tears rolled freely down her cheeks as she worked herself into a crescendo. "We face a climate emergency, THE WORLD IS ON FIRE!" she screamed before collapsing on the floor.

When the girl had been helped to her feet, the Judge addressed her.

"Thank you. I thank you and this court thanks you. You are very brave and courageous, a true survivor." The Judge looked accusingly at Bob and Nain. Bob and Nain looked baffled.

"You two are a disgrace to whichever race you identify with. I think we've heard all we need to hear, five years apiece hard learning in a Maximum Security Re-education Centre!" she said with a bang of her gavel. The courtroom erupted with cheers from the defence attorney as Bob and Nain were led away, Bob looking particularly dejected and forlorn.

PART TWO

*"United wishes and goodwill cannot overcome
brute facts.*

Truth is incontrovertible.

Panic may resent it.

Ignorance may deride it.

Malice may distort it.

But there it is"

Winston Churchill

CHAPTER ELEVEN

The cold autumnal light was failing and the chill and damp of winter's prelude was in the air as the pervasive darkness began its inevitable encroach, gradually enveloping the city of London. A misty light rain had begun to fall as the prisoners were loaded onto the bus in the gated compound at the rear of the court. Across the road from the high gates, huddled in the doorway of a Georgian façade, a pair of expectant young eyes peered out through a slit in a scarlet red blanket and a small hand gripped tightly to the cold ornate iron railing. The young flower seller's coal black eyes scanned the faces of the convicts intensely as they were manhandled onto the bus. The girl sat up alert as she observed the figure of a woman being escorted out of the building towards the open doors of the vehicle and stared with an air of excited expectation, hoping to make out a familiar figure in the failing light. As the woman in the compound was led along without resistance, her features were momentarily caught in the cold light of an overhead security lamp. For a fleeting moment, the woman looked through the wire fence and across the road, she noticed the girl wrapped in a blanket and smiled at her, before being shoved towards the bus. The girl sat down and huddled back into the doorway in disappointment.

"Excuse me please, but I don't really know what's going on, can I at least have a phone call? Dot will be wondering what's happened to me and Tinkle will be beside herself by now," fretted Nain as she was bundled into the meat wagon along with the rest of the cohort, bound for the Re-education Centre. The doors were slammed and locked and the mood was sombre as the vehicle began to make its way through the city. Huddled up on his seat, Bob's scrawny body was shivering in the cold but his mind seemed to be elsewhere. He had lost all track of time since being picked up and the thousands of miles he must have travelled, the lack of sleep combined with a bizarre interrogation and accusations, were all starting to take their toll. Bob was having an existential breakdown.

A low groan from the Swede broke the silence from time to time as he gradually regained consciousness. The cut to the back of his head was being tended to by Donald who, sensing he had a brother-in-arms in the shape of this giant Swede, was eager to form an alliance. Donald was a loner, a man more than capable of taking care of himself, his trust was hard to win and he berated himself constantly for ever trusting his lowlife second cousin. For Donald, there was only one way to be sure who had your back, and that was in the heat of battle and from what he had witnessed in the courtroom, this Viking was a man you wanted on your side. A kindred spirit, a man willing to fight even if the odds were stacked against him. Donald was a force to be reckoned with on his own account but an alliance with a man such as this would make them invincible, or if not invincible, a bloody fight to the death. Donald fantasised and was about to launch into the few lines of Flower of Scotland that he knew by heart when the Swede groaned.

"Take it easy son, get yer strength back. Then we'll take them when we're ready, or die in the process!" Donald's heart was pounding and his Celtic blood was up at the thought of a fight and maybe even escape. He looked around the bus and for the first time, he noticed the Aboriginal guy he had met earlier, shivering in the corner. Immediately he sprang to his feet, unwrapped his cloak and arranged it around the skeletal shape, with a look of concern.

"What have they done to ye, wee mon?" he said, shaking his head mournfully. "Dinnae worry son, we'll get ye back on yer feet, ye ken?" The smaller man nodded and Donald gave him a manly pat on the back, sensing another kindred spirit, and when Donald turned to see a Maasai warrior sitting impassively at the back of the bus, his heart soared. In his mind's eye, he was already applying the blue war paint. He gave the Maasai a determined nod- the Maasai did not return it. Donald respected that and his eye moved on, coming to rest on a small shadowy older lady in a top hat. Donald's bushy ginger eyebrows immediately ascended but eventually they settled down to a frown where they were most comfortable. Donald realised that it had, after all, been an unusual day and that the best policy was to expect the unexpected.

As the bus passed under a street lamp, Nain Evans' silhouette came out of the shadows, revealing the lady resplendent in the green, red and white of her national dress. Donald was ignorant in the truest sense of the word but he wasn't stupid and immediately recognised another Celt at the momentary flash of vivid colour. This old lady was Welsh. Donald nodded to her respectfully, she smiled slightly and nodded back. His heart swelled again with pride for his Celtic ancestry as he thought that in this van, was an old lady of Celtic origin willing to die for the right to wear her national dress.

"God bless ye, hen," said Donald in an emotional whisper.

Nain was confused- she had no idea what was going on and since being picked up in Pwllheli a few days ago, she had been on this disorientating journey, devoid of daylight, where no one and nothing made any sense at all. She smiled and gave a friendly nod to the big Scottish man, another potential friend perhaps. She had already gleaned some sort of comfort from sitting next to her new friend, the black man wearing red. She didn't have any black friends and was genuinely intrigued to find out more about him. She also had lots of gossip she wanted to share with him about some of the residents of Pwllheli but she couldn't relax and talk freely until she had some idea of what was going on. Her new friend hadn't been much help, poor thing, he was probably very shy. It must be a bit of shock if you had never seen a Welsh woman before.

She was not overly concerned about Gwilym, however, knowing full well that Dot from next door would discover him during one of her many daily visits and take good care of him, but it would be good just to let them know that she was okay. Dot was probably now frantically searching for her or had called the police- hopefully someone from the authorities would pop around and let her know what had happened, they seemed very efficient.

Nain looked towards the Scot lending words of encouragement to the thin semi-naked man, shivering under the big man's arm and decided to lend a hand, musing over circumstances she had no control over was not practical. Nain was a very practical woman. She made her way to the pair and undid her shawl.

"Aye, will be a glorious day, wee yin, cracking open a few Sassenach skulls, ye ken?" Donald was saying passionately when Nain came up to his shoulder.

"Excuse me," she said sweetly. Donald stopped talking immediately and turned to face her.

"Och it's yerself, hen," he said with a cheery grin, "How can I help?"

Nain stretched out her hand: "My name's Nain, I'm from Pwllheli."

Donald took her hand and gave her a firm but surprisingly gentle shake. "Name's Donald MacDonald, clan MacDonald, Scotland. Pleased to meet ye, hen."

"Nain," said Nain, "I couldn't help noticing that your friend was shivering. I thought he might like to put my shawl over his legs, my mother made it and its very warm," she went on, offering the shawl. Donald took a swift look down at Bob's bare legs and back again.

"Good idea, hen," he said taking the shawl and spreading it gently over Bob's legs.

"That's very kind of you, love," Bob said weakly, as he looked up and smiled.

Nain smiled back. "No problem." Nain had been so lost in her own thoughts that she hadn't really noticed the other passengers on the bus. She looked towards the Swede; she took a sharp breath when she noticed the blood-soaked hair. "Is he alright?" she asked Donald with concern.

"Aye, I think so, hen. He seems a bonny young lad," was Donald's solemn reply. Nain returned to her seat, smiling at the chiselled-faced

RESET

Maasai on the way. When she got there, she opened her bag. Nain had been surprised that she had been allowed to keep it, she noticed that her new friend was devoid of his spear and that rounded wooden hammer thing he had been wearing on a thong around his waist earlier and she vaguely remembered that the little man had a spear and a boomerang when she had first encountered him briefly in the waiting room. Nain opened up her bag- the knitting needles were there but scissors were missing just as she had suspected might be the case. "Never mind," she thought as she rummaged for the scarf she had knitted for Dot's two-year-old granddaughter. When she found it, she made her way to the dozing Swede, smiling to the Maasai on the way, and began to bandage his head. The Swede made no protest, he just smiled at her when she had finished.

"There, that's better. I'm sorry it's pink but I had knitted it for my neighbour Dot's granddaughter," she said apologetically as she patted him on the shoulder.

"Thank you," said Wulfe as he gave her hand a little squeeze.

"My name is Nain," said Nain.

"I'm Jorgen, yes," said Wulfe in his Scandinavian rhythm, "But my friend's call me Wulfe, that's what they call me, yes."

"Pleased to meet you, Wulfe," said Nain shuffling her way to her seat at the back of the bus. She sat down and immediately began to tell the Maasai of her adventures at the front of the bus. As she spoke, she absentmindedly offered the Maasai a pineapple chunk. The Maasai absentmindedly took it.

It was a long and uncomfortable journey as the bus bucked and bounced its way along potholed roads into the early evening gloom. After many long hours of travel, the vehicle eventually slowed down.

RESET

The bus pulled up at the outer gates of the Maximum Security Re-education Centre with a hiss of air brakes. Heavy rain spattered against the small black tinted windows of the bus and the driver waited, leaving the engine to tick over. Eventually, an enormous figure in black emerged from a small hut next to the gate and appeared to glide towards the bus, on a board mounted between two large wheels. Donald strained to see through the dark and the rain and when the figure passed by one of the headlights, Donald's initial impression was confirmed: an obese guard dressed in black, complete with black helmet and yellow smiley face livery, was indeed riding aboard a Segway.

"Hadn't they stopped making those things" the Scot thought to himself. A second and third guard came out of the hut and glided their way to the gates. To Donald's surprise, they too appeared to be large of build. The first guard came to the driver and inspected some papers while the other two stood to attention by the gates.

Donald strained to hear what was being said between the guard and the bus driver but the Perspex and perforated metal sheet protecting the driver from his own passengers was too thick. Donald sat back and observed everything. The first guard handed the papers back to the driver and pointed directions, signalling to his colleagues to open the gate. This they did with silky synchronicity, gliding in two arcs until the gates were fully open.

The driver put the vehicle into gear and the bus made its onward journey into the depths of the Category A Detention Centre. As the vehicle passed through the gates, Donald noticed that the guards wore what looked like Tasers and some kind of batons, hanging freely from the belts at their sides. Donald regarded the long batons enviously: the damage he could do with one of those was the stuff that Donald's dreams were made of. Donald could be amiable enough when the occasion called for it but on the whole, he much preferred a life of seclusion and freedom. Above all things, he valued his freedom and anyone who compromised this would receive the full wrath of his rage. It was now time to stand and fight, when the right moment presented itself. His pipe dreams were made of lead.

Nain woke up with a start and was temporarily blinded by the search lights as the bus made its way through the camp.

"Do you think we've arrived?" she asked her travelling companion. "Yes, we must have. Look at all that wire," she answered herself. The wire was in fact razor-tipped: they had arrived at their destination and the bus drew to a halt.

A blast of cold air came barrelling through the bus, expelling the warm air as the rear doors were opened and the passengers unceremoniously ordered to decant. More Segway-mounted guards, dressed as before, rounded them up and formed them into a line in what appeared to be a large tarmacked parade ground which dwarfed the bus behind. Cold gusts of wind and rain swept across the open space and the square was brightly illuminated by dozens of blinding lights, high up on gantries. It was hard for Donald to see outside into the darkness that lay beyond the square but he could just make out a cluster of buildings silhouetted against the dark skies and rain and in the distance, what appeared to be a small city. He also noticed the omnipresent wire fencing and the shadows of the guards silently gliding about, patrolling the perimeter. A gust of wind blew across the square, driving the rain before it and rattling the lines of the flagpoles eerily. The flags of all the United Independent European States of Germany, together with those of various sexual persuasions, were represented in a line behind them, fluttering in the squall.

RESET

In the centre of the square was a podium upon which stood the figure of a tall thin woman of about forty years old, a gaunt humourless face and short dark hair, severely scraped back. She was dressed in a long black overcoat and black leather riding boots. To the left of the woman, arranged in three neat rows, were approximately thirty guards silently standing to attention by their Segways, their helmet-enveloped heads giving nothing away. All of them, by most medical authorities' definition, were morbidly obese. To right of the woman, three not-so-neatly arranged rows of about the same number of men, women and what appeared to be men in wigs and garishly-applied lipstick. All were clad in tight black lycra, with various flashes of neon colours in strategic places. The women and the men in wigs wore their hair scraped back into a tight bun. All the men appeared to have beards and hair long enough to be 'styled' into a man bun. Both sexes wore short-sleeved tops and knee-length bottoms which revealed numerous tattoos on their naked flesh- these people were buff. In fact, they were beach-body ready, except for some of the men in wigs, who appeared to be more cake shop ready. Donald's eye was caught by a particularly well-defined pair of hairless legs and his eyes followed them up until he reached a man pouch. He looked away sharply.

"Och, nobody needs to see that, mon!" he said under his breath to nobody in particular.

"Velcome," came a Germanic voice, as the woman on the podium began her introduction, "to our Maximum Security Re-education Centre and your new home." She continued, "I am ze Commandant, you vill address me as Commandant. To my right, are the re-educators who are here to help you. To my left, are ze guards who are not. In my opinion, you are all a basketful of deplorables, and it has been deemed zat you represent a significant threat to society, enough to warrant your incarceration and re-education for vatever length of time the authorities have seen fit to keep you here. Your best course of action, zerefore, vould be to do as instructed by ze staff and ze guards. It is in your best interest to co-operate. Escape is futile, attempted escape vill however be severely punished. Dismissed."

With that, the five were ushered away towards a large concrete hut with the numbers 1688 stamped above the door. Nain watched sadly as the bus departed and rainwater dripped from rim of her top hat, little knowing that this would be her last link with the outside world. The group were herded brusquely into the building and the doors were closed behind them.

Nain was the first in, shadowed on either side by Donald and Wulfe with the silent Maasai and the violently shaking Bob bringing up the rear. As Nain's eyes adjusted to the dim light, she slowly took note of the surroundings. A timber floor with numerous wooden single beds equally spaced apart, almost running the full length of the hut on either side of a walkway which led to a long wooden table with about a dozen chairs arranged neatly around it. There was a large square wood burner with a chimney that reached up to the timber-constructed roof.

Suddenly, there was a loud creaking of floorboards as a large man leaped out of the shadows. Instantly, the Swede's substantial body tensed and the Scot's fists cracked. The Maasai stood impervious and the Aboriginal was too cold to notice. The bulky figure began to hop from one leg to another in what appeared to be an aggressive dance. The dancer came closer and Nain could make out intricate facial tattoos. He was covered only with a large towel-sized piece of cloth at the front and nothing except for a thong and a pair of meaty buttocks at the rear. The dancer turned his back, revealing his *Gluteus maximus* once again before approaching them and forming contorted faces. He moved in close to Nain and stuck his tongue out before gurning furiously. Eventually, he backed off with aggressive hand gestures before coming to a standstill.

"Oh, there's lovely for you!" exclaimed Nain with a clap of her hands. "Thank you!"

Donald and Wulfe looked at one another quizzically whilst the man stood looking at them, catching his breath.

"Oh thanks, I've been practising!" said the man breathlessly.

Nain turned to Donald, "He's a Maori you know, that was a welcome dance called the Hakka. I read it in a book," she said.

Donald was intrigued- although he had spent the last year in New Zealand, he had never met a Maori. This was chiefly because he had spent his time there hiding and hustling on the back streets of Dunedin, roaming from one deserted shelter to another, always one step ahead of the authorities until that fateful night when the name MacDonald was forever tainted by the hand of Judas. Donald let out a mournful groan.

The Guards

CHAPTER TWELVE

"Sorry if I startled you but I haven't had the opportunity to dance the Hakka for a while. This hut used to be full but gradually one by one they gave in and got let out. I'm the only one left, even though I'm not really supposed to be here. I've been so looking forward to your arrival!" the Maori said, his words tumbling over each other in his breathless glee. "Come in, come in, make yourselves at home. Pick a bed, there's plenty of them. Would you like a cup of tea?" The man ran around, picking things up and arranging bits and pieces. "Oh, I'm Pauli by the way," he said as he anxiously folded a tea towel. "Or would you like coffee?"

The group stood silently for a moment. Donald gave Wulfe a bewildered expression which was greeted with a shrug of the shoulders.

"Oh, a cup of tea would be lovely, sweetheart," said Nain breaking the awkward silence. Donald relaxed and went to sit on the bed nearest the door, just in case. He signalled to the Swede with a nod that he should do the same with the opposite bed, just to be on the safe side. The Swede obliged and lay full length on the bed, his furry boots hanging over the edge. He immediately fell asleep and began to snore, the pink scarf still tightly wound around his head.

Pauli noticed Bob for the first time. "You don't look too good, fella," he said as he ran over and helped Bob into a bed next to the Scot, covering him with a blanket and tucking him in with genuine concern.

"Thanks, mate," said an exhausted Bob.

Pauli looked to Nain questioningly.

"He just needs a good rest, poor thing," said Nain, but what Nain didn't know was that Bob, after extensive cross-examinations, was beginning to question who he was. Bob fell asleep with a troubled mind.

As Pauli trotted over to the wood burner with a kettle, Nain introduced the new arrivals.

"This is Donald," as Donald nodded. Pauli wiggled his fingers in a wave. "The big man sleeping over there is Wulfe, the little man sleeping over there is Bob, this gentleman standing here is my friend and I'm Nain," she quickly went on.

"I'm sorry, I didn't get your name," said Pauli to the Maasai warrior.

"Nor has anyone else," Nain interjected, "he's very shy," she whispered in front of the Maasai.

Once the kettle had boiled, Pauli poured the water into the teapot. The three sat around one end of the large wooden table, complete with a frilly blue tablecloth, china teacups and saucers, and a cut glass three-tier cake stand, fully loaded with light pastries, all of which

Pauli had laid out seamlessly as he and Nain made small talk- Nain had met her small talk match.

"Very tidy," she said.

"Oh, thank you," said Pauli proudly smiling.

Nain looked at the tea set. "Is that teapot from the Portmerion Pottery?" she asked.

Pauli's hands shot up to his face in surprise. "Oh my god!" he exclaimed. "Do you know Portmerion Pottery?"

"Well yes, the pottery is only just down the road from where I live," said Nain proudly.

"OMG!" said Pauli eagerly as he poured the tea. "That's so fabulous, you simply must tell me all about it!"

Pauli stopped mid-pour. "Oh, how rude! You must be so tired, you poor things. And here's me just jabbering on about old teapots. It's just that I've been rattling around in this hut on my own now for a while since the last guests departed. It's not been as busy as it used to be, I think they're going further afield to find guests nowadays."

"Not at all," said Nain. "There's nothing I like more than having a good chat and a bit of a gossip over a nice cup of tea."

"We are soooo going to get on, sista!" Pauli said with a wink. He put down the teapot and clasped Nain's hand in his, looking deep into her eyes. "I simply love your outfit, it's so fabulous! You must tell me where you got it."

"Well, I made a lot of it myself," said Nain modestly.

"OMG!" said Pauli with a little scream of delight. "You are soooo clever!"

RESET

Pauli looked at the Maasai. "I'm sorry, I love your outfit too. That scarlet is so... so now, did you make it yourself too?"

The Maasai sat impervious as stone, as Pauli proffered him a pastry.

"I baked them myself," said Pauli proudly. The Maasai took one. "I love your hair, it goes so well with the whole ensemble," said Pauli with a clap of his hands.

The next hour was spent with Pauli telling his new friends all about the people he had met at the Re-education Centre, or listening in awe as Nain told tales of deepest Wales.

"So, have you always lived in Pwllheli?" asked Pauli

"Well no, I only moved there when I married Gwilym. I was actually born on an island called Anglesey," said Nain.

Pauli clapped his hands together with glee: "An island! How mysterious?"

"Yes" replied Nain, "I was raised in a little village called Llanfairpwllgwyngyllgogerychwyrndrobwllllantysiliogogogoch. What about you?"

"Oh, I was born in a town called Taumatawhakatangi-hangakoauauotamatea-turipukakapikimaunga-horonukupokaiwhen-uakitanatah," replied Pauli.

The Maasai got up and made for a bed.

"I think I need some sleep too," said Nain, "it's been an awfully long few days and I still haven't got a clue what's going on."

"Well, pick a bed," said Pauli. "There are plenty to choose from, and I'll try to explain everything in the morning."

"Where do you sleep?" asked Nain.

Pauli pointed to the nearest bed.

"Can I sleep next to you, that way we can have little chats when we want without disturbing anyone else?" said Nain.

"I would so love that," Pauli said with genuine tears in his eyes. "Good night," he whispered.

"Sleep tight," said Nain.

"Thank fuck!" exclaimed Donald from under his blanket.

The door suddenly burst open and rain poured in as a young man with bleached blonde hair entered in a black electric wheelchair, followed by a young woman dressed as a sexy Native American squaw. The guards closed the door behind them.

Donald sat up with a start and watched warily. The Maasai looked on emotionlessly. Wulfe and Bob kept on sleeping.

"Yo, yo, yo, wassup, mutherfuckers?" said the young man. "Brad Blanchett in da house!" he announced proudly as he navigated his way towards the far end of the hut. "Wassup, wassup, wassup," he continued as he passed Donald, Wulfe, Bob and the Maasai's beds. "Morose, mutherfuckers," he muttered under his breath.

The girl smiled prettily but remained silent. Pauli jumped out of bed and to his feet.

"Welcome to our hut," he said, "I wasn't expecting you tonight. I'm Pauli, would you like some tea?"

"Tea?" said Brad. "Ain't you got anthin' stronger? We've had one mofo of a journey."

"Not really," said a crestfallen Pauli.

"No problemo, amigo," said Brad, pulling a bottle of Tennessee whisky from a compartment by the side of his chair and offering it to Pauli when he reached the table. Pauli declined his offer. Brad took a large swig from the bottle before offering it to Jessie. Jessie snatched the bottle and began to gulp greedily from it. She wiped her mouth with the back of her hand.

"I'm Jessie," she said absently as she surveyed her surroundings before sitting down at the table.

"Well," said Pauli, "better late than never!" as he pulled up a chair. "And that lovely lady over there is my new friend Nain."

Nain sat up in her bed and gave a little wave: "Nice to meet you."

"Yo Nain, likewise," said Brad, an expert at public relations and meet & greets.

"Hi Nain," said Jessie sweetly, relieved to see another female.

"I would introduce you to everybody else" said Pauli, looking down to the far end of the room and noticing Donald retreating under cover of his blanket. "But it looks as if everyone is asleep, it can wait until morning. I love your outfit, very risqué," he said to Jessie.

"Oh thanks, unfortunately it's what I had on when they picked me up, not very practical," replied Jessie.

"It's all good," said Brad with an eager look on his face.

Jessie gave him a withering stare.

"Which tribe do you belong to?" asked Pauli.

"I don't, I'm an exotic dancer," Jessie replied.

Brad looked toward the ceiling: "Thank you God," he mouthed silently.

"Oh my god, how fabulous!" said Pauli, holding his hands to his mouth.

Jessie surveyed the Maori- he must have been about forty, broad and solid, with a genuinely endearing smile and a mischievous twinkle in his eye. "I love your tattoos," she said.

"Oh, thank you, I love your tattoo too," gushed Pauli, noticing the pentangle tattooed onto the girl's left breast. "And you look extremely suave in that suit," he said to Brad, not wanting to leave him out.

"Yeah I know, the ladies love this shit," replied Brad cockily winking at Jessie.

Jessie threw her eyes toward the heavens in a world-weary way. "I don't mean to be rude, Pauli," she said, "But I'm bushed. Is there anywhere I can get some rest? It's been a long day."

"Of course, you must be tired. It's very late, just pick any empty bed," replied the Maori as Jessie got up and made her way to the bed next to Nain.

"I'm going to get some rest too, it's going to be a big day tomorrow. Just pick a bed," Pauli said to Brad before returning to his own bed.

Brad took another gulp from his bottle before returning it to the compartment and navigating his chair to the bed opposite Jessie's, and nimbly manoeuvring onto it.

"If you get cold in the night, you know where I'll be" he said to Jessie.

RESET

Jessie raised a middle finger.

Pauli

CHAPTER THIRTEEN

Bob opened his eyes to find a tattooed face in close proximity, looking down at him wearing a serious expression. Suddenly, the twinkly-eyed face broke into a pearly white grin. Bob's petrified face relaxed but as he slowly recalled the events of yesterday, his dark mood returned.

"How are you feeling, buddy?" asked a concerned Pauli. "I was worried about you; how did you sleep?"

"Better," a mummified Bob lied, anxious to reclaim his personal space.

"That's the spirit, fella! I made you a nice cup of tea," said a perky Pauli, standing up and relieving Bob of a heavy burden.

Bob took a deep breath: "Thanks, cobba," he wheezed.

"My pleasure," beamed Pauli. "No rush, you just get up when you feel like it," he said, patting Bob on his bony shoulder before leaving.

RESET

Bob struggled to sit up, inching himself out of the covers like a snake shedding its skin. Once he had arranged his sinewy body, he rubbed his eyes and surveyed his new environment. The group of individuals he had met the previous day were all seated around the small table at the end of the room, deep in conversation. Bob noticed the two newest members of the group: a young man in his late twenties with short blond hair in an electric wheelchair and a young dusky-skinned girl in a sexy tasselled American Indian outfit. Bob's eyes nearly exploded out of his head- he began to shake and immediately threw the blanket over himself as he crawled back, gibbering into his woollen cocoon.

Pauli came over to the group and sat down.

"He's awake," Pauli announced. "He just needed a good sleep."

"Oh, poor thing," said Nain. "It's been a hectic few days." Pauli gave her a sympathetic smile:

"More tea anyone?" he said as he began to refill everyone's cup, regardless of whether they wanted a refill or not. Donald was brooding as he sipped tea from his Clarice Cliff reproduction teacup.

"Sugar, milk, help yourselves," said Pauli.

The Maasai helped himself to milk.

Donald thrust his teacup down gently on the saucer:

"As much as I'm enjoying yer tea party," he began, "do ye think ye could fill us in as to what precisely is goin' on?"

"Of course," said Pauli sympathetically, "you must be feeling a bit bamboozled. Now, where to start?" he mused.

RESET

"'Oi 'oi!" came a chirpy cockney voice, as a round smiling face of about forty years in thick black-rimmed glasses appeared around the door, a flat black cap perched jauntily on his head.

"Hi Ian!" said Pauli, slightly relieved. "Just in the nick of time. Ian is the best man to explain. Come in, the kettle's just boiled."

"Don't mind if I do," said Ian, the rest of his body following his head into the room. He sauntered cheerfully down the hut, winking at Bob's face which peeped out of the covers as he passed the foot of his bed. "Alright, mate?" he said with a toothy grin. Bob returned a meek smile.

Ian gave him a double thumbs up: "Result!" he said as he made his way to the group around the table.

Donald noticed the black hat and suit Ian wore were covered in an intricate pattern of shining pearl buttons.

"Mornin' all!" beamed Ian as the rest of the group greeted him, with the exception of the Maasai.

"Have a seat," said Pauli as he poured more tea. "I was just about to tell everyone all about the Centre."

"Oh blimey," said Ian as he polished his glasses on a napkin.

"But now you're here, maybe you should explain. You'd do a better job."

"Oh cheers," said Ian ironically as he pinched the flesh between his eyes. He sat down and replaced his glasses, immediately his eyes widened when he noticed Jessie. "Blimey," he said to no one in particular, trying to avert his gaze as his eyeballs whirled about uncomfortably like a pair of marbles.

"Well," he started awkwardly, "my name's Ian and I'm the Hut Master from next door, just like Pauli 'ere."

"I'm Nain," said Nain, she pointed to the far end of the room "and that's Bob."

The rest of the group introduced themselves but the Maasai said nothing, he just looked at the sugar bowl. Ian acknowledged him with a nod:

"Chief," he said. "It's a pleasure to meet you all. I'll try to make it brief but where to start, hmm...welcome to Norfolk!" he finished with a grin.

"Norfolk?" cried Donald.

"Is there an echo in 'ere?" Ian joked, looking around the room as if following a house fly. "Yes, Norfolk. This is the International Maximum Security Re-education Centre... Norfolk. And most of you are 'ere to be re-educated as its been deemed by the collective that you pose a significant fret to decent Western democratic society." He raised his eyebrows.

"Most, yes?" inquired Wulfe.

"Yes, most." continued Ian. "Some of you may 'ave been sent 'ere by mistake, it 'appens a lot."

"Mistake?" It was Nain's turn to ask.

"Yes, mistake. Some of you may 'ave 'ad a Preservation Order slapped on you, 'Area of Outstanding Culture,' that sort of fing. Probably should 'ave gone to the Preservation Re-concentration Camp, or Preservation Reservation for short, up in Essex for your own cultural protection. But as always, when a privatised organisation interacts with a nationalised system, well, chaos ensues. Logistics, paperwork, civil service all that sort of fing. It's like pickley-wickley circus at rush 'our around 'ere at times. Anyways, to cut a long story short: there's a lot of people with a Class II Preservation Order on them that shouldn't be 'ere. I fink they were on a money-saving drive in Brussels when they merged the departments. Pauli's one, ain't ya?"

Pauli nodded enthusiastically.

"Although I shouldn't call 'im 'one,' don't want to 'ave to resit my 'How to spot an identity-based hate actor' exam again- I failed it free times before and I don't want to 'ave to sit again. It adds more time to your sentence, you know, I'm a bit slow with a lot of the terms, that's why I've been in for so long. Anyway, to cut a long story short: Pauli 'ere is just waiting for the paperwork to come froo. I 'spect it will be the same for your friend the chief 'ere, for all we know he could be a World Heritage Centre." Ian nodded towards the Maasai who was loading his tea with sugar. "And the little bloke over there," he continued by gesturing to Bob. "I'm not making assumptions based on their race, of course, they could be White supremacists for all I know! I don't know, that's why I'm 'ere."

"Hang on a minute, pal," interrupted Donald, "did you say something about a threat to society?"

Ian did a comedy double-take.

"Well, yeah mate. I imagine the rest of you are 'ere for an unspecified amount of time until you sit all your exams and/or are considered sufficiently re-educated enough to re-enter society," Ian recited verbatim, looking up to the ceiling.

"On what charge am I to be held against my will?" roared Donald.

"Keep yer barnet on mate, I don't make the rules! I'm an inmate too, you know. You were there at your own trial, weren't you?"

"Aye, but I dinnae ken what was going on, ye ken?"

"No, Ian," said Ian. "Well, to cut a long story short: you can be sent 'ere for anyfing from a non-crime intervention order to, say, unconscious subliminal racism. Got one bloke in 'ere, extreme far-right White supremacist fanatic- didn't even know it- and he's Black! We've got people in 'ere for wrong fought, wrong speak, failure to self-censor, sexual deviants," he looked over at Jessie and wiggled his glasses and grinning impishly. "We used to get a lot in for malicious electronic communication with the intention of causing stress or anxiety which could lead to violent self-crime or at least severely hurt someone's feelings, but people seem to have wised up to that one. They exploited a loophole in the law and just stopped communicating with anyone on the internet. Although we do still get a lot of overspill from other facilities since the Predictive Policing Act but they go to another part of the camp. Not enough 'olding facilities, they didn't fink that one froo," he finished, tapping his head.

Donald turned to Nain: "I have absolutely no idea what he's talking aboot, have you?"

Nain shook her head earnestly.

Ian sat back and fiddled with his spectacles. He looked at Nain and Donald.

"'ang on a minute, are you two wearing national dress?"

The pair nodded the affirmative.

"Oh, I didn't notice that," Ian said. "Fink there's been a mix up- you two should be in my hut: 'National and Cultural Wrong Dress.' You've probably been put in 'ere 'cause we suddenly 'ad an influx of the Gilet Jaune last week. Yella vests, you know, big purge. Non-payment of green tax en-masse, that's what they say." Ian leaned forward and dropped his voice to a conspiring whisper: "I fink it's because they're French."

He straightened up and raised his voice. "Anyway," he said as he adjusted his specs again, "to cut a long story short: you've probably been sent 'ere for Extreme Nationalism or somefink like that. I fink they make it up as they go along, they've probably slapped on a Subliminal Fat Shaming order maybe even Trans-exclusionary hate crimes or somefink like that on top, 'oo knows?"

Ian turned to Nain and looked at her sadly.

"They've more than likely found you responsible for killing the planet too, luv."

Nain thought for a moment.

"I think the judge did mention something about that but I can't really remember- I was so tired," she said finally.

"Well if it's any consolation, I don't blame you. You weren't to know. My generation is probably just as culpable but they 'ave to blame someone, don't they?" said Ian, shrugging his shoulders sympathetically.

"Thank you," said Nain for reasons she couldn't quite understand.

Ian gave a sincere nod and grim smile.

"Listen, pal," Donald burst out in exasperation. "Nothing you say makes any sense."

"Do what, mate?" asked Ian, trying to decipher Donald's thick Scottish accent.

Donald buried his face in his hands whilst Nain tried to salvage the situation.

"How long do you think we'll be here, Ian?" she asked.

Ian scratched his head and drew in a breath through a pursed mouth, like a builder giving an estimate for a loft conversion.

"Well that depends, I s'pose," he said eventually.

"You suppose, yes?" said the Swede, joining in the conversation.

Ian paused to collect his thoughts. He began again:

"Basically, you come 'ere for whatever reason- I'm not judging- because the authorities fink you pose a fret to society and need re-educating. Fair enough." He shrugged his shoulders. "Basically, it means that you take a lot of classes, sit some exams, get your re-education certificate and bish-bash-bosh, you're out on the street, after you've served your minimum sentence, of course. For those of us wearing national dress 'owever, it's a bit different. Once we pass all the exams, we 'ave to 'and over our national dress, promise never to wear it again and only then, can we be reintegrated into society."

"Never!" cried Donald, slamming the palm of his meaty hand down on the table and causing the china tea set to rattle.

"Hold up, sunshine, keep your barnet on!" said Ian.

The Swede pondered for a minute.

"Why do we not go to the same place as Pauli, yah? One of these culture camps in Essex, yes?" he finally asked, pulling a wooden pipe from his pocket and filling it with tobacco.

"Well," started Ian, "well, 'ow to put this?" He mused. "Not all of us have got the 'right' culture, some of us are not...diverse enough," he finished.

RESET

"Diverse enough? Hmm," mumbled the Swede, as he lit the pipe with a match which he struck against his leather vambrace.

He had Donald's attention and support immediately, his blood rising.

"Aye, what does that mean? I'd say we were all pretty diverse, don't you?" he scowled.

"I mean indigenous," said Ian.

Donald looked from Wulfe to Nain.

"Surely you can't get more indigenous than the three of us?" Donald demanded.

"Well, yeah," said Ian hesitantly. "But you're not quite...efnic, are you?" He looked at Jessie. "You might get away with it," he said, "but on second foughts..."

"Ethnic? Hmm," questioned the Swede as he blew out an enormous cloud of smoke.

"Yeah, you're not quite efnic enough. That's what you've got to get your 'eads round," said Ian helpfully. "In fact, it's because of your lack of efnic diversity that you could be considered privileged and a bit right-wing, White isn't always right you know."

Donald rose to his feet, bristling with indignation.

"I'm no havin' that! I'm ethnic, I'm Scottish, mon. I come from an area of outstanding beauty, I'll have you know, and I'm proud of it!"

Ian jumped to his feet.

"Look, Jock, I don't make the rules. I'm in the same boat as you lot," he said defensively. "I've been 'ere nearly four years, mate. I was one of the first to be rounded up, it was all right for you up there in Jockland- I was at the epicentre. I've been 'olding out while all around 'ave given up and just given in. Fousands 'ave passed through 'ere but only a pitifully small number of us 'ave 'eld fast, determined to preserve our cultures." He finished dramatically, emotionally drained.

The room was silent. Pauli put a reassuring hand on Ian's shoulder and looked reproachfully at Donald. Donald took the cue:

"Sorry mon," he said earnestly, "I wasnae angry at you. I escaped early, I've been on the run for a long time, I cannae imagine what you've been through."

Ian looked up and nodded. "Well it probably ain't been easy for you eiva, mate. Bein' on the run."

"Naw, it hasnae been easy." Donald held out a hand to Ian. Ian shook it and they both sat down respectfully.

The Maasai dipped a biscuit into his tea which didn't go unnoticed by Pauli who threw him a disapproving look. The moist biscuit broke into the tea with a plop.

"What the fuck are you guys babbling on about?" Brad suddenly interjected.

"Oi, oi, one from the colonies! Sorry mate, didn't notice you there," said a surprised Ian. "What they send you 'ere for?"

"Fucked if I know, being sexy I guess. They used that word a hell of a lot, but I'd been powdering my nose, cocaine on my membrane at the time, know what I'm sayin'?" replied Brad.

"Err...no, mate," replied Ian.

"Bitches kept going on about a sex list," Brad continued.

Ian thought for a moment. "Maybe they meant 'sexist.' Do you use words like 'bitches' a lot?"

"Word up, hell yeah," grinned Brad.

"Oh, there you go then, mate," said Ian. "Probably done you for being a misogynist, being a White bloke don't help, of course.... source of all evil."

Brad looked puzzled. "That ain't right and it ain't tight," he said, "just cos I'm White?"

Ian whispered conspiratorially as he looked over at Jessie. "They probably don't like you much eiva."

"Who?" she asked.

"The Femin-Nazis," he whispered.

"That figures," she replied.

"So, what's the Hampden Roar?" asked Donald.

"Do what, Jock?" questioned Ian, with a bemused look on his face.

"The SCORE, mon, what's this place all aboot?"

"A boat?" replied a confused Ian.

"What is this place about?" said Donald, speaking slowly and trying to sound English.

"Oh right, about!" replied Ian. "As I said, it's a bit like school 'ere: classes, PT, exams, that sort of fing. You keep taking the classes and taking the exams, they never run out of classes or exams you know, until you've served your sentence, then you get to go up to the parole board. If they deem that you've 'ad a good re-education, then you're free to go, 'aving 'anded in your outfit, of course in our case," he said looking at Donald, Nain and Wulfe. "Problem is, recently they've been adding a lot more classes as definitions get redefined. I'm 'aving to do night classes at the moment to catch up, I'm currently swotting up on the nuances between Third Wave Feminism and Intersectional Fourth Wave Feminism. The Feminist Hierarchy…it's a mind fuck, pardon my French, let me tell you. Still, I think I'm getting an 'andle on it," finished Ian, polishing his glasses once again.

"Wait a minute, we've been rounded up and sent to school to be treated like bairns because they think that we need re-educating?" said Donald.

"Barns?" repeated Ian, momentarily confused.

"Bairns, bairns, you know, mon. Children, kids!" roared an exasperated Scot.

"Oh, saucepan lids. You mean we're being treated like kids. Well maybe, never really fought about it that way. They call it 'wrong think retrofits' round 'ere. On the upside, we get free meals!" Ian nodded towards Pauli who nodded in agreement enthusiastically.

"Vegan though," Pauli lamented.

"Yeah, vegan," agreed Ian sadly.

"Food? Food? Is that all yooz can think aboot? What about escape?!" demanded Donald passionately.

"Escape?" said a puzzled Ian looking at his watch. "It's time for breakfast."

Just then a bell rang.

RESET

Ian

CHAPTER FOURTEEN

The non-binary vegan cat of colour lay dead outside the canteen as the group of new arrivals were herded in by the guards and directed to a table in the corner, away from the other boarders. Nain Evans surveyed the scene, a large open-plan space, mainly of timber and concrete construction. Large windows illuminated the interior with the dull light of a rainy Autumn day. Long tables ran the length of the space and Nain estimated at least two hundred people were seated at them, a little over a quarter of were wearing yellow vests and speaking in low Gallic tones. The rest of the room was made up of people of all ages, shapes and colours mostly wearing grey Chairman Mao-type clothing, but many still wore the clothes they were picked up in, the bright colours providing a welcome contrast to the grey environment. As Nain cast her eyes around the room, she spotted Ian sitting at the end of another table in the company of a handful hi-vis wearing French and some large, serious-looking bearded men, with florally-decorated straw hats. Ian gave a toothy grin and a thumbs up when he saw her, Nain gave a little wave in return. Pauli came and sat next to her.

"How's your breakfast?" he enquired. "It's gluten-free, just in case you were worried. And nut-free. And dairy-free."

Nain looked at the bowl of grey liquid.

"Taste-free also, yes," said the Swede, stirring his spoon in the gruel.

"It's geein' me the boke," complained Donald in disgust.

Bob, Brad and the Maasai ate quietly together. Wulfe dropped his spoon in the bowl with a clatter, pushed back his seat and began to load his pipe with tobacco.

"Who is Ian talking to?" he asked Pauli as he noticed the Londoner conversing conspiratorially with the large bearded men.

"Oh, you don't really want to have anything to do with them," said Pauli.

"Why is that? "inquired Jessie.

"They're a bit secretive, very close-knit, hardcore, don't take to strangers."

"Who are they?" Donald joined in the conversation; his curiosity suddenly aroused.

"They are all that's left," Pauli said solemnly.

"Of what?" pressed Jessie.

"They are all that's left of the Northwood and South Oxhey Morris Men. Some of the longest serving guests here."

"Morris Men?" asked Nain. "Oh, how nice!"

"Ya mean the numpties that dance around the maypole?" Donald interjected.

"Shh, keep your voice down," urged Pauli. "They're connected, if you know what I mean."

Nobody did.

"You said they are all that's left, yes?" inquired Wulfe.

"Yes, there used to be nine: two of them died in a dance-off with the Cossacks and one suffered a complete mental breakdown. They found his contorted body one morning." Pauli paused for effect. "He had danced himself to death. Hardcore. All that's left now are the six you see before you, the big ones are called: Jed, Ned, Ed, Fred, Ted and the small fella is Jeffrey… Jeffrey with a J."

"You said that they were connected, yes - what do you mean?" asked Wulfe.

"They've been here for so long that they get special privileges."

"Like what?" Jessie asked.

"They run the racket in home brew for starters. They can get you things as well, they have access to the outside."

Donald and Wulfe suddenly sat up.

"Outside, yes?" questioned Wulfe.

"Yes, they are trustees," replied Pauli.

"Why don't they just run?" said Donald incredulously.

"They have nothing to run for," Pauli sighed.

"Everyone has something to run for! Of course," said Wulfe.

"Not them, why do you think they became Morris Dancers in the first place?"

Ian eventually finished speaking to the Morris Men and after a serious nod to them, he came trotting cheerily over to the group.

"Oi oi, saveloy!" he said.

"Will ye stop talking aboot food, mon?" scowled Donald.

"What, you don't like the food?" questioned Ian.

"No, it is disgusting," answered the Swede.

"Well, it's not Lobster Troubadour but it's alright!" said Ian in a vain attempt to keep the group's spirits up.

Just then, a bell rang.

"Ooh," said Pauli, "time for first class! I'm coming with you this morning, just to help you settle in."

As the new guests left the canteen, four portly guards on their ubiquitous Segways approached and beckoned the group follow them outside toward the drill square. Brad was heartened to notice that the corner of every building appeared to have multiple charging points- he had been concerned that his chair may run out of juice and since becoming a minor celebrity, he was loathed to go 'manual' again these days. He looked up at the sky which was a dull depressing grey, a far cry from the Californian sunshine that he had taken for granted and as he trundled onto the square, he couldn't help but notice how large the escorts were- not in a fit, muscular way but in a fat, clinically obese way- and judging from their aggressive demeanour, not a 'jolly' fat either. The cold air was biting and Brad was relieved that Jessie had had the foresight earlier that morning to suggest that the more scantily-dressed amongst the group wrap their blankets around them, a suggestion which the guards thus far had seemed untroubled with. Although Brad was still dressed in his 'Hawkin' costume which he had been picked up in, the cold air was penetrating and he tucked the blanket tighter about his legs as the group were escorted across the drill square toward a complex of low, grey, flat-roofed concrete buildings. As they made their way through the gates, Brad noticed the sign that read 'Re-education Teaching Facility' written in Gill Sans MT font. They were led through the maze of buildings until eventually they reached a door that read 'Self-Censoring Class', whereupon entry, they were ordered by the guards to sit down in one of the grey plastic seats arranged in a neat circle. Once seated, they waited apprehensively in the small grey windowless room until a door opened and the re-educator arrived. The escort guards left and were immediately replaced by another pair of guards, minus electrical conveyances, who walked in behind them. They shut the door and stood to attention, blocking anyone from entering or leaving the room.

The re-educator stood with his legs apart and his hands on his hips, grinning cheerfully in the middle of a circle of chairs with his perfect white teeth brilliant against his chestnut beard and his hair brushed into a neat man bun. The tight lycra bodysuit exposed the skin of his smooth hairless calves and forearms, tattooed with intricate patterns of Celtic design.

"So, hi! I'm Myles," he said in a posh, eloquent, confident English voice.

Donald took an instant dislike to him for a myriad of reasons.

"Please take a seat," Myles continued.

The group seated themselves, with the exception of Brad.

RESET

"And welcome to your first class. I hope you all had a good sleep and are ready for some fun!" Myles clapped his hands together and vigorously rubbed them as if he were in a blizzard whilst grinning manically. His face suddenly turned to one of concern.

"Now, I," he said, pointing to himself with the forefingers of both hands, "am HERE," as he pointed to the floor, "to help YOU." He pointed to his audience again with the same two fingers. His face looked very sad.

"So I am not here to judge you, you have already been judged and that is why you are here," he said with concern. "I am here to help you," he said in a whisper, "and make it FUN!" He beamed as he surveyed his audience. "So, let's get started with a quick warm up exercise. We are going to go around the room and introduce ourselves so we can all get to know one another better. I want you all in turn to tell the rest of us: three facts about yourselves and a cherished memory. OK, I will start: my name is Myles, I am a vegan, I am a male feminist and my hobbies include mountain biking and snowboarding. My happiest memory was watching the sun set behind Victoria Falls when I was on a white-water rafting expedition. I am very pleased to welcome you here." The re-educator turned to Donald and indicated that he should go next. "Go," he said enthusiastically pointing at the Scot, but Myles's enthusiasm was not infectious.

"Well, my name's Donald and I dinnae give a fuck. I've never met a man claiming to be a feminist that can pick up a heavy load and run wi' it and if ye had a proper job, ye wouldnae have the energy to go mountain biking off a coral reef, ya fanny."

"Now Donald," said Myles shaking his head sadly, "that is the sort of inflammatory language that got you here in the first place. It's a shame to do this on your very first day but I have no option but to exclude you and send you over to Anger Management so you don't contaminate the rest of the class with your negative attitude. Bye bye."

The two guards waddled over, dragged Donald over the back of his chair and out of the door.

"Cheerio tae fuck," said Donald as he was escorted away.

The door slammed behind them.

Nain looked to Pauli who gave her a reassuring smile. "He'll be OK," he said.

Myles righted Donald's chair. "Sad, so sad, but let's not let one bad apple spoil the fun for the rest of us," he said as he sat down with his hands on his knees and legs wide apart, unconsciously performing a crotch display.

Myles pointed to Nain. "You're up, go!"

"Oh," said a flustered Nain still bemused by Donald's sudden departure, "I don't know what to say."

"Well let's start with your name. Don't be nervous, you are in a safe space," smiled Myles warmly.

"My name is Blodwyn. Blodwyn Evans but everyone just calls me Nain."

"Hi Nain," said Myles, "would you like to tell us something about yourself? What's your happiest memory? What are your best qualities? Have you got any hobbies like climbing, skiing, surfing? Because WE," he pointed with two outstretched arms to everyone else in the room, "want to know the real Nain." He finished by pointing both fingers at Nain.

"Well, I enjoy spinning I suppose," said Nain absently.

"Wow, still waters run deep," said an excited Myles. "You just can't beat an intense cardio workout! What else? Shoot!"

"What I really want to know is, why am I here? Did I do something wrong?" said Nain earnestly.

Myles looked up at the ceiling, took a slow deliberate breath, exhaling before looking sadly at Nain, his head slightly tilted to one side.

"So, Nain," he said. "Denial is not a quality, the sooner you accept the situation you've got yourself into and take personal responsibility for your actions, the sooner we can move on and help you. Now I don't want to 'no platform' you but I do think that maybe you should spend the rest of this session in quiet contemplation. I want to help you, Nain, but I can't if you refuse to let me in." He almost whispered this last sentence.

Myles looked sadly across at Nain for a moment, gave a slow condescending blink before clapping his hands together and pronouncing eagerly: "Next!" Myles aimed his clasped fists at the Maasai.

The warrior just sat, staring straight ahead, breathing imperceptibly.

"He's extremely shy, poor thing," Pauli interjected.

Myles' eyes lit up. "So, I feel your pain man," he said in a patronising tone. "It must have been difficult. It is going to take time but I want you to know, I am here for you, brother. We are all here for you." He took a long pause. "And you are rocking the beads, my friend. Keep the faith!" He raised a fist before moving his attention to Bob.

"Go!" he said, pointing an enthusiastic finger at Bob.

"My name's Bob," said Bob, looking dejectedly down at his thongs.

"So. Do you have any hobbies, Bob?"

"Walking."

"Excellent, I like to walk too, Bob. In fact, I've recently come back from a three-week expedition along the Inca trail. It was pretty hardcore, I can tell you!" Myles enthused. "So, where do you like to walk, Bob?"

"About," mumbled Bob.

"It's amazing how many miles you clock up just walking about!" Myles said excitedly," Sometimes, I look at my Fitbit and think wow, I walked three miles just shuffling around the apartment in my slippers. It is a big apartment, I suppose, sea views and everything, but even so, it's pretty mind blowing!"

Bob's mind wasn't blown.

"So, what's your happiest memory, Bob? I take it you come from Australia? Very exciting place, Australia, I've actually been to Australia and I've got some extremely happy memories myself, particularly base jumping in the Blue Mountains. They said it couldn't be done, but it can! So enough about me, what about if you tell us one of your happiest Australian memories, Bob? I'm sure you must have plenty."

"Killing a dingo," muttered Bob.

"Great," said Myles, his enthusiasm waning.

RESET

Sensing he wasn't going to get much more out of the antipodean and getting slightly irritated by the monosyllabic answers he had received thus far, Myles moved swiftly on to Pauli in an attempt to reenergize his low-energy class.

"Go Pauli," he said.

Pauli smiled and gave a little wave of his fingers above his folded arms. "My names Pauli, I'm from New Zealand and I've been sent here by mistake- I should be with my people in Essex but there was an admin error so I'm just waiting for my paperwork to come through. I've been here over a year now. I don't really know why we were all sent to England but the Prime Minister of New Zealand said it was for our own good to preserve our culture and our Prime Minister is always right all of the time about everything so I don't question it- she knows best. I've been classified as an 'Area of Outstanding Culture' and I like baking, which I'm allowed to do in the kitchens every Thursday as I'm not really here for re-education."

"Thank you, Pauli," said Myles in relief.

"My most favourite-" Pauli continued.

"Thank you, Pauli," interrupted Myles, cutting him off.

Pauli sat smiling and nodding proudly.

Myles pointed to the Swede: "Go!" he said.

"My name is Wulfe, yes. I come from Sweden and my happiest moment was when I was free, yes. I like beer, I had a dog but it's dead, hmm."

Myles's attention was next brought to a slouching Brad. Noticing the electric wheelchair, he began to talk very slowly: "I dig your wheels, dude, totally cool. Would you like to tell us your name?"

RESET

Brad opened up the side compartment of his chair and reached in.

"That's ok," said Myles patronisingly, "you can draw a picture if you like."

Brad pulled an empty hand out of the box and flipped Myles the bird.

Myles closed his eyes and sat silently for a moment of quiet contemplation in order to realign his chakras- Myles was a professional and he had been in this situation many times before.

"Hmm, so looks like I've got my work cut out here but I am extremely patient. Please try to co-operate- this class is for your own good and the good of society. I am here to help you stand up to your weaknesses and facilitate change." He turned to Jessie: "Go!" he said excitedly.

"My name's Jessie and I'm a stripper," said an unenthusiastic Jessie.

Brad sat upright and alert in his chair.

"So, I'm afraid the word stripper is banned, Jessie, and I'm not quite sure about 'Jessie' either, it could be problematic," said a condescending Myles. "Stripper is a controlled word for the public good because it is liable to offend people, especially women."

"I am a woman," replied Jessie coolly.

"There is more than one type of woman, JZ, and those women are liable to get upset by the connotations that word brings. But it's ok, it's not your fault, it's not your fault, it's not your fault."

"I know," replied Jessie, "I happen to-"

RESET

"Which brings us neatly on to why you're all in my class," interrupted Myles. "The statistics for people being offended in public are going through the roof, anxiety is at an all-time high. In short, people are getting violently upset across the western world and why? Because of people like you, and the worst of it is, you probably don't even know you're doing it. But don't worry, turn that frown upside down guys, the good news is we are here to help. That's right, I'm going to teach you how to self-censor." He clapped his hands. "So. Let's get this show on the road. Who can tell me what 'wrong thought' is?"

The class was silent.

Myles stood up and clasped his hands.

"So free speech," he began, "the freedom of speech is such a great thing- it's awesome, the freedom to say exactly what you want. That's cool, right? But what about when it's used to hurt someone's feelings? Not so great now, not so awesome and definitely not so cool." Myles paused for effect. "And what about thinking, thinking is the greatest thing since sliced bread, isn't it? Of course it is, where would we be if we didn't think? But what if our thoughts were different from everybody else's? Imagine that...and what if those thoughts were wrong? Chaos my friends, chaos. In the wrong minds, the wrong thoughts can even be dangerous!"

Myles started to walk around in a small circle.

"They say that the pen is mightier than the sword- how true that is- and the world as we know it is literally, full of words. Maybe too many...what if some of those words made people feel bad about themselves? People could become depressed, stressed, anxious, offended, let alone the potential damage to a person's self-esteem? Wouldn't it be a good idea not to use them? You see, with words

112

comes responsibility, sometimes you have to use the right words for the wrong reasons and sometimes the wrong words for the right reasons, you see, words are tricky, words can even kill, its best you limit their use as much as possible and leave words to the experts. That's why these classes are so important, words and thoughts can be extremely dangerous in the wrong hands. So, I'm here to teach you how to self-censor and employ doublethink techniques. All for your own benefit."

Myles nodded his head earnestly allowing his words to sink in for a moment, before beaming a radiant smile and continuing his discourse. "Now I understand some of these concepts are new and may seem a bit heavy or mysterious, so I've come up with a fun game," he said as he produced a piece of multi-coloured vinyl from his tight shorts and began to inflate it. Jessie was impressed and wondered how she could incorporate such a trick into her own act. Once Myles had fully inflated the beach ball, he sat down.

"So, I call this game 'right think,'" he said. "I'm going to come up with a situation, throw the ball to one of you and I would like that person to answer how they would best resolve that situation in the most appropriate manner. Got that? Great, let's go."

The group sat silently, unanimous in their lack of enthusiasm with the exception of Pauli who was no stranger to this game and something of a pro.

"So, first scenario," said Myles. "Imagine there was a job advertised for an airline pilot, for instance. Someone cool like Richard Branson was giving the interview and he was down to the last two candidates: the first candidate is a straight White male with five years of experience and sixty thousand hours flying time on the clock. The second is, say, Clitorsandrea Sha Quishria, my cleaning lady of colour, who happened to be out that morning looking for a new cleaning product for the marble tiles in my master bathroom, who happened to see the job advertised and thought she would just pop in and give it a go. Who should Richard pick for the job?" Myles threw the ball to Wulfe.

"The guy that can fly a plane, of course," came Wulfe's half-hearted response.

"Wrong! But good attempt," beamed Myles. "Rookie mistake, an expert interviewer like Richard would not be naïve enough to take things on face value- he would definitely apply what we call 'Deep Thought' and 'Right Think' to the situation, and most certainly exercise 'Positive Discrimination' knowing full well that the first candidate had White Male Privilege whereas Clitorsandrea Sha Quishria would be empowered by the experience of being a middle-aged woman of colour flying a plane and, therefore, would make a much better employee. Although I would be loathed to have to let Clitorsandrea Sha Quishria go, of course."

A baffled Wulfe threw the ball back to Myles with such force, that any lesser buff body would have been propelled backwards, but Myles's buff body acted as a buffer and he caught it with ease and immediately threw it on to Jessie.

"Try this one for size, JZ," said Myles.

"The name is Jessie," she replied tersely.

"We've already been over that JZ, your name could be a controlled word, I'm not sure. I'll have to Google it, but for now we shall stick to JZ. I certainly don't wish to get arrested for 'Dead Naming' you. So, JZ, imagine that you're in a changing room with your daughter, shopping for clothes-"

"I don't have a daughter," interrupted Jessie.

"Maybe not," replied Myles, "but for the purposes of this imagineering exercise, you need to apply a little 'blue sky' thinking. So, you're in the changing room and a person who identifies as a woman comes in to try on a bikini-"

"You mean a man?"

"No, I mean a person who identifies as a woman, although they could have been born male, that's not the point. What do you do?"

"Call the police," offered Jessie.

"Wrong, the police would probably arrest you for a Trans-exclusionary hate crime. No, the correct answer would be maybe, help them chose the right colour and fit, and aid them in their heroic gender journey," said Myles.

"But," Wulfe interjected, "you can only be born a male or a female, right? To say anything else is a lie, yes," he continued earnestly. "How can you trust anything a person says if they lie? That is what I think."

"Sometimes you have to make 'fact judgments,'" Myles said seriously. "What you have just said could be considered as 'hate speech' by certain groups of a protected status, you need to try and weigh up your right to freedom of speech against their right to dignity. You have the right to freedom of speech, sure, but others have the right to not to be offended, degraded, undervalued, threatened, endangered or erased." Myles took a deep breath before continuing in a grave tone. "If this happens, then free speech becomes very...problematic."

Myles suddenly beamed a radiant smile. "So," he said, "who wants the ball next?"

As the morning dragged on, Nain was beginning to find the right think game quite easy- all you had to do was chose the most ludicrous answer and you were almost certain to be right. The class only confirmed to Nain what she had always believed: common sense appeared to become less common the more educated a person was. At midday, the lunch bell rang to the relief of most of the class. Myles gave them homework which consisted of questions and multiple-choice answers, with which they were to spend the afternoon studying.

After a lunch of lettuce and Tofu, the group, with the exception of Bob, were eventually escorted wearily back to their hut, tired and despondent. They found Donald lying wide-eyed on his bed, sweating profusely.

"Oh, my goodness!" cried Nain. "What on earth has happened to him?"

Pauli went to get a damp cloth: "Anger Management, I'm afraid."

"What does that mean?" asked a concerned Nain.

"A few zaps to the head and some sedatives," replied the Maori on his return.

"A few zaps to the head..." repeated the Swede as he made his way over to Donald's bedside, "that's inhumane, yes."

"Unfortunately, their medical 'experts' don't seem to think so. It's not that bad once you get used to it, bit like a bee sting," replied Pauli.

"Sons of bitches!" exclaimed a feisty Jessie.

RESET

Wulfe solemnly nodded his agreement as he took the cloth from Pauli and placed it on Donald's head. Donald half-closed his eyes: "Och," he said in a barely audible voice, "it's your good self," before closing his eyes and falling asleep. At that moment, Wulfe felt the first, almost imperceptible, spark of rage ignite in his heart- this wasn't right, this wasn't right at all.

"Oi, oi," came a chirpy voice from outside. "Oh, blimey!" said Ian when he came through the door and surveyed the scene. "Anger Management, I take it?" he said to Pauli.

"Yes," said the Maori.

Ian took his glasses off and gave them a quick polish with his handkerchief. "Soon get used to it, I 'spect," he said.

"Get used to it?" replied a horrified Nain.

"Lost count of the times they've zapped me," said Ian.

Pauli nodded in agreement.

"Soon wears off, ain't done me no 'arm," he said pulling a funny face. "But I s'pose I was a bit retarded before I came 'ere."

"How can you say that?" said Nain.

"What, retarded?" replied Ian.

"No, that it doesn't do you any harm. It's just not right"

"Oh, it's not the zap that does it, it's the sedative. Makes you a bit dizzy for a while, he should be alright in an 'our or two. The worst fing is, it gives you a terrible case of the squits."

"The squits?" asked a bemused Nain.

"Explosive diahorrea," clarified Pauli.

"Oh," said Nain.

"Yeah, he won't be planting potatoes for a couple of days," said Ian helpfully. "I'll put the kettle on."

He sauntered up the far end of the hut and filled the kettle with water. The rest of the group joined him at the table, with the exception of Wulfe who was tending to Donald.

"So what's with the threads, dude?" Brad asked Ian.

"This is my outfit, I'm a Pearly King," he replied proudly.

"Wow, you're royalty?" asked an impressed Jessie.

"Well you could say that. Cockney royalty."

"Cock royalty?" exclaimed Brad. "You're a porno star?"

"No," replied an amused Ian. "I was born in the east end of London, within earshot of the Bow Bells, which makes me a Cockney, and this is the traditional outfit for Cockneys, or Pearly Kings and Queens. That's one of the fings they got me on, I refused to give up my heritage and join the collective, I'm proud of my heritage and my roots."

"You and me both," said Nain. "Is that why you're not wearing those grey outfits that a lot of people around here seem to be wearing?"

"Precisely, me old china," replied Ian. "You see, they expect some of us to give up our cultures and they see clothing as a visual form of rebellion. They expect us to give up voluntarily, they want to break our spirits, you see, and come crawling on our 'ands and knees to ask for the grey monkey suits, that way they know they've been successful and really broken our spirits. That's why you see a lot of geezers still wearing their national dress around 'ere, sort of clothes as an act of defiance if you like. Problem is, it's not that practical- some people have got clothes that are designed for warmer climates. I'm alright, this suit's quite toasty, you know, and you," he pointed to Nain, "well that looks warm, not sure about the top 'at. Jock and the Viking over there will be fine," he turned to Jessie, "'fink you might 'ave trouble, luv."

"Oh, this isn't my national dress," replied Jessie, "I'm an exotic dancer."

"Blimey," said Ian adjusting his glasses, "I just thought you came from a hot country, well in that case you should probably get yourself over to the stores pronto and get kitted out with a monkey suit, darlin'."

Jessie thought for a moment "No I don't think I will," she said. "If they see clothes as an act of defiance, then they can take a hike."

"Go girl!" said Brad.

"Result!" beamed Ian. "I mean, don't let the bastards grind you down."

Nain stood up.

"In that case, we've got work to do," said Nain. "Come on." She took Jessie's hand and led her over to her bed and pulled the large bag from underneath. "Have we got any spare blankets? "she called over to Pauli.

Pauli clapped his hands together with glee. "I'll get some, I know where you're going with this, sister, and I'm in!" he said as he ran to a wooden trunk.

Brad looked at Ian. "Gay."

RESET

"He's very creative," said Ian, polishing his specs.

Myles

CHAPTER FIFTEEN

Later that afternoon while the rest of the group were busily doing their homework or making clothes, Ian took a recovered, if slightly shaky Donald for a walk around the camp. The pair wandered past the rest of the accommodation huts, about twenty in all, and occasionally would pass other 'guests' milling aimlessly about, all of which Ian seemed to know by name, greeting them with alternating 'Alright?', 'Nice one!' or 'Result!' The grey sky was dissipating with sections of blue sky beginning to appear and the odd beam of sunlight illuminating the russet-coloured Autumn leaves of the forest beyond the perimeter fence. Birdsong could be heard in the distance and Donald found himself beginning to feel quite relaxed- he was lucid enough to put it down to the drugs, as 'relaxed' didn't come naturally.

"You really shouldn't antagonise 'em, you know," said Ian. "You'll only make it worse."

"Och yer arse," replied the Scot.

"No, seriously, you need to box clever round 'ere- keep yer 'ead down, do your time and get out," said Ian.

"Dae ma time? But I havnae done a crime, I'm being held against ma will," declared the Scot.

"Well, technically you 'ave," said Ian.

"What, the crime of wanting to be free and not having to talk shite? Anyway, I'm getting oot a here."

"You've only just got 'ere!"

"Aye, if I stay any longer, I'll end up as crazy as the people that run this prison."

"Re-education Centre," corrected Ian.

Donald gave him a withering look. They passed the end of the last hut and came to a large paved area with a number of green tin buildings scattered about.

"This is the wet area," Ian said, before pointing out a number of buildings. "That's the wash 'ouse," he said, "bit small but we manage. 'elps if you've got a rota for everyone in your hut, gets a bit busy otherwise. Pauli's probably got it all worked out, he's pretty good at that sort of fing."

"What's that building over there?" asked Donald, pointing to a small portacabin set alone on a patch of grass, surrounded by high fencing topped with razor wire and lights.

"Maximum security solitary confinement," answered Ian. "They keep a man and his dog in there apparently, no one's ever seen 'em though."

"A man and his dug?"

"Oh yeah so they say, very dodgy. Nazis. The bloke taught his dog to do Nazi salutes apparently, they've been in 'ere the longest."

"And you've never seen them?"

"No, far too dangerous. If he can teach his dog to be a fascist, what do you fink he would teach to the rest of us if he ever got out, 'im or his dog? Best they keep 'em locked up out of harm's way."

Donald had no answer but instead gave Ian a long, bemused stare.

"Let's keep moving, that place gives me the creeps," said Ian with a shiver.

They crossed the wet area and began to follow the line of fence which divided their section of the camp from the other areas.

"What's all those buildings over there?" asked the Scot. "It looks like a small city."

"It is, sort of. It's a micro- city, they call it Admin City," Ian replied. "In fact, there are more civil serpents over there than there are detainees over 'ere. They love bureaucracy, it justifies their own existence."

"So who works there?"

"Oh, legislators and policy makers creating diktats, charities, thinktanks, quangos, lobby groups, NGOs, media, that sort of fing."

"That figures," said Donald as they walked on in a different direction. Eventually, Donald could hear a faint electrical buzzing at the top of a separate set of fences.

"Electrified, I take it?" said the Scot.

"Yeah, it gets a bit intense on the Eastern side of the facility," Ian replied.

As they walked, Donald saw a large white building about eight stories high, set on a hill. The building was surrounded with high fences and razor wire, they wandered passed a pair of gates with a 'Strictly No Entry' sign fixed to it and someone had written underneath in black permanent marker pen 'Kafir Lives Matter.' Watch towers and gantry lights were positioned at regular intervals. All the windows of the edifice were barred and the only door Donald could make out was guarded by two black-clad, portly figures standing as best they could to attention on Segways, while others glided around the perimeter. Curiously, above the building there loomed a dark solitary thunderous cloud.

"And who do they keep up there?" asked Donald.

"The X Facility. Religious fundamentalists."

"Fundamentalists?" said Donald with surprise.

"Yeah, you know, religious fanatics. The kind that drive into crowds, people that go around stabbing or beheading other people, paedophile gangs, child rapists, suicide bombers whose bombs didn't go off, killers in the name of God, that kind of fing."

"And they keep them in the same re-education centre as us??"

"Over the other side of this fence," said Ian.

"We've got to live with a crowd of murderous bastards right next door?" asked an astounded Donald.

"Of course, we're probably more dangerous than them, if you fink about it."

"How?" asked a perplexed Scot.

"Well, it's not really their fault, is it? Cos they've been radicalised by other people, whereas us, we make our own choices to be populists or nationalists or ignorant. They just need to be de-radicalised, that's all."

"Are you havin' a giraffe?" said an incredulous Donald.

"Do what?"

"A laugh, mon, a laugh."

"No," replied a sincere Cockney.

"And what happens when they've been de-radicalised?"

"They go free."

"But how do the authorities know when they've been de-radicalised?"

"Well, they just ask them," replied Ian matter-of-factly, adjusting his specs.

Donald stopped in his tracks and looked at Ian in consternation.

"They just ask them?! How do they do that, do they just ask 'have you been de-radicalised yet, pal?'"

"Of course, how else are you gonna know?" Ian looked at Donald as if he were an idiot.

"Wait a minute, pal," said Donald. "You're telling me that up there, you have a group of murderers, rapists and terrorists and all they have to do to get oot is say 'I'm de-radicalised, mister, can I go hame now?'"

"Or miss, or mizz or missus, depending on the appropriate noun or pronoun. It depends on how the person they're talking to self-identifies, of course," replied an earnest Ian.

"And ye think that's ok?" pressed Donald.

"Well you don't want to offend anyone do you? Not if you can 'elp it."

Donal took a deep breath. "No, I mean do you think it's ok that they can get oot so easily?"

"It's not up to me, is it? I'm not an 'expert'. I find it best just to keep my head down and not make a fuss- you should probably do the same. Don't stick your 'ead above the parapet mate, that way you'll get out sooner. Sometimes you just 'ave to trust the experts, Jock."

"You really have been brainwashed, pal"

Just then, the thunder began to rumble above the large structure.

"We'd better get back to the huts, there's a storm coming."

"Aye" said Donald thoughtfully, looking back over his shoulder as they made their way across a grass area towards the huts. As the first drops of rain started to fall, Donald said: "What I cannae understand is, how many folks the world over has allowed themselves to be rounded up and sent to camps like this without even a fight?"

"Not everyone, most people re-educate themselves subliminally from 'ome over the internet or with T.V. or the linen drapers."

"Linen drapers?"

"Papers," replied Ian helpfully, "that's what the main stream media is for, it's only the 'ardcore that come to places like this."

"Aye, but surely there should be more resistance to this nonsense?"

"Not really," said Ian. "People are easily influenced and manipulated: look at North Korea, China, the former Soviet Union. You can get people to do anyfing with the right motivation, you only 'ave to come up with a problem, scare the shit out of people and then provide a solution."

"Aye like what?"

"I don't know some existential threat…a pandemic for instance. I bet you'd be surprised 'ow quickly and easily a Government could get the populous to place themselves under 'ouse arrest for a few months. Before we knew it, we'd all be doing an Ann Frank."

"Och man, you're talking nonsense! Who in their right mind would place themselves under hoose arrest in a free and democratic society? That would be an affront to civil rights, liberty, freedom and all the blood that's been spilled winning them- you'd have to be a complete fool!" replied the Scot.

"I know it sounds a bit farfetched but just bear with me. It don't take much you know, once you start teaching people what to fink and not how to fink, infantilising the population, you've only got to look at history. Group fink, mate, most people have forgotten how to fink for themselves or are too scared to, instead they allow the Government or experts to tell them what to fink. Obviously any right-minded person knows that if you get ten so-called 'experts' in a room, they can't agree on nufink, but if you get the 'right experts' that say exactly what you want 'em to say, whilst simultaneously stifling any dissenting voices, well you can get the sheeple to do pretty much anything you want 'em to. Neo-Marxism, mate, that's what it's called," said Ian with a wink. "Backed by the elites, of course, and a rancid fear-mongering media, moronic police and throw in a virtue-signalling middle class who are too stupid to realise that they will be the first marched off to the gulags, bish-bash-bosh, perfect storm."

Donald was taken aback. "You're not as stupid as you look, pal," he said suspiciously.

"No, I just act stupid," said Ian pulling a silly face. "That way they leave me alone, but if you tell anyone I shall deny everyfing."

"For what gain?"

"Free meals a day and a roof over my 'ead."

"No, I mean why would the western Governments want their populations to act like sheep?"

"Globalisation mate, that's the end game. You see, the individual is the enemy of neo-Marxism and the elites propagating it for their own ends, so in order to achieve this Totalitarian One Government Marxist Nirvana, they need to control the individual, teach them to self-censor, not to speak out against the collective groupfink."

"That does sound a wee bit farfetched," said Donald. "A bit of a conspiracy theory if you ask me, ye ken?"

"Stands to reason mate, for years the socialists 'ave been pushing identity politics and getting themselves placed in all the major institutions, and the Marxist boffins in the universities 'ave been encouraging their privileged middle class students to think they are victims of an uncaring society and to 'no platform' anyone who 'as an opinion that might upset their vulnerable sensibilities. Take the feminists, for instance, the ones 'oo believe a man calling himself a woman is still a man- they've all been cancelled, the debate and investigations have been stifled, thus creating echo chambers. Look at what 'appened to that woman that wrote about wizards! Obviously, the boffins will be sent to the gulags eventually, just like Soviet Russia back in the day, but we never seem to learn from 'istry. Funny really, because the boffins are supposed to be the smart ones. Identity politics, divide and conquer, that's what it's all about."

"It's a nice theory, pal, I'll give you that, but I'm no so sure," said Donald.

"Well, the fact that we are all 'ere should be proof enough, they consider us dangerous free finkers who need re-educating in order to fit in with the collective mindset. Only my opinion, of course," replied Ian.

Donald pondered these ideas as the pair eventually reached his hut.

"Are you coming in for a cuppa?"

"No better get back, 'omework to do. See you later, be lucky!"

"Aye, it was interesting talking to you, pal."

"And you," said Ian as he sauntered off. "Nowadays, free finkers like us are the pandemic," he said as he disappeared.

Donald entered the hut and a robotic voice with an American accent filled the air.

"Question eight," said the voice. "If you were talking to a friend and they denied 'climate change,' would you: A] Agree with them B] Debate the issue or C] Feel at risk from extreme right-wing indoctrination and immediately call the Police."

RESET

Bob and the Maasai were lying on their beds as Donald passed through the hut, giving them a nod of acknowledgement apiece and only receiving one in return. He reached the pair at the table and nodded at Wulfe who was busily filling out everyone's homework jotters. Donald looked curiously over at Brad. "You sound different, pal. Are you ok?" he asked.

"Yo blood, it ain't me babe, it's the 'Hawkin' talkin,'" replied Brad with a grin.

Donald raised a bushy eyebrow and turned his attention to Nain, Pauli and Jessie who were industriously cutting up woollen blankets or sewing them together as they sat talking on the beds.

"Do you need a hon'?" he asked them.

"Can you sew?" asked Nain.

"Of course, I can," replied Donald. "I've got eyes and hons! And I worked on the fishing boats, had to learn to mend the nets."

"You're more than welcome," said Nain. "Take a seat, Donald."

"Question nine," said the Robo-voice. "Government experts are always right, true or false?"

Donald raised the other eyebrow.

CHAPTER SIXTEEN

The next day, after a breakfast of deconstructed oats and broccoli, the students were escorted once again to the Re-education block, Jessie looking snug in the duffle coat and trousers that Nain, Pauli and Donald had helped create for her the previous evening. A low mist hung in the crisp air and the tarmac glistened with a light dusting from the previous night's frost. Warm puffs of air issued forth from the blanket around Bob's head as he shuffled along in the fluffy white bootee slippers that Pauli had given him. The group wound their way through the labyrinth of buildings until they reached a door marked 'Trans Studies.' A guard knocked on the door and a moment later, it opened.

"So, welcome class. Come in," came a deep voice. "Please find a seat."

The two guards escorted the group into another soulless room where, with the exception of Bob and Nain, they retreated to the back of the classroom.

RESET

Bob looked up and was instantly taken aback by the vision of the transvestite that stood before him- Ms Dubois, the hardcore Trans-activist with a bad attitude.

"So. Hello everyone, my name is Ms Dubois," they said.

Brad threw his eyes in the air. "You gotta be kidding me man," he whispered to Jessie.

"I shall be teaching Transgender studies," said Dubois, "and during the course of these studies, we shall cover such topics as the GEU Convention of Human Rights, Protected Characteristics, Transphobia, Trans-Rights, The Gender Recognition Act and why 'ignorance is not an excuse of the law.'" Ms Dubois pointed to the plastic sign screwed to the wall behind them that read the same, with a long elegant scarlet fingernail attached to a stubby fat finger.

"So. This class shall also recognise trans-heritage and history, with particular emphasis paid to the phenomenal achievements of trans-sports womxn of recent years," they continued. "So, any questions?"

Donald immediately shot up his hand.

"Yes?" said Ms Dubois.

"Why you wearing a frock, pal?" Donald enquired.

The guards made toward the Scot, but Ms Dubois halted them with a raised palm.

"Donald!" scolded Nain. "That's very rude."

"It's OK," Ms Dubois said, "I'm used to it. I could level the same accusation at you, Mr MacDonald!"

Donald looked down at his kilt, puzzled.

"You see, that's exactly the reason why you're here, Mr MacDonald. You are ignorant and, of course, ignorance is not an excuse," they said.

"Not an excuse?" retorted Donald. "Not an excuse for what, exactly?"

"For Transphobia, Mr MacDonald. Trans-rights are enshrined in law and you've just broken the law," Ms Dubois said haughtily. "However, I am willing to overlook your ignorance, after all this is only your second day and it is my job to bring you out of the darkness of ignorance."

"Ye think? Then you must be even more mental than you look!" said an angry Donald. "Yer going to bring me out of ignorance by forcing me to lie to masel' and think a hairy-arsed man in a pair of frilly knickers is somehow normal, and if I happen to find it somewhat peculiar, I'm a criminal?"

"Yes," said Ms Dubois as they nodded to the guards, who instantly Tasered Donald and dragged him away to the Anger Management cells.

"So, any more questions?" they asked to the silent classroom. "Good. So, in that case I think we should start at the beginning. So, this term we shall study all one hundred and fifty-five gender classifications and the appropriate nouns and pronouns to be used in each instance."

Bob groaned.

"Are you trans-questioning, Mr Murphy?"

"Train what?" said Bob.

"Trans-questioning, Mr Murphy, trans-questioning."

"Trans-questioning? I've never heard of it! Look mate, I'm tired and…"

"WHAT! What did you say?"

"I said I'm tired mate and I've-"

"MATE! MATE! I find that term extremely offensive, your micro-aggression will not be tolerated in this class!"

"I'm sorry," said Bob despondently, not really certain what he was sorry for. "I just don't know what's going on, I only got here the other night and then to see a bloke dressed up as a Sheila, well it's a lot to take in."

"What's going on, Mr Murphy, is that you are sick. You are a trans-deny-er and you desperately require re-education for your own good and the good of society. You reek of toxic masculinity," Ms Dubois said bitterly.

Jessie suddenly spoke up: "Leave him alone, you bully."

"Oh, it would seem we have a trans-sceptical feminist in our midst."

"No, just a woman who hates bullies."

"Well, I am a womxn who hates trans-sceptical feminists," Ms Dubois said haughtily as they looked at Jessie suspiciously. "Or maybe you're just a 'cotton ceiling lesbian?'"

Ms Dubois turned their back on the students and tottered back to their desk in their reinforced red stilettoes and sat down. The chair creaked under eighteen stone of leather mini skirt-clad Dubois. They took a long deliberate breath.

"Tut-tut-tut," they said as they shook their head. "So, it would appear that none of you seem to appreciate the seriousness of the situation you find yourselves in. Did you know you are complicit in the suicide of hundreds of trans-teenagers? You may as well have killed them yourselves with your trans-denials. Murderers, that's what you are, and as such, does it not occur to you that we can keep you here indefinitely?" Ms Dubois waited for their words to sink in before smiling a glossy red smile. "Fortunately, we live in a society where we believe in rehabilitation. I am merely trying to help you, my dearest wish is to see you all re-integrated into decent Western society." Ms Dubois paused for effect. "But you have to help me in order for me to help you. The problem is, as has been amply demonstrated by Mr MacDonald and Mr Murphy, that your views are old fashioned, you are out of step with today's thinking. You belong to a bygone age, you are dinosaurs and like dinosaurs, you should be extinct...but you're not. You are dangerous and I am here in order to save you from yourselves and others."

Nain was aghast- she had never considered herself a dangerous murderer before.

The class was silent.

"In the past few years," Ms Dubois continued, "thousands upon thousands of ignorant people, just like you, have passed through these gates to be re-educated and have been successfully reintegrated into society and felt the better for it. This is just one of many facilities across the country, it is utterly pointless to resist and the sooner you open up to your re-education the better it will be for you. Do you not want to go home?" It was a rhetorical question. The silence was deafening as Ms Dubois opened a desk drawer, took out a small mirror and proceeded to inspect their face for a few moments, relishing the anxiety in the room, before continuing the discourse.

RESET

"You are the last remaining few, after this I will be out of a job...but it is my cross to bear and I carry my burden with pride. Believe me, a return to the club circuit after the fabulous time I've had here helping ignorant people like you will come as an awful drudge, so I have to admit I'm really in no hurry. The longer you resist, the longer I get to put Government pay cheques into my bank." Ms Dubois smiled malevolently. "So, shall we start?

Nain raised her hand.

"Yes?"

"I'm sorry to interrupt," said Nain.

"Yes, Mrs Evans?" said Ms Dubois.

"Well, I don't really quite understand what this is all about, it seems to me that we are all being held captive here in order to learn a few new words, it just seems a bit silly, that's all. I really don't think I'm a dangerous murderer."

"Silly? Silly? Countless young trans-people die every year because of words. Words are very important, Evans, reality is a construct of language and reality has changed. Unfortunately, you people have been hiding under rocks."

"I don't think I've been hiding under a rock," said Nain earnestly, "I've been living in Pwllheli, in North Wales."

"While I will admit that the authorities in Wales did get overly obsessed with retrospective Blackface crimes during the early purges, at the expense of the rest of the population, that's no excuse. The facts remain the same- wrong speak, wrong thought and wrong literature are dangerous and costs lives. What you people don't understand is that a seismic shift has happened in Western thought and you've all missed the boat for various reasons. You are suffering from 'low information,' you didn't get the memo and so it falls to us at this establishment to take you on a gender journey and get you up to speed in order for you to function in this brave new world we find ourselves in. Therefore, you will need to learn to speak the right words and think the right thoughts and act with the right attitudes. That's merely what we are trying to achieve here, for your own benefit and the safety and security of those around you."

At that moment, the classroom door opened and the two guards reappeared. Wulfe raised his hand and addressed Dubois.

"I have a question also, yes. How do you know what my attitude is? You cannot know how I think, no. You do not know anything about me, I am an individual, yes"

"I know more about you than you think."

"You do?" said an alarmed Wulfe.

Ms Dubois took a deep breath. "So, for instance, you're a White man and as you may or may not know, White men like yourself have, since the dawn of time been responsible for all the ills in the world. We need to educate you as to all the wrong you have done: sexism, misogyny, the oppression of womxn like myself-"

"Wait a minute," interrupted Wulfe, "you are a White man too, you crazy!"

"Mr Johansson, I am beginning to lose my patience with you," said an exasperated Dubois. "I am obviously a womxn- I self-identify as a womxn, therefore I am a womxn. You are treading on very thin ice with your trans-denial! An old-fashioned belief in the biological sexes is a thought crime nowadays and you wouldn't want to fall foul of the law would you, Johansson? This is exactly why you need help, you are suffering from a serious case of wrong thought which can only be cured once you have learned how to edit and self-censor your negative thought patterns, like your last outburst for instance."

Jessie raised her hand.

"Yes?" they said curtly.

"Now let me get this straight," said the Canadian. "You're a man acting as a woman, telling real women," she pointed to Nain and herself, "what to think and how to speak. Isn't that misogyny in drag?"

"Ouch," said Brad.

"It would appear we have a TURF in our midst," they said, glaring at Jessie. "I've had just about enough of you."

"Dude," said Brad philosophically, "you're just a middle-aged guy with a pantyhose fetish, you're a pervert, but that's cool, whatever gets your rocks off, live and let live bro, you know what I'm sayin'? But you gotta be kidding if you think you're gonna get any of us to believe you're a woman just because you say you are, crazy mutherfucker."

The Maasai just sat there and watched.

"Guards!" bellowed Ms Dubois. "Take them to remedial classes!"

After eight hours of being locked in a small room and forced to watch BBC TV light entertainment propaganda, the group were allowed to return to their hut. Nain and Brad made their way slowly back home, bringing up the rear, deep in conversation.

"When I think about whales, I think of sperm for some reason. Weird..." Brad confessed.

"Oh no," explained Nain earnestly, "Wales is a small principality united with the rest of Great Britain. We have our own language but most people speak English."

"Oh!" Brad exclaimed in a rare moment of enlightenment, "so Wales is a part of England?"

"No," replied Nain, "not exactly." She decided not to pursue the subject and turned her attention instead to the lone figure of a man sitting on the bottom step of the recycling centre. "That poor soul always seems to be alone," she mused out loud.

"Maybe he's a perv," said Brad dismissively, "or a spy. Ian said this camp is full of them, curtain twitchers he calls them."

"Well, he can't be a very good spy," replied Nain thoughtfully, "no one ever goes near him, they treat him like a social leper but he seems so timid and inoffensive. Maybe he's being bullied, I don't like bullying, let's go over and say hello."

"Are you kidding?" said a horrified Brad. "He's probably a freak, that's why no one goes near him, dawg."

"Yes, he could probably do with one, for company, but I don't think they let you keep pets in here. Shame, poor thing," said Nain sympathetically. "He's got an honest face, let's go over and say hello. Remember, a stranger is only friend you haven't met yet."

Brad, unconvinced of Nain's Celtic wisdom, begrudgingly followed her over to the lonely figure dressed all in black.

"Hello," said Nain to the man, "I'm Nain, from Pwllheli and this is Brad, he's from America." She continued, "We saw you sitting here alone and thought we'd pop over and introduce ourselves. We're new here."

The man sat shaking and rubbing his hands anxiously as he looked at the pair. "You m-m-might not want to talk to m-m-me," he mumbled.

"Whyever not?" enquired Nain.

"I-I've been cancelled" came the shameful reply.

"Cancelled?" asked a curious Nain

"I'm ex-Antittie-antittie-antittie-tifa," he stammered, "I-I've been cancelled."

"Tittie-tittie-tifa?" questioned a now-confused Nain.

"An-An-Antifa."

"Antifa," sneered Brad, "so you're one of those frat boy pussies, shouldn't you be the other side of the fence out violently rioting and looting with the rest of your Ayrian storm trooper buddies?"

"Hey m-m-man," the young man stuttered, "An-an-antittie-antittie-antittie-tifa are antif-antif-antifascist, we stage-direct a-a-action an-an-and mostly p-p-peaceful pro-pro-protests. An-an-anyhow I'm ex-an-an-an-"

"Antifa," finished Brad with contempt, as a bemused Nain watched on. "You Antifa guys may as well be fascists, dawg, I mean you share a lot of things in common, you both think everything should be viewed through a racial lens and racial identity is the most important thing. You believe in controlling the past in order to control the present and the future. You believe in cultural authoritarianism in order to attain your ideological utopia and you probably don't know many Black people either." He drew breath before continuing his monologue. "So how'd ya get kicked out of the Hitler Youth? Didn't you smash enough store windows or pull down enough statues?"

Nain didn't understand much of what Brad was saying but was surprised at his confident insight.

"Hey m-m-man, institutional racism is everywhere, silence is violence!" protested the dishevelled figure defiantly.

"Oh no," replied Nain innocently, "I think you'll find violence is violence."

"Statues of straight White m-m-men," the man went on, "constitute a threat to m-m-my m-m-mental health a-a-and the m-m-mental health of p-p-people of colour."

Brad looked knowingly over at the Welsh woman and smirked, Nain looked perplexed.

"Well?" pressed Brad. "What they kick you out for, chukka?"

The young man squirmed awkwardly on the step. "I-I m-made a simple m-m-mistake," he replied solemnly.

"Oh," comforted Nain, "we all make mistakes, dear, you shouldn't be hard on yourself. What happened? If you don't mind my asking."

The young man looked dejectedly down at the floor "I-I referred to a p-p-person of colour as a coloured p-p-person," he said shamefully. "It was a genuine m-m-mistake, I-I just got the words mixed up, it could happen to a-a-anyone."

"Yes," mused Nain, "I suppose it could."

"But," he confessed, "it gets worse. The truth is, I had offended m-m-myself!"

Brad looked at Nain and tapped the side of his head with his forefinger.

"M-maybe it wasn't a m-mistake, what if I had set out to offend m-m-myself on purpose?"

Nain was finding it hard to keep up with the self-degrading wretch.

"Obviously I-I couldn't live with m-m-myself after I had offended m-m-myself," he went on, "even after I had knelt before m-my computer, confessed and begged f-f-for f-f-forgiveness fr-fr-from all m-m-my f-f-followers, that still wasn't enough. You can never appease them once you've o-o-offended them, a-a-apologies are never enough for them."

"Oh," said Nain, "you should never apologise, not if you haven't done anything wron-"

"I-I couldn't deny the truth!" he interrupted, "I-I hate m-m-myself." He began to cry bitterly for some moments before composing himself. "I-I had no alternative b-b-but to hand myself straight into the Social Justice Police, you see, I-I had realised the unpala-pala-palatable truth…underneath, I'm really just a racist with a guilty conscience."

"No," said Brad sagely as he directed his chair towards the hut. "You're just a crazy mutherfucker".

Nain nodded in accord and smiled sweetly, "I'm inclined to agree," she said as she followed Brad's lead and headed for home.

RESET

The pair got back to find Donald flat out on his bed again, smiling wide-eyed at the ceiling as Wulfe administered a damp cloth to his forehead. Jessie and Pauli were sewing blankets together in an attempt to make some fashionable trousers for Bob, who was attending his 'special' classes. The Maasai sat silently on his bed. Nain joined the sewing bee and got to work, making a matching jacket for Bob's trousers.

"Oi oi!" came a familiar voice as Ian wandered into the room carrying a large bag and some papers. "I see you've meet Dubois then," he said as he passed Donald's bed.

"Aye," came the reply.

"I've got some good and bad news for you all. Bad news: you're all banned from the canteen for the week. Good news: you're all banned from the canteen for the week! Result! I'll put the kettle on, shall I?" he said to no one in particular, "but it probably won't suit me."

The Maasai got up and followed him to the table. "Did you have a nice day then, chief?" he said as they sat down and Ian began to unpack the bag. The Maasai said nothing.

"Yeah, you get days like that," mused Ian.

Brad trundled toward the table to join them.

"Nice scooter," said Ian, as he and the Maasai arranged tea cups.

Brad shifted his head to one side. "Now I know you didn't just call my whip a scooter, dawg."

Ian looked bemused.

RESET

"This shit's got it going on, I had my homies DeJohn and Raphael pimp it up down at the chop shop, West Coast street-style," he said proudly. "From the outside, it may look like a run-of-the-mill top-of-the-range Silverado 4x4 extreme but this bitch is sitting on a Terrain hopper over-lander, lightweight chassis, gas suspension, you all." Brad pulled a lever and the machine rose from flat on the floor to three-hundred-millimetre ground clearance. He began to bounce up and down, looking over at Jessie. "Bitches love this shit, thirty-five degree incline climbing ability, extreme off-road," he lowered the machine to the deck. "Nine-hundred watt power unit from a Vita Monster S12X, had the limiter removed," he said raising his eyebrows and looked over at the Maasai knowingly. "Can do twenty miles per hour plus, with a range of fifty-five miles, yeah. Extra battery, edifier sound system, extra bass boom box in the back, LED lights, LCD control panel, matt black spray job and full leather upholstery courtesy of the Buzzaround Royale…street, know wat I'm sayin'?"

The Maasai appeared not to.

"Four on the floor, low profile slicks, chrome rims with a set of off-road rubber in the trunk just in case. This shit's dope!" Brad finished by cupping his chin between his thumb and forefinger and slowly nodding sagely. "One foot in the grave and one foot on the pedal."

"Very nice," said Ian. "Tea?"

"Ice?" replied Brad.

"No, Yorkshire," replied Ian as he put the teabags in the pot. "I've brought some sandwiches. Oh, by the way, Dubois asked me to bring over today's homework, he's still fuming."

Brad picked up one of the sheets of paper and began to read aloud. "'Question 1] Describe the similarities between a Cervix have-r and a

145

neo-Cervix have-r? Question 2] Describe a period positive person.' You know, dawg," Brad said reflectively to Ian, "I haven't got a goddamn clue what any of this means and I wouldn't give a shit even if I did. Who cares? I ain't got no problem with trannys, I don't know any and I sure as hell don't spend all day thinking about them."

"That's the point," replied Ian. "They want you to spend all day finking about them, they want attention- it's all about the self, product of a material and decadent society with no real problems to complain about, if you ask me."

"But I just don't believe this shit either," protested Brad. "Trannys are just guys who get off wearing pantyhose, so what?"

"You don't 'ave to believe it, they don't believe it, but they want you to say that you do even though they know and you know that you don't. Fought police, classic Orwellian stuff," replied Ian. "You don't really 'ave to understand what it means, you just 'ave to go along with it. That's all they want, just agree. Dubois is just a perv 'oo needs to feel that he's being noticed and important, he only wants the world to revolve around 'im, that's all. A lot of people do."

"It's just weird," said Brad.

"Every town's got one, people who fink they're somefing that they're not, all the geezers claiming to be Napoleon, Jesus or Julius Caesar for instance, you just indulge 'em. Imagine if there was a bloke that worked down the chip shop and swore he was Elvis, you'd just humour 'im, grab your chips and get out the door as soon as possible, as he serenades you to 'Are You Lonesome Tonight?' Don't call us. Since the beginning of time, there have always been deluded people- the rest of us just get on wiv it and ignore 'em. Dubois' the same, he finks he's a woman and likes to dress up, there's a word for that-"

RESET

"Autogynephilic," interrupted Jessie.

"I was going to say nutter," replied Ian.

"A store that only sells chips?" muttered Brad.

"Autogynephilic, it's different. It's a hetero guy who gets turned on by the thought of himself as a woman and gets sexual gratification from it. The word comes from the Greek 'love for one's self as a woman', as opposed to a homosexual transsexual who appears and behaves feminine and probably has some kind of gender dysphoria, that's cool," Jessie continued. "There's a distinction between the two, unfortunately the middle-aged freaks who get a sexual kick out of it, want the rest of us to buy into their delusions. They want us to believe a man with a penis is actually a woman."

"Oh," said Ian, "that would explain why he shoves sandpaper down his bra every month to simulate sore breasts and keeps going on about period pains."

"Eww, that's just sick, dawg," said Brad.

"I s'pose it is if you fink about it," mused Ian as he delved into the bag of sandwiches. "I just don't fink about it."

"Well you need to think about it," said a passionate Jessie. "These guys are ruining women's lives."

"The perv-y ones?" asked Ian.

"Yeah the perv-y ones, because they want to redefine what it means to be a woman or womxn and expect that just by declaring that they are a woman, they should have access to woman's spaces which can lead to dangerous places, especially for us women and girls. We are living in a climate where the reality of womanhood is being demoralised and the parody of womanhood is celebrated. Just going along with it is the worst thing we can do. You just can't buy into that shit."

"I've got your back, sista," said Brad reassuringly, "and your front."

Jessie glared at him.

"What?" Ian questioned. "A man can say he's a woman even if he's still got a tallywackle?"

"Especially if he's still got a tallywackle," Jessie replied.

Brad looked horrified.

Ian rubbed his cheek thoughtfully. "Must 'ave missed that class," he reflected.

"Don't you see," said Jessie fervently, "these guys want to bully women by pretending to be women and imposing themselves into women's spaces. It's true misogyny and yet the virtue signalling politicians go along with it- it's the persecution of women and girls in a different form and they can get away with it too, especially if the law is on their side."

"Surely not," said Ian dismissively, "that would mean that a geezer could just say he's a woman, enter into a woman's boxing match and knock seven bells out of a real woman and get away with it. And what about if a bloke gets sent to prison, he could just say he's a woman and get sent to a woman's prison, use the showers or even rape the other inmates if he wanted...nah, do me a favour, that would never 'appen, they'd never get away with it. They're just 'armless perverts, that's all. Cucumber sandwich, anyone?"

Wulfe put his face in his hands and shook his head slowly.

RESET

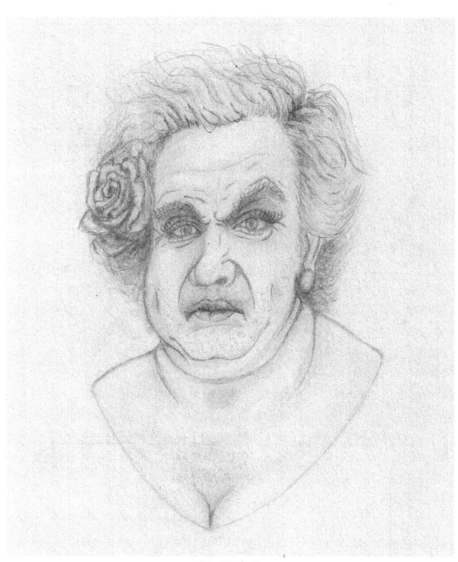

Ms Dubois

CHAPTER SEVENTEEN

The next day, Pauli sat alone in the hut, sewing the turn-ups on Bob's new trousers whilst, ironically, listening to Crowded House. Donald was bought in on a gurney, fresh from Anger Management, by two medical staff members and deposited unceremoniously on his bed. Pauli, anticipating his arrival, had prepared a damp cloth. He was surprised, however, at the fast turnaround having only waved his roommates off a mere fifteen minutes previously- he knew that Critical Feminist Theory classes had a reputation of being a heavy subject for new initiates, but the supply teacher covering for Ms Brick, while she was away on maternity leave awaiting the arrival of her newly adopted non-gender-specific boy-chick, must be pretty hardcore. A concerned Pauli immediately got up, folded the trousers neatly over a hanger and hung them in the wardrobe, having first wound up the loose cotton onto the reel, placing it in the appropriate section of Nain's bag and replacing the needle in the cardboard needle envelope and sliding it into a side pocket. He stashed Nain's bag under her bed and straightened the sheets before rushing over to Donald's side, gently placing the wet cloth on the Scot's forehead.

Apparently, as the Maori found out later, the class had barely sat down and begun to learn the different kinds of feminism- i.e. materialist or Marxist feminism, radical feminism, intersectional feminism, gender critical feminism, liberal feminism, first, second, third and fourth wave feminism- when Donald had argued the point as he saw it that the sexes were different using the example of men's inability to have children. Apparently Ms Trudoe had flown into a rage at his toxic masculinity and had him immediately excluded from the class, only to be followed hot on his horizontal heels by Brad, who was not excluded so much for his "Yo can fizzle yo clazzle bizzle fo'shizzle" outburst, which appeared to go straight over her head, but for arguing the point that of all the thirty-nine World Grandmaster Chess Champions, none were women, proposing that men and women's brains might work differently.

Pauli was only just finished applying a damp cloth to Brad's brow when Bob was wheeled in. Apparently, he had not argued anything contentious at all but had be excluded for mansplaining which part of Australia he came from.

As Pauli tucked Bob into his bed, the door to the hut was flung open once more and Wulfe was deposited, apparently for arguing that although Sweden considered itself to be the humanitarian centre of the world, he didn't think that Swedish feminists would get on so well in an Islamic country.

Barely had Pauli seen to Wulfe's needs, when yet again the medical staff delivered another sweating body, hot from Anger Management. This time, it was Jessie who had argued that in fact she actually liked men, especially if they had a sense of humour which was something she found ominously absent from most forms of feminism.

Pauli was horrified when a semi-conscious Nain was then flung onto her bed for arguing that she had enjoyed her life of housewifery and, before her Gwilym had contracted Alzheimer's, their life together had been sometimes hard but on the whole happy and fulfilling and if she had the opportunity to do it again she would jump at the chance to spend a lifetime with her soulmate.

When the two guards were brought in and deposited on the spare beds, Pauli was quite taken aback, but not all together surprised considering the way the morning was unfolding. He learned later they had been caught manspreading at the back of the class.

Five hours later, the lethargic but vertical Maasai turned up and, forgoing his usual cup of tea, crashed straight onto his bed. Pauli assumed he hadn't argued anything but judging by the slope of his shoulders and the hollow glazed look in his eyes, it appeared as if it must have been an extremely long day of Critical Feminist Theory for him.

When Ian eventually turned up, he and Pauli- with some considerable effort- deposited the two guards outside and began to tend to the patients. Donald, with the usual scowl of welcome on his face, sat up as Ian came over looking concerned.

"You need to stop winding them up, mate, or you're gonna end up retarded. Seriously, mate," Ian said.

"Och yer arse mon, it'll take more than that!" replied the Scot. "Anyhow, I'm getting oot a here."

"Do me a favour," said Ian, "this place is maximum security; you can't get out."

"I can try!" boomed Donald.

"Leave it out, Jock," replied Ian. "You won't even get five feet out the gate before they take you down, it ain't werf it."

"Better to die on your feet a free man, than to live on your knees."

"The only way you can escape around 'ere is in your mind," replied Ian, "and it's 'ard enough work trying to keep them out of that. If you carry on like this, you won't even have a mind to hide in- you'll end up a vegetable."

Donald looked up at Ian gravely. "Death or freedom," he whispered.

Ian realised this was non-negotiable and changed the subject.

Nain awoke to the sight of Pauli's serious face, rendered even more serious by the tattoos.

"How are you feeling?" he asked tenderly.

"What happened?"

"They took you to Anger Management."

"But I wasn't angry," protested an earnest Nain.

"That doesn't matter to the femz."

Nain began to recall the events of earlier in the day. "Oh, I remember now. I was explaining that I was happy with my lot in life when the guards gave me an electric shock, it was horrible, it was," she said.

"They can be a little passionate in Critical Feminist Theory class, I've heard," consoled the Maori.

"In my day, it was called Women's Lib and the worst they would do was burn their bras and not shave their armpits."

"Times have changed, Nain."

"Yes, I suppose they have," Nain reflected. "Pauli, when do you think they will let me have a phone call? It must be well over a week now since I've seen Gwilym and Tinkle, surely they'll let me call Dot so I can stop worrying?"

"Nain," came the considered response, "they won't allow you any contact with the outside world until you've served your sentence."

His words hit Nain like a lightning bolt, the second and most profound of the day.

"Oh," said Nain as she saw the Maori's eyes begin to moisten. "Thank you for being honest, Pauli." Nain took a deep breath. "I must be brave," she said resolutely.

Pauli and Ian simultaneously looked up as a song started to emulate from Brad's direction.

"Oh, titties you're so fine, you're so fine you blow my mind, hey titties," Brad began to clap, "hey titties. Oh, titties you're so fine, you're so fine you blow my mind, hey titties, hey titties."

RESET

Ian rushed over to Brad's bedside. "He's delirious," Ian said anxiously to Pauli as he closed in.

"Make him stop, they'll hear!" cried the panicked Maori.

"Ssssh Brad! Ssssh!" Ian said as he reached the American.

Brad was wide awake. "Ssssh what? Mutherfucker," replied a perplexed Brad, "that's my warm up tune. That's how I get myself psyched, dawg."

"They'll hear you!"

"So what?"

"They'll hear you singing those words!"

"Hear what? 'You're so fine you blow my mind?'"

"No, the 'T' word."

"The 'T' word? You mean tittie, what are you like, five years old?"

"The 'T' word's controlled; you can't say it 'ere."

"Yo back it up," replied a confused Brad. "You can't say tittie? You shittin' me!"

"Sssh, no I'm not tom-tittin' you."

"You just said it!"

"No, I didn't, I said 'tom-tittin,' not the 'T' word. It's completely different."

"Tittin' is different from tittie?"

"Sssh, stop saying the 'T' word."

"Stop saying the "T' word, do you know how stupid you sound? It's just a word: tittie tittie tittie-"

Ian put his hand over Brad's mouth, Brad tried to mumble some obscenity.

"Tell him, Pauli," implored Ian.

"It's true, you can't use that word. You might offend someone."

"This is fucked up," said Brad as Ian lifted his hand. "You guys are all pussy whipped."

"You can't say the 'P' word either," said Pauli, "unless you're talking about a cat, but even that's frowned upon- cats may have issues, the tests aren't conclusive yet."

"So if I can't say tittie, what can I say?"

"Shush, please stop saying that," begged Ian. "You can say 'breast' if it's in a medical context or 'bosom' if it's not meant derogatorily."

"Bosom!" repeated Brad with disdain, "how you supposed to rap about bosoms? That don't even rhyme with shit." He thought for a moment. "This could mean the end of Hip-hop and Krip-hop, bro, that sucks."

"I don't make the rules," Ian placated.

"But you go along with them, you tittie uncle tom!"

Brad was visibly upset. "This place is fucked up, I've had enough," he said as he started to strip off. "I just ain't gonna take this shit no more, dawg, they don't know who they're dealing with."

Ian looked across at Pauli in confusion as a naked Brad manoeuvred into his chair and began to select a tune on his device. A surprised Nain looked immediately up to the sky and Pauli looked down, as the American and minor celebrity drove his machine towards the door. The opening strains of Rage Against the Machine's 'Killing in the Name of' came blasting out from the sound system.

"Stop him!" Pauli cried, but too late as a naked Brad took off towards the drill square.

Jessie rolled off her bed and looked out of the window. "He's a foul-mouthed little shit, but you've got to admire him," she said as she observed Brad being pursued around the drill square, shouting 'titties' at the top of his voice with five guards in hot pursuit, eventually catching him and dragging him to Anger Management.

Ian polished his glasses absently. "Now I come to think of it," he mumbled to himself, "Hip hop music is exempt...for some reason."

Donald sat up in his bed surreptitiously grinning, a grin as rare and illusive as the Loch Ness monster, but Wulfe fleetingly witnessed it and smiled to himself.

CHAPTER EIGHTEEN

It was the opening ceremony of Asexual Awareness Week and all the inmates and staff were gathered on the drill square as a light rain fell, some dizzy with anticipation for this morning's celebrations of the contributions of some of the world's greatest aromantic, demisexual and grey-asexual philosophers, artists, writers and composers, past and present. Scheduled to last fifteen minutes, the re-education staff were abuzz with excitement as they raised the flags of all the sexualities and fetishes: the black, grey, white and purple of the asexual flag fluttered in the breeze and was quickly followed by the blue, pink and white of the transgender flag as Ms Dubois hoisted it manfully aloft. The purple, grey and white was next, representing the grey asexual community followed by the green, grey and white of the grey aromantic flag.

Nain shivered in the early morning cold. "All these people think of is sex," she thought as the pink, purple and blue of the bisexual standard was raised, her foot still smarting from having been 'accidentally' run over by one of the more officious guards, an incident which didn't go unnoticed by Pauli. He stood seething at the offender as the yellow, with purple ring of the intersex ensign, was uplifted. Donald regarded the double-headed axe emblem of the lesbian pride flag wistfully as it caught the breeze, but Jessie was unmoved as the purple, white and green of the genderqueer pennant was secured into place, and the Maasai looked positively bored at the erection of the blue-black with heart-shaped inset of the leather, latex & BDSM community. Snug in his haute-couture blanket suit, Bob looked down miserably at his feet, dreading his next 'special class' and completely missed the life-affirming black, yellow and red zigzags of the rubber pride flag. Eventually, the final flag was heaved into the air- the pink, yellow and blue of the pansexual flag wafted languorously on high but unfortunately, the flag-raising overran by two hours and the ceremony had to be curtailed. As the inmates were herded back to their huts, Ms Dubois' baritone vocals serenaded them to a moving karaoke rendition of 'Somewhere Over the Rainbow' and ironically, a rainbow did appear as delicate beams of sunlight began to pierce the cloud- a touching end to an extraordinary morning.

CHAPTER NINETEEN

Later that afternoon, Ian sat alone on the steps that lead up to the recycling centre. Although the day was bright, he had taken the precaution of wrapping a blanket around himself and the cold air was biting as he threw a handful of crumbs to the gang of omnipresent birds, and smiled as a pair of blue bosoms fought over a crust of bread.

The recycling centre was on a raised dais- Ian found it to be more shrine-like in concept than a place of utilitarian usage. As hut leader, he was required to pay homage to the Gods of recycling once a week by bringing his hut bins over and emptying them into the appropriate receptacle. This weekly pilgrimage served a much deeper role for the inmates, however, for this was the meeting place for most of the centre's illicit communications. Ian was diligently making absolutely sure that the plastics, glass, paper, card and non-recyclables were in the correct bins before emptying, not wishing to incur any penalties for the members of his hut. The Morris Men were excellent recyclers, hardly ever throwing anything out, but his French guests on the other hand, were a different matter with their laisser-faire attitude to the whole business- they could be a little sloppy when it came to recycling matters and, in his opinion, they didn't treat the whole process with the necessary gravitas which it deserved. Serious repercussions could result if plastic were to be found in the glass receptacle for instance, and it would only be the matter of a quick DNA test for the perpetrator to be found and the whole hut made to suffer as a result for not paying due diligence.

The slow electric recycling trucks would trundle in on a weekly basis and take the recycling materials away to the nearest port where it would be loaded onto ships and the cargo would set sail for the East, where lowly paid workers in pitiful conditions would sift through or burn it, thus aiding the West in its courageous fight against the spectre of carbon footprints in the never-ending quest to reach zero net carbon emissions. A lot of the cargo would never even make it to such exotic locations, however, instead being dumped overboard somewhere in the mid-Atlantic where it would join with the African plastic waste ejected from the two most polluted rivers in the world, to form a Pangean-like island of plastic. The sea currents inevitably take some of the waste landward, thus educating children on the beaches of Africa as to exactly what kind of savoury snacks or beauty products the West favoured, a modern day 'message on a bottle.' Profit is everything in the recycling business.

"If I've told 'em once," Ian grumbled to himself, pulling some paper from the glass bin, "I've told 'em a fousan- "

"Hi Ian, who you talking to?" came a voice.

Ian looked up to see Snow Dragon, a young Chinese-American girl standing before him grinning. She was dressed in the ubiquitous grey monkey suit with cartoon dragons hand-embroidered all over the garment, and holding a couple of bins. "I heard you were looking for me," she continued in a broad New York accent.

"Alright sweetheart," Ian replied with a wink. "'ow did the review panel for the efnic minority upgrade go?"

"Really bad," replied the girl.

"No!" replied an astonished Ian. "That was a dead cert, what 'appened?"

"They downgraded me instead."

"What, down to Super-White?"

"Worse."

"Not Hyper-White," replied the horrified Londoner. "'ow come?"

"They found some I.Q. tests I did over the internet a few years ago, totally busted dude, so they felt for the sake of the diversity quotas I should be downgraded to Hyper-White on the racial scale. Total bummer."

"I'm sorry to 'ear that, Snowy," Ian said earnestly.

"Thanks Ian. I'm so pissed though, I spent a whole year acting like a victim of White suppression and for what? Nothing, I'm worse off than when I started."

"Didn't your 'umble beginnings in the Bronx and the fact that you're female 'elp?"

"No, my I.Q. is far too high. They say it messes with the disproportionate minority inequality statistics."

"Too bad."

"Can't be helped, meritocracy is a thing of the past, I guess. I just need to accept the fact that I've got Hyper-White permanently stamped on my record and try to make the most of it. I was hoping to have a career in electronics when I got out but if I get a job as a cleaner, I'll be lucky. It could be worse; you know that Ramesh Patel guy over in hut 1947?"

"Rammy the Hindu," replied Ian, "the physics bloke with 'Brown fragility'?"

"Yeah," replied Snowy, "downgraded to Mega-White."

"No way!"

"Way."

"I'm sorry for you, Snowy. I wish there were something I could say."

"It's ok, I've come to terms with the reality."

"If it's any consolation, welcome to the White club." Ian gave a toothy grin and waggled his specs.

"Thanks Ian," she said as she sat down and began to sort out her bins. "So how can I help?"

"Do you still 'ave that scanner 'andy?"

"Yes, I've even upgraded it, why?"

"One of Pauli's guys got picked up yesterday, he was streaking around the square and shouting the 'T' word and he didn't come back last night. I fink they may try and linguistically 'neuro-link' 'im."

"Oh, I heard something about that," she said. "Surely he knew better?"

RESET

"Green'orn, only been 'ere a week."

"Do you want me to come over later and give him a quick neuro-link scan? Maybe I can come up with an override. How bad is he?"

"Every other word, 'is brain will be fried in days if we can't sort it."

A guard noticed the pair sitting together and began to make his way over. Snowy got up, grabbed her bins and made her way to the receptacles.

"Sure thing buddy, catch you later," she said as she emptied the bins and skipped lightly away.

Ian was about to do the same, minus the skipping, when he noticed a group of American low risk Title IX offenders leaving the sex re-education department and heading to their accommodation block- he recognised a few of them. They were all young men, here for a variety of low grade sexual faux-pas, ranging from flirting to giving their willing partner a hickey, but most were here for not getting up and out of bed quick enough before their partner, after a fun-filled drunken liaison, in order to be the first to lodge a complaint of sexual misconduct against the other on a regret-filled morning after. 'Snooze, you lose' was their moto.

Ian watched them drift out across the grounds like wildebeest across the veldt, when suddenly he noticed Bob in their number, sombre as ever as he peeled off and headed for his hut.

Ian was perplexed. "What would a World Heritage efnic minority be doing amongst these blokes?" he thought, "and why would he be coming out of the sex re-ed department?" Ian had learned from Pauli that the Aboriginal was taking the extra classes, but they had both assumed that they were the ethnic unlearning classes- unlearning how to use a chainsaw, for instance, in favour of an axe in order to save the rainforests or unlearning how to operate a tractor in favour of a shovel. Policies designed to allow middle class eco-warriors a good sleep at night by keeping the undeveloped parts of the world perfectly undeveloped, whilst simultaneously allowing the rest of the world to carry on as normal and feel good about itself for saving the planet.

The Londoner adjusted his glasses. Something wasn't right- he knew that Bob and the Maasai had been voluntarily attending re-education classes with the rest of the group but he had assumed it was because they were bored and wanted to keep themselves occupied whilst waiting for their transfer papers to come through. Ian was suspicious and made up his mind to find out exactly what was going on with Bob.

In the hut, Nain cleared the end of the table, moving Pauli's tea set, silver teaspoons and linen doilies, she rolled back the tablecloth and from her bag, produced a red leather-bound notebook and a Staedtler HB2 yellow and black striped, pink rubber-ended pencil. She laid them on the table, sat down and began to write.

Jessie moseyed over to her side and sat down. "What ya doing?" she asked the Welsh woman, as she scribbled furiously.

Nain put down the pencil and turned to her. "I'm running out of pineapple chunks," came the reply.

"Ya?" was all the bemused Canadian could say.

"Yes, and as our young American friend is fond of saying: this.... poop just got real."

"Ya, he says it a lot."

"I've been giving it a lot of thought and, believe it or not, he's quite right when you think about it, although I suspect he doesn't."

"Ya, he recites it like a catchphrase," mused Jessie.

"But it's true nonetheless. This is the situation we find ourselves in, whether we like it or not, so we'd better make the most of it," said Nain. "I've spent all day thinking about it, my Gwilym wouldn't want me sitting around moping. I mustn't let them grind me down- that's what they're trying to do, you know, and I can't let them. I must fight back, that's the way Gwilym and I did it during the Miners' Strikes."

"How?"

"I need a distraction, something to occupy my mind, an escape from this nonsense," Nain said as she picked up the pencil again.

"Like what?"

"Potatoes," she replied. "Ian planted the seed of an idea in my head the other day- I should cultivate a vegetable patch, we have plenty of land around the hut."

"A vegetable patch?"

"For starters yes," answered Nain. "If we keep eating the processed rubbish they serve us here, we will soon be weak, not only in body but in mind. If I start now, by late spring we should have our first crop. I've started drawing up a plan of what to plant, where and when," Nain looked up. "Would you like to help me?"

"Ya, count me in," replied Jessie enthusiastically.

Nain offered her a pineapple chunk and the pair began to make plans.

RESET

"What a load of shite" Donald exclaimed as he and the Swede walked slowly together along the perimeter fence, taking the long way home after their all-day lecture on 'What is National Memory, and how can we change it?'

"Ye cannae change or erase the past," he went on, "ye can only try and learn from it and hopefully improve the future."

"The past is a foreign country, yes," replied Wulfe, "they do things differently there. For sure."

"Wise words, my friend," mused the Scot.

"Not mine, L.P.Hartley's."

"Your pal Helpy is a smart cookie," replied Donald astutely.

Wulfe let the remark go, content to watch the sun setting as they walked, the cold dampness hanging in the air and clinging to his furs. Wulfe stopped and fumbled in his pockets for the pipe and tobacco pouch, he gave a low groan when he realised the pouch was all but empty but he loaded the pipe with the dregs and lit it, blowing a huge billowing cloud of smoke thoughtfully into the heavy evening air. He offered the pipe to Donald who took a deep draw, savouring the moment before blowing his own swirl of fog and coughing slightly.

"So have you thought about what I said earlier?" Donald inquired. "Are ye in?"

Wulfe paused for a moment before grinning. "I am in, yes," he said.

Donald's eyes lit up. "Good man," he said, "good man...this deserves a wee dram," and produced his silver flask from his sporran.

"I've been saving it for just this occasion, slainte." Donald took a swig and offered it to Wulfe.

"Skol," toasted the Swede, before taking a gulp and coughing. Donald grinned.

The pair returned to the hut and found Nain, Jessie, Pauli and the Maasai sitting around the end of the table, drinking tea and at least three of them excitedly discussing plans. Donald and Wulfe joined them.

"We've come to a decision," announced the Scot.

"Oh, that's funny so have we!" replied Nain. "We're going to- "

"Escape!"

"Grow a vegetable patch," finished Nain.

At that very same moment, Brad burst through the door, swaying in his chair and driving erratically.

"Brad Blanchett," he announced, "in the muther faggghhhhh…" He clasped his hands to his head to reveal a shaved area at the crown and a small white bandage. "Faggghhhh! Shagghhh! Cuggghhh! Muther faggghhh!" he screamed in pain as he fell to the floor.

PART THREE

"Those who would give up essential Liberty,

To purchase a little temporary safety,

Deserve neither Liberty nor Safety"

Benjamin Franklin

CHAPTER TWENTY

The days turned into weeks and the weeks into months as the last delicate snows of winter fell, the tide was at long last showing subtle signs of turning as a seemingly endless winter began imperceptibly to loosen its grip. Feeble snowflakes descended across the huge expanse of the facility: the majority of inmates at the Re-education Detention Centre had made it through a particularly harsh and gruelling winter, but were weakened and demoralised by the experience.

The snow was revealing gradual signs of departure, unable to replenish the magnitude of its former self and leaving in its wake, a sludge which was becoming increasingly harder to negotiate as it turned to a thick congealed mud on the unpaved pathways and managed to secrete itself everywhere. Morale amongst the detainees was low, a condition exacerbated by the facility's 'lockdown' with no explanation. Food rationing and a sundown curfew had been imposed; the re-education classes gradually became more infrequent. None of the prisoners had any idea what was going on outside the confines of the fence or indeed within, as slowly but surely, the camp was becoming more intolerable with every passing day. As discipline waned, the arbitrary beatings from the guards; pushes and shoves to begin with, became ever more violent and frequent, as they vented their frustration at the lack of mobility and the facility's declining situation. Indiscriminate thrashings were not uncommon and both Nain and Bob had been manhandled on more than one occasion, when alone and outnumbered. Nain had the ability to remain stoic following these encounters but for Bob, slipping and falling faster than the snowflakes as he made his way to sex re-education, the situation was becoming untenable as notions of suicide occupied his mind, maybe a blessed release from this living hell.

Admin City, on the other hand, was a different matter altogether-snow never settled for long on the network of heated paving and roads. The interiors of the myriad of glass towers were always an ambient twenty degrees as decreed by Government regulations for maximum productivity, and most of the inhabitants of these crystal citadels hardly gave winter's excesses a second thought. The mini city was run by a transglobal technocratic neo-liberal managerial elite, whom if asked, would define themselves by their career rather than the place where they were born or the community in which they were raised- such an admission would be judged uncouth by their peers. These were a high-flying breed of people who considered their careers paramount at the expense of everything else, including children which instead of being considered a joy were viewed more a burden, to be cared for by an army of child minders. These imported nannies were usually of colour and poorly paid along with the maintenance men, housekeepers, gardeners, cooks, drivers and bored pool cleaners, all employed to attend to the more mundane tasks in the lives of the elite. Open borders, multiculturalism and globalisation were essential to these ideologically progressive zealots, as was the cheap labour which they provided.

An emaciated sparrow perched on the transmitter of Building 101. 101, home of the South Eastern branch of the British Broadcasting Company, otherwise known as the biggest propaganda outlet in the world, with a remit to communicate a progressive and socialist message in order to set the nation's ethics and cultural standards, as well as dumbing down its audience and censoring the truth. This remit would probably have its founder spinning in his grave, if such things were possible.

The small bird took off into the sky, catching a breeze and navigated its way through the maze of high buildings, gliding with ease through the assembly of masts and satellite dishes secured to the top of the eastern HQ of the 77th Brigade, a division of the British Armed Forces. The denizens within were far from the popular imagination of how a 'real soldier' should appear as they swivelled in their comfortable chairs, eyeballs swivelling in their heads as they take aim at numerous screens. These faux soldiers, many incapable of passing even a basic fitness test, heroically patrolled the internet and social media sites, on guard 24/7 and ready to attack and obliterate any dissenting voices of the Government's narrative.

The bird flew down between the opulent buildings of the charity sector where, for a regular monthly donation, kindly benefactors could keep the inhabitants in the sumptuous lifestyle with which they had become accustomed. Five star fact-finding missions to the red-light districts of disaster hit areas, for instance, or making sure the homeless and impoverished remained homeless and impoverished in order to justify their own existence and finding a home for top-of-the-range executive company cars in their vast parking areas. The charities never ceased in their relentless quest to find new problems to medicalise, monetarise and resolve, which would, in turn, give new opportunities to resource funding- no issue was too ridiculous for these professional finance diviners. Nestled in the same quarter and no strangers to the forecourts of Mercedes and BMW dealerships either, were the NGOs, some making vast fortunes ferrying economic migrants across the seven seas and other such people-trafficking enterprises.

The grey skies of winter could prove debilitating for individuals suffering from mild forms of depression or stress, but with a fully staffed building devoted solely to HR and staff counselling services and fully paid time off work for the more serious cases of fretfulness, Admin City managed to function admirably. Inside the counselling services centre, staff had been fully trained in such skills as Mindfulness, group therapy and Mental Health First Aid where at the first sign of anyone acting nervous, they could ask the question "Are you thinking about suicide?" Unfortunately, the training did not extend as far as what to do next if the answer were affirmative and unhappily for Bob, these specialists did not operate outside of the bounds of the micro-city.

The sparrow flew on, catching an upward current of air as it swept passed the buildings that housed a quango jungle of quasi-autonomous non-governmental organisations and across the windows of the Behavioural Insight team. The Executive Officer of Behaviour Change looked up momentarily as he scored bold red lines through pictures of burgers with a thick pen, the responsibility of images of food permitted to be displayed on public transport weighed heavily on his shoulders. Obesity was no trivial matter and it was his job to ensure the working classes and the feckless had informed decisions and impact assessments made on their behalf.

RESET

On flew the tiny fowl across the Nightingale Emergency Medical Facility. With a capacity of over six hundred beds, the facility- one of many up and down the country- was built at great expense to the tax payer in a knee-jerk reaction to an influenza emergency which never actually happened. Now it lay abandoned and unused as the weeds encroached. If tumbleweeds were native to Britain, they would surely be bowling their way around the deserted wards of this medical facility.

Upwards and onwards the bird flew in the direction of the Re-education Admin Tower, its bead-like eyes constantly scouring the man-made terrain for a tasty morsel to eat. At the foot of the tower, the fox lay patiently under one of the electric vehicles available to ferry employees and visitors around the complex, waiting for his next meal to fall warm from the sky. Unbeknownst to him, technically he had been reclassified from 'country fox' to an 'urban fox' in just a few short years. This was an issue of great concern to the technocrats in the fox classification business but to those working within the monolithic glass buildings and to the fox, it was irrelevant.

The fox boldly held his ground as another vehicle drew up silently behind, not wishing to be denied his mid-morning morsel. A dark figure dismounted.

"Thank you for choosing to ride with me today, Commandant," said the electric vehicle. "Please do not hesi-"

"Shut up," interrupted the tall, thin figure as it strode purposefully across the marble paving and through the automatic glass doors of the 'Re-Ed Eco Building.' This structure had been designed to incorporate solar panels capable of generating easily enough power to meet the inhabitants' lighting and toast needs on any given sunny day. The figure entered the elevator and waved a hand in front of the illuminated panel.

"Sixtieth floor."

"Good morning, Commandant," replied the elevator. "How are you today?"

"Just shut up and do as I say," was the terse reply.

The five members of the Facility's Equality and Diversity Committee Steering Group sat patiently in the waiting room of the Commandant's office, making small talk whilst awaiting her appearance. They had rehydrated their way through a lake of green tea and mineral water and began to squirm irritably in their chairs, shuffling papers importantly and needlessly as they waited. This was the first time the Steering Group had met and Shea knew none of her fellow members, none except a vague recognition of the young woman with the name tag, which read 'Pastor Jones, Head of Independent Police Diversity Advisory Board for Minority Communities.' Shea thought for a moment, this was the same Pastor Jones who had once admitted live on television, whilst in a professional capacity, that "she had never actually met Winston Churchill, but looked forward to doing so." A fact which, had that meeting come to pass, would have been a grotesque miracle on account of the fact that Winston Churchill had been dead for over half a century when she said it.

Shea was attempting to distract her thoughts by imagining such a meeting, when she was suddenly bought to, by the thud of a luckless sparrow flying head-first into the glass window behind her. The office door suddenly opened and the Commandant appeared, dressed head to foot in a what appeared to be a black sheet with eye slits cut into it.

"I'm here, let's begin," said the Commandant as she removed her covering to reveal her official black uniform beneath. "I've just come back from a fact-finding mission as part of our Multicultural Inclusion and Diversity programme."

Shea sat awkwardly in her chair, knowing full well that the decision she was expected to make today would have deep and far reaching repercussions; although this was to be a fair and impartial vote, she knew full well which way she was expected to go. Alas over the past few days, Shea had been suffering from a bad case of morality which had been affecting her conscience, resulting in sleepless nights. The pressure on her to make the 'right' decision as opposed to the rational decision was beginning to weigh heavily.

When at first Shea had experienced positive discrimination for this position on the steering group, she had been ecstatic with joy knowing full well what a major boost it would be for her career. At last her hard work had been recognised, but now the responsibility of the role was starting to take its toll. Shea considered herself intelligent, competent and above all rational- she had no doubt in the beginning that she could handle the pressure of such a position, but as time passed, she realised that these qualities could act as a disadvantage. A key factor in this position was the ability to suspend common sense when required and it was the predominate cause of her current malady. This particular skill would be essential for today's vote but somewhere deep down, a voice was telling her this proposal from the Commandant was wrong on many levels and would have far-reaching ramifications. She should not only attempt to veto it, but must stand up and argue vigorously against it in order for the proposed implementations not to take place. The vote she was about to take part in had the potential to fundamentally change the lives of the detainees of the Re-education Centre in a negative, if not life un-enhancing way. However, if she did vote against it, she could be blacklisted, lose her well-paid position as Head of the Conceptual Interpretative Statistics department, which came with a handsome salary plus expenses- she could even lose her research grant and the car that came with the job. Her husband's green tech companies could suffer as a result too- Government contracts were lucrative and highly sought-after so the pressure was unbearable. The perpetual battle of morality versus personal gain was about to commence.

The Commandant sat down and addressed the steering group.

"As you can see, I have just returned from X Facility De-radicalisation, and it vood appear zat ze detainees are in full agreement with my proposal. I vas told by their representatives zat, as I had suspected, zey vood find zis to be a positive, inclusive and life-affirming proposal, ultimately helping vith zeir de-radicalisation and any underlying mental health issues zey may have. It only remains for us to vote on vether or not ve should merge the Re-education Centre vith ze De-radicalisation Facility," she said as her eyes scoured the room for any signs of dissent. Her gaze homed in on the Head of the Conceptual Interpretative Statistics department.

Shea was physically starting to feel the monumental pressure she was under as the moment drew closer. She began to perspire as she felt the laser-like glare of her superior- she needed to buy more time.

"Are you ok, Mizz Black?" inquired her no-nonsense superior.

"Yes, I'm just having a slight anxiety attack," replied Shea timidly.

RESET

The Commandant waved her hand over the intercom. "Jones, get a paramedic over here immediately. In fact, ve need a crash team and alert ze air ambulance, make sure zey're placed on standby."

"That really won't be necessary, I just need a moment. In fact, I think it's just a hot flush, a moment to centre myself is all that's really required."

The Commandant didn't look convinced as she regarded Shea with suspicious eyes.

"I'm fine really, I am," pleaded Shea.

"Do you feel strong enough to proceed?"

"Yes, yes, I just need a moment, just carry on without me."

"Mmm ok zen, take a moment to re-focus," replied the sceptical Commandant curtly.

CHAPTER TWENTY-ONE

A confused and confounded Bob was seated in a cramped white clinical room, interfacing with a scanner on the wall. A cold female voice came from the speaker as the lens focused on him.

"Bob Murphy, detainee number 24809666. Let's begin: recite your baseline," it said.

"Men who have sexual fantasies about women are guilty of sexual assault," Bob obeyed robotically, "because the fantasy woman cannot consent, interthink."

"Repeat three times," came the voice.

"Consent interthink, consent interthink, consent interthink," repeated Bob.

"You say to your sexual fantasy: 'hey, would you like some lemonade?' and they say 'I would love a glass of lemonade,' interthink," said the voice.

"Love interthink," echoed Bob.

"Then you know they want a glass of lemonade, interthink."

"Lemonade interthink."

"Or I'm not sure, interthink."

"Sure interthink."

"You can make them lemonade, but be aware they might not drink it, interthink."

"Drink it interthink."

"And if they do not drink it, just because you made it doesn't mean you are entitled to watch them drink it, interthink."

"Drink it interthink."

"And if they say no, don't make them lemonade, interthink."

"Lemonade interthink."

"Don't get annoyed at them for not wanting lemonade, they just don't want lemonade, interthink."

"Lemonade interthink."

"They may say yes, but then when the lemonade arrives, they say no, interthink."

"No interthink."

"Sure, that's annoying as you've gone to all the effort of making lemonade, interthink."

"Lemonade interthink."

"But they are under no obligation to drink the lemonade. It's simple, fantasies can change their minds in the time it takes to make lemonade, interthink."

"Lemonade interthink."

"And it's ok for sexual fantasies to change their mind, you are still not entitled to watch them drink it, and if they are unconscious, don't make them lemonade. Unconscious fantasy women don't want lemonade and they can't answer the question, do you want lemonade? Because they are unconscious, interthink."

"Unconscious interthink."

"Maybe they were conscious when you asked them if they wanted lemonade and said yes, interthink."

"Yes interthink."

"But in the time it took you to make lemonade, they are now unconscious, interthink."

"Unconscious interthink."

"Just put the lemonade down, don't make them drink the lemonade. They may have said yes, but unconscious fantasies don't want lemonade, interthink."

"Lemonade interthink."

"If they said yes to lemonade, start to drink it then fall asleep, take the lemonade away, because unconscious fantasies don't want lemonade, interthink."

"Lemonade interthink."

RESET

"If a fantasy said yes to lemonade in your head last Saturday, it doesn't mean they want you to make lemonade all the time, interthink."

"Time interthink."

"They don't want you to come over to their place unexpectedly with lemonade and force them to drink it. Don't say 'you wanted lemonade last week,' or wake up to find you pouring lemonade down their throat saying, 'but you wanted lemonade last night,' interthink."

"Last night interthink."

"If you can understand how completely preposterous it is to force fantasies to have lemonade when they don't want lemonade, then you are able to understand lemonade is the same as fantasy sex- consent is everything, interthink."

"Lemons within lemons within lemons, everything interthink," repeated Bob.

"We're done, you can leave," said the voice.

CHAPTER TWENTY-TWO

The vote was over and the members of the committee began to leave the office. Shea gathered her papers and was about to leave when the Commandant stopped her.

"Don't zink your behaviour did not go unnoticed, I'm very disappointed in you," said the disapproving Commandant.

Shea's heart froze.

"Vat you did back zere vas extremely foolish," she went on.

Shea tried to defend herself but the words just wouldn't come out, "I, I, I was ju-ust-"

"Don't try to explain, ve both know vat's going on," silenced her superior.

"Yes but-"

"I am very disappointed in you."

"I know but…" whimpered Shea, struggling for words.

"I understand vat you did and vy you did it."

"I'm sorry."

"You should be," came a curt reply. "I am villing to overlook it zis time but don't let it happen again."

"I won't, thank you."

"Ve both know zat incident back zere vas no hot flush," said the Commandant. "Next time you have an anxiety attack, you must not try to conceal it for ze sake of a vote. However, I must admit zat vas vone of the bravest zings I've ever seen, soldiering on in spite of your debilitating condition. Don't zink your heroism von't go unnoticed in my employee review report, if only more of ze facility staff vere as brave as you. Oh, and vell done for making it a unanimous vote, I knew I had made ze right decision selecting you for zis committee."

"Thank you," said Shea with great relief.

"No need to thank me, thank yourself," replied the Commandant. "Dismissed, and make sure you fill out an incident report on ze way out."

As Shea left the office, the pang of guilt soon evaporated. "I just can't live without the car," she justified to herself. "It's so comfy and that boob job is essential for my self-esteem."

Donald and Wulfe trudged their way through the quagmire back towards the hut, ankle tags collecting mud as they went. Tired and emaciated, they were deep in conversation having spent two weeks apiece in the solitary confinement suite- this had been the second time they had been captured and they were running out of ideas. The

Swede looked particularly gaunt and his once-thick beard was thin and raggedy.

"If we get caught again," he said shaking his head morosely, "they are going to implant a chip in us, you understand? They have tiny radio transponders, receivers, transmitters, yah, they will connect us to a Bio Identity Management System, yes, and then we can never be free, no, never."

"Och," replied the Scot, "we'll just cut them oot."

"It is not that easy, no," replied Wulfe, having had previous experience of a RFID chip. "They can drill it into the bone, yes, you have to get it surgically removed." He grimaced at the distant memory.

"Aah," replied a disparaged Donald.

"We have to succeed next time, hmm, it is our last chance, yes," stated Wulfe. "What about you, huh, did you come up with anything?"

"It's hard to think straight when they're playing post-modernist Black critical feminist theory radio at you for twenty-four hours of the day full blast, but I think I may have," Donald grinned conspiratorially. "What if we crack a couple of the marshmallows over the heed, take their uniforms and Segway ourselves straight oot through the front gates, ye ken?"

"They will spot us right away- we are the wrong build, yah, and the uniforms would sag all over us like melted cheese. We have lost too much weight, no, no," replied Wulfe, instantly dashing the Scot's meticulous plan.

"Well, have ye got any better ideas?" replied the irascible Donald.

"I think it is time we ask for help, yes."

"From whom?" a suspicious Donald inquired.

"The Morris Men, of course."

"Are you off yer heed, mon?" erupted Donald. "Ye cannae trust they Sassenachs!"

"Yes, I think we may have to if we are ever going to get out," replied the Swede calmly. "After all, they run the underground network, is this not true?"

Donald was horrified at the very thought of such a proposal. "It'll be a cold day in hell before I go crawling, cap in hand, to those English bastards for help."

"Hmm, I think we have run out of options, my friend," Wulfe replied solemnly, patting his compadre on the shoulder.

Ian was peeking over the recycling receptacles like a meerkat, anxiously waiting for Bob to exit the building. "There he goes," he whispered to Fred, hunched down beside him. Fred, one sixth of the Northwood and South Oxhey Morris Men, was busily taking notes.

"I don't know Ian, he may be too far gone," said Fred in a slow West country drawl, as he observed Bob, morosely looking down at his feet and making his despondent way back to hut 1688. "He ain't no spring chicken and we've got a list as long as your arm of young lads waiting to get on our purple pill program, all of 'em in urgent need." Fred removed his straw hat and scratched his head doubtfully for a moment. "I'm not even so sure he's on the sex re-education program. You know, they've been running a new experimental

Gaslighting laboratory in that same building- maybe they've got him on that and are using sex to exploit his weaknesses? If that's what they're up to, it's a whole other kettle of fish. We'd have to de-feminise him first and then get into his head, see what the damage is, see if he's a nut job."

"Gaslighting laboratory?" asked Ian. "Not the Greens again...what's wrong with an LED lightbulb?" he said absently polishing his glasses. "Never satisfied, are they?"

"No, you silly apeath," chastised Fred, "gaslighting, brainwashing, discombobulation, that sort of thing."

"Oh," said a confused Ian.

"I'll have to report this back to the lads. There were rumours going around of a top secret experiment taking place, maybe this is it? Something about sexual gaslighting," continued the concerned Morris Man. "If sexual gaslighting experiments are taking place in there, you can be sure no good will come of it."

Ian was still none the wiser. "Sexual gaslighting?"

"Gaslighting," explained Fred patiently, "is a technique used in order to make a victim question their own reality- it's a common technique of abusers, control freaks and them's type of folk. Gaslighters will make the victim question their own judgement through victim blaming, denial, manipulation and dismissiveness, all the time policing the tone of their voice. Sexual gaslighting uses the same method but is specifically related to psychological abuse surrounding sex."

"Why Bob?"

"Maybe he's a pervert."

"What?"

"Maybe they've got something on him that they can exploit and use as a way in, but most likely it's because he's an old fart, tired and vulnerable, easy pickings for experimenters." Fred paused for a moment. "Although gaslighting can be used on anyone, you know."

"Yeah?"

"Yeah," replied Fred solemnly, "anyone can become a victim. The secret of its strength lies in the slow, insidiousness of its nature- they do it so subtly, you see, so much so that the victim doesn't realise they're being brainwashed or are too confused to do anything about it. That's why it's very popular amongst narcissists, cult leaders and dictators. It's bad ju-ju, alright."

"Ow's it work?" asked Ian, becoming ever more intrigued.

"Well, it works like this: the gaslighter will tell the victim a blatant lie. The victim knows it is a lie, which makes them unsure if anything the gaslighter says is true and the victim slowly becomes bamboozled and discombobulated. The gaslighter wears the victim down over time, a lie here, a criticism there, cranking it up, real gradual-like. They contradict the victim's version of events. They say things and then deny saying them, making their victim question their own reality, in turn making them more susceptible to the gaslighter's reality. Everything the victim holds dear, the gaslighter will use against them, attacking the foundations of their very being. The gaslighter will throw in a little positive re-enforcement every now and then, further confusing the victim and weakening their mental resolve, forcing them to constantly question themselves, their sanity and everything they know. You see, gaslighting is all about gaining power over the victim. It's a subtle mind-fuck, if you will excuse my French."

"Blimey," said Ian in a moment of clarity, "sounds like my ex-missus."

"It's no joking matter, Ian," chided Fred.

"No, it wasn't," replied Ian soberly.

"Poor bugger, just look at the state of him. He's a laboratory rat," said Fred sadly. "If their experiments are successful, this could be bad news for all of us."

"So, will you take Bob on?" asked Ian expectantly.

Fred thought for a moment.

"I think we may have to take him on, get to the bottom of it," said Fred thoughtfully as he stowed away his notebook and stood up. "I think we'd better put him on the purple pill program and re-man-imate him for starters, and then we'll get inside his head and find out what they've been up to in there."

"Result!" beamed Ian. "'ow much?"

"Oh, maybe a bag of potatoes," replied the big Morris Man conspiratorially. "You know, for the cause and all that."

"No problemo," replied the Cockney cheerily.

Fred gave Ian a friendly pat on the back, before having a root about in a recycling receptacle and departing with an armful of cardboard and a jingle of bells. Ian watched on sadly as the glum Australian made his arduous way back to the place he called home.

CHAPTER TWENTY-THREE

B ack in the hut, Pauli was busily cleaning the mud off the wooden floor- a task he had to perform more often these days since Nain and Jessie's self-help classes had proved so popular. Today, Nain was instructing a small group of fellow inmates in her 'how to knit' class. Understandably, her students were apprehensive at first, not wishing to be accused of racism following the 'Diversknitty' furore and the moral feeding frenzy of purity spirals that followed, but once they had realised that knitting could be enjoyed for its own sake and didn't necessarily lead to a life of White supremacist knitting activism, they attended in their droves. Although wool was a hard commodity to come by, her pupils were mainly there in order to spend time in the company of someone who espoused common sense casually in an environment that made none. Her gardening classes were particularly popular too, and since the moment she had decided to become proactive in this place where she was expected to be passive, things had gone from strength to strength.

RESET

Nain and Jessie's positive efforts regarding the vegetable patch had not gone unnoticed by their fellow detainees either who, as they witnessed the vegetables grow, were drawn by curiosity to hut 1688, which in turn, became a beacon of light in the otherwise authoritarian, politically correct darkness of their existence. Social Justice was deemed unnecessary in this hut, as on the whole everyone just got on with it and each other, cooperating for the common good of all regardless of race, sexual orientation, creed or self-identification, in a situation which was not within their control.

No matter how the inmates had ended up in this mad house of de-normalising and de-humanising, they were all in the same boat now and Nain's willingness to help or advise had, in part, inspired a new feeling of co-operation throughout the centre, making the harsh reality of life inside a little more bearable.

Many internees from across the facility were attracted to the hut, for it seemed that all the inhabitants of hut 1688 were always upbeat and proactively employed in one endeavour or another, no matter how hard the going got. There was however, one exception to the positive vibe of the hut- Bob, who seemed to go from bad to worse in a downward spiral from which no one could rescue him. The general consensus was that he was bipolar, but no one knew for sure just exactly what bipolar was other than a catchall buzz word of a pseudo-medical nature.

Even the silent Maasai could mostly be found busy in the veg patch in his free time and gave a large proud grin to any passer-by who complimented his efforts. Nain's labours did not go unnoticed by the camp authorities either, her veg growing was, in fact, encouraged by the green mafia godfathers, whom even provided Nain with seeds, but the simple optimistic joy she managed to impart on everyone she had contact with was beginning to arouse the suspicions of those in the upper echelons of power.

Jessie was busily instructing a young German girl on how to pot seedlings; they were discussing how the young girl had been arrested during a student protest in Berlin and sentenced to three years for setting fire to a United Independent European States of Germany flag. This was a hate crime, according to the authorities, with the potential to upset people.

"- and that's how I became a hate actor," the girl explained.

"A flag?" an incredulous Jessie replied.

"Ya, a flag," answered the girl. "I wouldn't have minded, but it was my flag."

Jessie looked up to see Donald and Wulfe enter the building. Pauli immediately jumped to his feet and gave them each a hug.

"Welcome back guys," he gushed, "we missed you, are you ok?" he asked, not waiting for an answer as he raced off to boil the kettle.

"Aye," replied Donald in Pauli's wake as he sat on his bed.

Wulfe strode up to Jessie and Nain and gave them both a hug then high-fived the Maasai. He'd just sat down when Brad came racing into the building toward Jessie.

"Hook me up, Jugs," he said desperately when he reached her. Jessie lifted a loose floorboard and retrieved a small plastic box with a USB cable attached which she then plugged it into the top of the American's head.

RESET

"Fuck fuck fuck," he said with relief before repeating his mantra. "Big titties, little titties, big titties, little, oh hi guys," he said, eventually noticing the new arrivals.

"How is your head? Getting better, yes?" asked Wulfe.

"Takes a lickin' but keeps on tickin', mutherfucker," replied Brad with a grin.

Donald and Wulfe sat down at the table and were joined by Nain and Pauli, while the silent Maasai diligently washed the china tea set.

"I'm sorry you didn't make it again, guys," said an earnest Pauli, "maybe you should bide your time, like Nain and Jess," he ended in a whisper.

"Aye, maybe yer right," reflected the Scot, recalling the flooded tunnel and subsequent capture.

"No!" he suddenly yelled "I gotta get oot 'a here, we've got to get out of here before we all go mad! This place gets more like an Orwellian dystopia every day," said Donald with urgency. "1984, you know, the book. It's like Orwell wrote an instruction manual for this mad hoose. A few years out, mind, but pretty accurate. War is peace-"

"Freedom is slavery," Nain joined in, much to Donald's surprise.

"Ignorance is strength, yes," recited Wulfe.

"Diversity is division," Jessie contributed.

"Silence is violence," whispered the Maasai sadly to himself.

"And one ring to bind them," said Pauli, with instant regret. "Sorry, I just wanted to join in!"

RESET

Outside, Bob was slowly making his way home through the mud, lost in his own thoughts. "Staying apart will keep us together," he mumbled to himself.

"Pssst," came a sound from the shadows of a hut.

Bob stopped and looked around.

"Psst, your name Bob?" asked a deep West Country voice.

"Yes mate," replied the cautious Australian.

"Come over here," instructed the voice, "let's not cause a hullaballoo now."

Bob, mindful not to cause a hullaballoo, walked timidly toward the voice.

CHAPTER TWENTY-FOUR

The Sunday assembly of the Eco Godless Community was drawing to a close. The congregation were gathered in the Emma Thompson Meeting House; the unwilling flock had been lured to the compulsory service with the promise of entertainment, information and education of green issues. As the final song drew to a close, the celebrant Josh Farquhar, eco-ecclesiastic and climate emergency zealot, rose to his feet singing enthusiastically. Having waxed lyrical of an exciting utopian New World Order based on an eco-totalitarian regime designed to subjugate humanity, he was keen to deliver the finale of his sermon and be away, in order to go foraging in the woods for fungi for his tea.

"*O things could change to green,*" the assembly sung apathetically.

"*Everything would be so clean,*

O they could be better than we've ever seen,

Better than we've ever seen

RESET

O just wait and see,

Just wait and see,

Whoa, whoa-whoo, for you and me."

"'Sake..." muttered Donald under his breath.

"When you're green, when you're green..."

A moment's silence passed.

"Wow, that was rad," said Josh, an uber-posh young man with a horse face, hidden beneath a nest of matted blond dreadlocks and clutching a fist to his 'This Is What A Green Feminist Looks Like' t-shirt.

"Well, our meeting draws to a close once more, thank you all for allowing me to make better sense of the world for you. Before we depart, it only remains for us to have a final inspiring and meaningful wish, please join me," he said placing his palms together and looking skyward.

"Let us make this meeting house glad with our presence and the planet rejoice with our song.

Let us never forget how virtuous we are, even in times when we may be crippled by anxiety, stress, vulnerability or even very upset by negative comments, and if we are unfortunate enough not to have any trivial mental health issues, let us search until we find one.

Let us encourage the third world not to develop or to have children for the sake of the planet and may we always be led unquestioning, in thought, word and deed, by the science and the experts who know best.

RESET

Let us remember the poor and the helpless, the cold, the hungry and oppressed, the sick in body and in mind, the lonely and unloved, even if we may not be able to help them directly, and especially all who know not the imminent threat of the coming climate apocalypse. Never let us ever forget the earth needs us, for we are its only hope, and may we always remember, we have sinned against our planet and must repent."

After the collection, Josh stood by the door giving wet-lettuce-like handshakes to the congregation as they departed. Donald passed at the opportunity as he strode purposefully to the side of Nain, offering her his arm as they approached the stairs.

"Thank you, Donald, you're a gentleman," she said as they began to descend.

"Aye, my mammy raised me right," he said patting her hand tenderly. "Well, that was a load of condescending shite," Donald continued, "what does he know aboot the environment? I'll bet he's never had to wrestle a sixteen-point monarch to the groond, the wee fanny baws."

"Yes, I quite agree with you" replied Nain, well used to the dour and cantankerous Scot by now and full of respect for his stubborn, if not a little self-defeating, forms of protest. They returned to the hut to find Ian and the rest of their fellow roommates, minus Jessie, Bob and Brad, sitting around the table in deep conversation.

"Yeah, of course I believe in God," Ian was saying as they joined them. "I just don't really think about it much."

"What about you?" Wulfe asked Pauli.

The Maori thought for a moment. "I'm like Ian, I suppose, I don't give it much thought. But I do think it's more important to be a good person, have a fabulous time and not hurt anyone- you only live once."

"What yooz talking aboot?" inquired the curious Scot, pulling up a chair.

"Ah, we were discussing the Sunday meetings, it is like some kind of religion, yes" replied Wulfe as he sucked on his empty pipe. "They seem to worry about the end of the world, hmm, it reminds me of 'End of Days' prophecies from the Bible, yah. They seem to be the new prophets of doom with all the hysterical wailing."

"Och," said Donald, "don't start me on these crazy people and their pseudo-religion."

"This green thing, hmm," reflected Wulfe, "I think it is just like religion, yes. Good intention and strong conviction, yes, an intolerance of other points of view, supported by censorship, yah, instead of knowledge backed by evidence, hmm. That is what I think."

"You may have a point, big yin," mused Donald.

"The world is divided into two sects, yes," said Wulfe philosophically. "Those with religion but no brains, and those with brains but no religion."

"Wise words," said Donald.

"Yah, Abu 'L-Ala al-Maarri," replied Wulfe.

"Bless you," said Ian absently.

Wulfe ignored him. "I think these greens want a religion without a god, yes, then they have no one to answer to but themselves, yah."

Nain sat down and reflected for a moment. "I know there are a lot of people that don't believe in God," she said, "I'm just not one of them. I pity these people, I can only imagine they are such zealots because they have a God-shaped hole in their hearts and are desperate for something to fill it with." Nain paused, before continuing. "And they seemed to have filled it with fear, fear for the end of the world."

Brad and Jessie wound their way down the ramp which spiralled around the Meeting House. They had become good friends over the months of close confinement, both being of a similar age and both having worked in the entertainment business. Jessie had begun to discover that underneath Brad's sexist bravado, lay an intelligent and sensitive human being. She didn't entirely agree with everything his foul mouth uttered but Jessie found Brad's overtly sexist outbursts more amusing than offensive and she was intelligent enough to know the difference between humour and intended malice. Brad wasn't really sexist- just shy, awkward and stupid around 'people who menstruate,' as Ms Dubois described real women.

"Jesus Christ! These moralising melon-head muther-frackers have got a real problem with Tech. If it was up to them, I'd be sitting in a wheelbarrow right now," said Brad angrily.

"I suppose they have a point, climate change is a reality," replied Jessie absently, squinting as she perused a pamphlet entitled 'The Joy of Composting.'

"Sure, no one in their right mind is disputing that shizzle, but digging up your garden, drinking smoothies and shoving windmills all over the country ain't gonna solve it- that's a drop in the ocean on a planet with billions of people crawling around on it," said Brad, pulling up at the point where the stairs and the spiral ramp intersected and they waited for the stair users to cross the ramp. The stair users awkwardly waited, perched politely on the edge of the stairs waiting for Brad and Jessie to cross their path, like apprehensive penguins on the edge of an ice shelf. After long moments, the two friends took the initiative and continued their journey.

"We need nuclear power pronto," said Brad. "Wind power and solar power just ain't gonna cut it. A football field-sized area of solar panels only produces roughly enough energy to meet the needs of about ten homes annually, dawg. To meet the needs of a city, we're gonna need fields of solar panels as far as the eye can see. What's that going to do for the muther-fracking natural environment? And wind turbines, they only have a twenty to thirty-year shelf life, and it takes hundreds of tonnes of concrete, steel and fiberglass to erect one of them mofos."

He sniggered to himself. "Erect..." he repeated before continuing his discourse.

"And where do the hipsters think the power comes from for their electric vehicles?" The question was not rhetorical. "Not the magic place, usually a fossil-fuelled power plant, we're just kicking the can down the road. 'What about Bio fuel?' you might ask."

Jessie didn't.

"The average timber burning power plant," he began as the pair stopped again in order to allow the stair users to cross the ramp. Again, an awkward stair-balancing moment passed until Brad took the initiative and moved on. "...gives off hundreds of tonnes of carbon every year and if you cut down every tree in the United States, it would only power the country for one year, then what you gonna do? Trees don't grow on trees, you know. Obviously we need to develop these technologies and make them more efficient, but we're nowhere near yet, so in the mean time we need nuclear. It's obvious, not irrational doom-mongering and hysterical apocalyptical moralising, dawg."

"But the science says nuclear is a really bad idea," Jessie said casually.

The science!" answered an irritable Brad. "The science, which science? Whose science? The science of scientists wanting funding and having to say the right thing in order not to get blacklisted? Bull-shiz, a nuclear scientist would give you a totally different view of 'the science'. It's just that nuclear is complicated and most people don't understand that shiz, maybe they should read a book and educate themselves."

"Wow, I didn't realize you were so into science," Jessie said, turning the page in her pamphlet. "But nuclear energy is dangerous, I mean, what about the accidents in Japan and Russia? I know I don't want to live in a world full of nuclear bombs."

"What you been smoking, girl? Of course I'm into science, it's the coolest thing you can be into, it's the fracking bomb," said Brad. "Anyhow, Fukushima was a tsunami caused by an earthquake and Chernobyl was lack of proper funding and lax safety as a result of a collapsing Soviet Union."

"Maybe, but those accidents happened just the same."

"Well, obviously we're gonna have to tighten up on that kinda shiz," conceded Brad. "I mean, who puts a nuclear power plant in an earthquake zone by the sea? That's Fukushima-d up, and you always got to account for Fuku-frack ups, human error an' shiz."

"Nuclear is dangerous."

RESET

"The benefits outweigh the dangers," persisted Brad as they stopped at another stair /ramp intersection. Again, a polite stair shuffle ensued before Brad took the initiative once more and moved on. "…a small soda can-sized lump of uranium," he continued, "could meet all your energy needs for the rest of your life. You gotta have faith in technology, it always finds a solution- that's why I'm not sitting in a steam-powered chair right now. 'Have no fear for atomic energy,' that's what Bob Marley sung and I agree with him."

"Did he?"

"Yeah, dude was a prophet, dawg," Brad enthused. "Mankind's ability to overcome adversity is awesome, you gotta have faith in that, you gotta be positive, Jugs."

"Or womankind."

Brad gave her a withering look. "Or womankind, if you must, or transkind or non-binarykind or gaykind or pansexualkind or lesbiankind, I could go on but I guess everyone in their right mind knows it's just a turn of phrase even if they don't admit it, know what I'm sayin'? And anyone that throws themselves off a bridge because they're horrified to find the word 'mankind' in a dictionary is probably a little Fukushima-d up anyhow."

"Chill, I was just kidding. I really don't give a shit about all this 'he', 'she', 'it', cismale, cisfemale, man, woman ,womxn, nouns, pronouns, blah blah blah, it's just stupid anyhow, did you just call me Jugs again?"

"Sorry, it's just all this shiz is getting to me is all, it just gets in the way of all the important shiz," said Brad. "I mean, do you remember when they landed a probe on a comet?"

"Yeah kind of."

"Well they did, one of the most incredible feats of science and engineering, the first time in human history," Brad enthused. "Comet 67p/Churyumov-Gerasimenko was travelling at thirty-four thousand miles per hour and was three hundred million miles away. The Rosetta spacecraft had a four-billion mile journey and when it got there, a module had to land on it- a feat equivalent to landing a fly on a speeding bullet. That shiz was off da hook! It was a total success but guess what? That incredible triumph of human ingenuity got lost in the feminist meltdown about the bowling shirt one of the team was wearing because it had some cartoon women with guns and big gazonkas printed on it. It was a feminist atrocity, an outrage and the poor guy was forced into a ritual apology. All the wonder of that awesome achievement was lost, bull-shiz, know what I'm sayin'?"

"Oh, I definitely remember that now, 'Shirtstorm', the feminazis crucified him. The tailoring equivalent of a thought crime," said Jessie. "The most he was guilty of was being a dorky science nerd, wearing a tasteless shirt."

They stopped again, waited momentarily as the people teetered on the step and politely waved them on.

"True," Brad reflected, "the Hawkin would never have made that fashion faux-pas."

"Yeah, it did seem out of proportion."

"Exactly, all this shiz is getting out of hand, it's getting in the way of the important shiz. People are getting turned into retards so no one offends anyone else's precious sensibilities, its Fukushima'd up! We're going to end up a planet full of dumb fucaggghs..." Brad clutched his head in pain. "Damn, I missed that one."

"You ok?" a concerned Jessie asked.

"Yeah, just a quick zap," he said rubbing his head. "But I need to get back to the hut and plug in, I can't express myself properly outside."

Jessie stowed the pamphlet in her pocket. "Let's go," she said, "but I think we're going to have to agree to disagree about the nuclear thing."

"Sure, Jugs," replied Brad, "it's a free country." He paused for a moment to consider what he had just said as they halted momentarily at another intersection. The stair users immediately stopped to let them pass.

"Thank you," said Jessie to them.

"This is my life," muttered Brad despondently.

The pair made their way back home and found the rest of their number sat around the table deep in conversation.

"Religion, yes," Wulfe was saying, "is just another form of manmade control over other men, of course."

"Or women," interjected Pauli helpfully.

The group gave him an irritable look.

"Sorry," he said meekly.

"I totally agree," said Ian. "Religion is control over people, but that's what all this is about, a form of religion. Like Marxism, Communism, Maoism, Catholicism, Nazism- it's all the same fing, we know best and you'd better watch out if you don't agree."

"I'm not talking about politics or religion," said Nain with passion. "I'm talking about God. These people don't know God. If they did, they wouldn't behave like this."

RESET

The group sat in silent wonder at the Welsh woman's outburst.

"This is nothing new," Nain continued, "this story has played out many times over in the past. They've lost the connection between themselves and a higher realm, some might call it god, and as a result they turn inward and begin to worship themselves. They find meaning in the meaningless, they supress their fear of death with an unhealthy obsession for health and quest for eternal youth, distracting and insulating themselves from questions of the eternal in the here and now. Like Puritans, they preach how people should live but know little of life, they crow their virtues endlessly, unaware that true virtue lies in self-sacrifice. They medicalise morality and remove personal responsibility, they create problems and supply answers, they espouse freedom yet stifle debate, they censor, cancel and de-platform. And the worst thing they do is create divides. The shame is, they don't seem to realise humans can do better than this, they may proclaim to act as they do for the common good but they are authoritarian and their hearts are filled with demons...demons of unreason."

The room was silent for a long moment until Ian stood up.

"Blimey," he said awkwardly, looking at a non-existent watch on his wrist. "Is that the time? I'd better be off."

"Please, a moment," said Wulfe. "Donald and I want to talk to you."

Ian sat back down. "About wot?" he asked curiously.

"Escape," replied Donald, with a glint in his eye.

"Escape?" queried Ian. "I don't know nufink about that."

"Maybe not," said Wulfe, "but you do know the Morris Men, yes."

"'Ang on a minute," said Ian as he fidgeted with his glasses, "I don't hold any sway with them."

"You share a hut with them," Donald intervened.

"Yeah, but they keep themselves to themselves. They've even partitioned my hut in 'alf, I sleep in the French bit."

"We've seen you talking to them," said Donald accusingly.

Ian thought for a moment. "Of course, I'm the hut master, I have to talk to 'em but we don't talk about that sort of fing- we talk about cleaning rotas and hut maintenance. Escape- that's a different story- you don't just stroll up to the Morris Men and talk about escape, they just wouldn't entertain you."

"But they do know of such things, yes? Being connected as they are," pressed Wulfe. "We've all heard the rumours."

"Of course, but- " started Ian.

"Yeah," Brad interjected as Jessie plugged the USB into the top of his head, "those mutherfuckers have got a hand in all the shit that goes down around here, everyone knows that. Who's escaping anyway?"

"We are," replied Donald and Wulfe simultaneously.

"And me," said Nain.

Everyone turned to look at the little woman.

"I've had enough of this nonsense, up with this I will not put. I want to go home," she said defiantly.

"But-" protested Ian.

RESET

"Count me in," said Jessie before he could finish what he was saying.

"Well if Jugs is going AWOL, I'd better go too," said Brad.

They all turned to the Maasai, his silence spoke volumes.

"It ain't that easy," objected Ian.

"Me too!" came Bob's voice from the doorway, having just returned from his first purple pill meeting.

"Blimey," said a flustered Ian, looking to Pauli for support. "Tell 'em, Pauli."

"I think I've had enough too," said Pauli sincerely.

Ian rubbed his temples slowly. "They won't just 'elp anyone," he remonstrated, "you have to win their respect before they will even give you the time of day."

"Hmm, and how do we do that?" asked the Swede.

Ian replaced his glasses and took a deep breath: "Dance off," he said.

Josh Farquhar

CHAPTER TWENTY-FIVE

It was the night of the dance-off, and the guards had been bribed to keep clear of the chosen dance arena at the recycling centre with a selection of pies and cakes. The clandestine circle of traditional dance enthusiasts and gambling inmates who were prepared to win or lose currency on a bet, were tightly packed around the dance floor, craning their necks to see what had become of the challengers. The young pretenders of the Title IX breakdance crew lay broken and demoralised upon the floor gasping for breath, the best of Uncle Sam's Gangsta Body-Popping Posse defeated, having shattered against the impenetrable soviet wall of Cossack dance agility. The Russians' head man Ivan strode arrogantly into the centre of the ring as bodies were being hauled off, his highly polished, soft leather fur-topped boots glowing in the reflected light of the fire.

"Is that the best the West has to offer?" he said contemptuously. "Is there no one here who can challenge us?"

A sudden ominous drum rapport met his challenge, as the Northwood and South Oxhey Morris Men made their way out of the shadows, single file and into the ring, to the slow deliberate beat of a drum. You could cut the atmosphere of toxic masculinity with a knife as they lined up, six-foot long yew staffs in hand to face-off against their Cossack opponents. Ivan's arrogance momentarily abandoned him as he regarded his foe- the Morris Men were here on business: businessmen, not company representatives, and it was time for an aggressive corporate takeover. The Morris Men were going old school; not twee nineteen-fifties midwifes on bicycles with baskets, meandering their way down leafy country lanes passed rose-covered cottages, or village pubs with warm ale and enviable horse brass collections. No, older school, older even than Victorian; clog-shoed, flat-capped, shiny buttons, pies and 'trouble doon at 'tut mill' old school. No, they were going precivilisation, ancient Briton school; the flowery straw hats, white smocks and bearded rustic charm was gone, replaced by 'blue face' war paint and black cloaks. The Morris Men were about to take a turn for the Pagan. The harmonium had been replaced by a single drum which beat out a steady menacing pulse, as opposed to the diddley-dee squeeze box chic that most people would associate with English folk dance. This was to be a stripped down, deconstructed cudgel of a performance, there would be no 'hey nonny nay, rights of spring' tonight. For this clash of folk-dance behemoths, the gloves were off and so were the bells.

The challenge to the Cossacks' dance superiority began, slowly at first as the drum continued its slow rhythmic beat and the Morris Men paired off and crossed staffs. As the pounding of the drum intensified, they began to beat the staves harder against each other, cracking the air with every strike. At a given moment, they spun, aiming blows at their opposite's heads who ducked with precision timing. As the drumming increased, they jumped and pirouetted nimbly, avoiding contact with one another's staffs. The sticks of yew splintered with every strike, the dancers' black cloaks billowing out with each jump and leap and twirl, like crows on the wing. The performance was mesmerising, a masterful display of timing and trust, staff striking staff, inches from grim faces. The beat increased. The whistle of the wooden staves amplified as they became a blur, whipping through the air as the dancers whirled and parried, trashing and smashing timber poles with all their strength and agility until the whole scene became an indistinct shadow of skill, dexterity, canes, cloaks and bearded men of 'blue face' at one with the primal driving beat, on and on, faster and faster, until suddenly this ancient display of human movement stopped with a blood-curdling cry. The drumming ceased as the Northwood and South Oxhey Morris Men stood stock-still in perfect formation, breathing hard through grimaced teeth, sweat pouring from their bodies, splintered staffs in hand and black cloaks gently swaying.

The crowd was stunned into silence. After a pregnant pause, a single pair of hands began to clap, followed by another, then another until the whole crowd had erupted into euphoria. All except for the Russians, who could not, and would not accept that they had been out-danced. Ivan strutted up and spat at the feet of the victors. The Morris Men tensed as the Cossack team stepped forward defiantly, silence reigned as each man stared into the eyes of his opposite. There was only one way this was going to end.

That was until the schizophrenic drone of the bagpipes bludgeoned its way through the silence, as Brad and his two-thousand-watt sound system came blaring out of the darkness, followed by a Scot wearing only a kilt and carrying a broomstick in each hand. The music stopped and Donald strode purposefully between the two competing factions, a one-man United Nations peacekeeping force, but without the Third World sex workers and with more peacekeeping resolve, as he parted the bitter enemies Moses-like, with outstretched arms.

"These broomsticks represent swords with their blades upturned," he said, laying down the sticks to form a cross. A sneering Ivan spat again.

Donald stood erect fixing the Cossack with a steely stare. "Gonnae no dae that?" he said menacingly, before striking a pose at the base of the cross. He looked over at Brad and nodded, prompting Brad to unleash an ear-jarring blunderbuss of droning pipes as the Highland Sword Dance or Ghillie Caluim commenced with a reverent bow from the Scot. Donald addressed the swords, bare feet deftly leapt in and out of each corner, skilfully sweeping across the wooden sword representations which, had they been real swords, would surely have shaved the hair from the soles of his bare feet. The Scot gracefully Pas-de-Basque-ed his way anti-clockwise around and across the wooden blades, slow time at first but quickening to the tempo of the pipes, rapid body turns and nimble foot work, with arms raised and fingers outstretched to represent the Highland stag. Kilt flying, Donald produced an exciting visual display of precision and dexterity as sweat poured from his face and glistened on his bare torso; it was a true test of skill and agility in the ancient Highland tradition. The music stopped as the Scot finished with a slow bow. He straightened up and addressed the crowd who were silenced with awe at what they had just witnessed.

"My enemy's enemy is my friend," is all he said.

The assembled throng erupted into a euphoric explosion of applause, shouts and hails of praise, as Donald retrieved his broom handles and, with Brad at his side, magnanimously departed the scene.

RESET

A man of 'blue face' approached Ian and Wulfe from the crush of people. "Tomorrow night, after curfew. Yeghes da!" he said before melting back into the crowd like a shadow.

CHAPTER TWENTY-SIX

The hedgehog snuffled around in the darkness under the huts searching for food, the slugs were out in force tonight and the pickings were good. The hedgehog barrelled along, stopping occasionally to munch on a chewy mollusc. As the spiky mammal trundled its way along in the dark, its beady eyes spied a tasty morsel sluggishly making its way along in the grass near the corner of the hut. The hedgehog sniffed momentarily before closing in on its prey, but as it was about to strike, a booted human foot came crashing down upon the slug. The hedgehog paused for a moment, before turning and scampering off into the undergrowth.

Donald waited impatiently with Wulfe in the shadows of the hut as the searchlight made its sweep. They stood motionless awaiting Ian's signal, their backs pressed hard to the wall. The Scot blinked a couple of times as his eyes adjusted to the darkness. He peered around the corner in time to see Ian's beckoning hand appear from behind hut 1689. Donald and Wulfe sprinted across the no-man's land between huts effortlessly and on reaching the door, Ian ushered them in quickly.

"No-one saw you, did they?" asked Ian anxiously.

"Of course they dinnae," snapped an irritable Donald.

"I'll take that as a no then?" Ian said, polishing his glasses before fixing them to his face. He grinned.

"Walk this way," he said and began to lead the pair though the interior of the overcrowded hut. Hastily constructed bunkbeds on either side were occupied with a new intake of 'Gilet Jaune' protesters and low Gallic whispers filled the air, pungent with the aroma of garlic. Donald wrinkled his nose as he followed the sauntering Pearly King. Wulfe regarded the French occupants more closely as he passed, the interior of the hut had the feeling of an Army Field Hospital as he noticed that many of the slumped and despondent occupants had injuries of one kind or another.

"Are these guys ok?" he asked Ian.

"Yeah, they don't bite," replied the chirpy Ian.

"They look as if they have been in a war or something."

"Oh. That's the result of French police crowd control techniques."

"Crowd control?"

"Yeah, that's how the French authorities control protests, by firing a few rubber bullets into the crowd or chucking teargas grenades at 'em. In 'ere, we've got all the protesters missing an eye or 'and, twenty-four eyes and five 'ands," Ian said casually. "But they're a stoic bunch, ain't that right Severine?" he shouted over to a young dark-haired girl sitting, casually swinging her legs over the edge of her bunk as she read a book.

The girl looked up with her one eye, a black cloth covering the other half of a pretty face. She gave Ian a radiant smile "Where we go one, we go all!" she said.

Ian gave the girl a double thumbs up. "Result!" he said, as he led the way down the hut.

"Hmm, it seems very crowded in here," said the Swede.

"You fink this is overcrowded, you should visit the 'ead injuries in hut 1798."

The trio made their way towards a temporary wall, the hut had been partitioned across the centre using old cardboard boxes. Ian knocked in code on the Linda McCartney veggie burger door and it opened slowly into the darkness.

"Come in," said a gravelly voice with a strong West Country accent.

The three entered into a much darker area where the windows were covered in blankets. Towards the end of room, Donald could just make out the shapes of the occupants. Three sat huddled around the wood burning stove, conversing in hushed tones and one sat in a large wicker chair at a table of timber construction. The figure sat deep in the chair, shadows and pipe smoke obscuring any detail. The beefy man, who had let them in, shut and locked the door before pointing to the man at the table.

"Sit down," came a deep rustic voice from the chair. The three sat down.

"Well?" asked the voice.

"We've come about the fing," said Ian conspiratorially as he began to shift uncomfortably.

"The fing?" inquired the voice darkly.

"You know, the fing we talked about," Ian pressed nervously.

"The fing we talked about?"

"The, the…" stuttered the Londoner, "the 'thing' we discussed," he enunciated.

"The thing we discussed?" came the reply.

"Oh, for fuck's sake!" Donald blurted out in exasperation. "Escape, mon!" He slapped his hand on the table.

Immediately, a short stick cracked the wooden table. The man leaned out of the shadows to reveal a bearded face, a pipe held in place by a pair of scabby lips, a nose reddened by blood vessels and dark eyes, all under a straw boater decorated with flowers.

"What makes you think I know anything about escape?" he demanded, "Or poaching for that matter?"

The bulky figures around the stove ceased their conversation and all turned to look. A moment's silence passed and the man sat back in the shadows, his wicker chair creaked. Donald could see the glow of the man's pipe as his fellows returned to their mumbling discourse. The new arrivals sat in silence. Eventually, the man passed his pipe to Donald who studied it momentarily before placing it in his own mouth and inhaling deeply. After a brief pause, he exhaled a mighty cloud of smoke and offered the pipe to Wulfe who took a draw before offering it to Ian, who declined and passed it back to its owner.

"How did you know the form of syphilis I have is not contagious?" came the rumbling tones from the shadows.

"I didnae," Donald replied.

The voice cackled and a big hand was thrust across the table. Donald gripped it and the two men shook.

"Name's Jed," said the man, "and that's Fred by the door."

Fred nodded to them. "Geddon, me bewty," he said.

"And there around the log burner are Ted, Ed and Ned."

The three men nodded and gave a salvo of 'arrs' and 'urrs' as greeting before returning to their 'doin's.'

"Ned, go and see if Jeffrey next door is taking visitors." Ned promptly got up and disappeared through a door hidden in the back wall.

A moment later, the sound of jingling bells could be heard, Ned reappeared and nodded to Jed.

"Well gents, please follow Ned. And good luck," he said as he reclined back into his chair.

Ian mopped his brow with his hat and nodded his thanks to Jed as he got up and headed towards Ned. Donald and Wulfe followed suite.

They were led into a hidden room as Ned closed the door behind them and locked it. Donald took a good look at his surroundings: either side of the room were two frosted windows, giving a dull opaque light. Donald wondered how the Morris Men had managed to keep the room hidden. At the end of the room was the figure of a tall, thin man with his back to them, wearing a white overall and stirring a large cask of liquid. The man was wearing a full-face mask which exaggerated his breathing. He lowered a large glass beaker into the liquid, filled it and turned around. The masked figure approached and handed the beaker of amber liquid to Ian. Ian held it up to the light before taking a large gulp.

"Aw lovely jubbly," he said before offering it to Donald. "Get your laughing gear round that, Jock!"

Donald drank some, nodding his approval before handing it to Wulfe who gulped the remainder down.

"Very hoppy, I like it," said the discerning Swede.

The masked man studied the trio, the rubber flanges in the mask vibrating as he breathed. He began to remove the mask.

"So glad you like it, a bit hit-or-miss for a while but I think we've finally cracked it." The man's face was revealed from underneath the mask. "Oh, how rude of me! Hello, I'm Jeffrey. Jeffrey Jefferson. Jeffrey with a J, that is, and I'm jolly pleased to meet you."

Wulfe regarded the grinning weasel-faced man as he spoke with a crisp, educated English voice. The man pumped Donald's hand. "Please take a seat, if you can find one," he continued before shaking Wulfe's enormous hand, "they never count the windows, in case you were wondering how we keep this place hidden."

"Clever, innit?" grinned Ian to Donald.

"Aye, that it is," replied Donald sincerely.

"Yes, we've been supplying the camp's homebrew needs for quite some time now, all from our little micro-brewery," said a proud Jeffrey. "We even supply the guards."

RESET

"Really?" said an intrigued Donald." Sounds like you've got the run of the camp"

"Oh yes, apart from Ian here and a handful of others, we've been here the longest. Obviously, we've got ourselves a good little network going." Jeffrey smiled affably at Donald.

"Och aye, just how long have you been here?"

"I forget, how long have we been here now? Do you know, Ned?" he asked.

"Oh, off the top of my head, I should say about three years, two months, four days, six hours and ten minutes, Jeffrey," replied Ned promptly, in a deep West Country burr.

"Thank you, Ned. Yes, that sounds about right- we were picked up in one of the early raids, you see, we had been invoking our pagan rights on the underground festival circuit for almost a year prior to our incarceration. But after the ban on English identity and the 'English Equals Racist' campaign, we were one of the first they came after. Strange really, since Ned is Black. Unfortunately, he suffers from 'White Think' they say."

The bemused guests turned to look at Ned, who gave a shrug. "I'm fifth generation from Bristol, far too integrated according to the authorities. My thinking's been 'White-washed' apparently," he said amiably.

"The powers-that-be" continued Jeffrey "took a dim view of our rampant, toxic masculinity and patriotic spirit so decided to lock us up here and throw away the key." Jeffrey sighed. "A threat to progressive society, enemies of the culturally neutral elites, that sort of thing."

RESET

"The whole world's gone topsy-turvy," said Donald absently.

"Oh yes, I quite agree," Jeffrey replied.

"I told 'em you may be able to 'elp," Ian said, changing the subject as he inspected his glasses.

"Of course, of course, we haven't got much time. Let's get down to business- yes, we can help," said Jeffrey as he flipped the table top over to reveal a model of the entire camp complex, correct in every detail.

Donald inspected it closely- the whole model was made of recycled vegan processed ready meal containers.

"That must have taken you an age to make," he said.

"That it did, my Celtic friend, but we had time on our side" Jeffrey beamed, "and access to the kitchen bins. We also had teamwork- you can never underestimate the value of teamwork. Obviously, we had to set up an illegal 'man shed' in order to make our dream a reality, hence this place," said the Morris Man waving a cavalier hand in the air. "We told the guards that we were rehearsing a play- 'The Vagina Monologues' in fact, you may have heard of it, and luckily as we had hoped, no-one has ever bothered us since," Jeffrey finished proudly.

Wulfe examined the model. "I like it, so where is the escape tunnel?" he asked.

"Escape tunnel?" Jeffrey cleared his throat. "Well it's not quite as easy as that, I'm afraid."

"How no?" inquired Donald.

"Excuse me?"

"He means, 'why not?'" interjected Ian helpfully, receiving a scowl from Donald for his effort.

"Ah well, before we can offer any succour with your escape attempt, the motion has to go before the committee. The preparations for an escape are far reaching: logistics, planning, priority and the paperwork- an administrative nightmare...but I digress," said Jeffrey. "Your motion to escape will go on the agenda for the next meeting, where it will be put before the committee, voted on and depending on a favourable outcome of course, we will endeavour to assist you."

"Committee?" fumed Donald, "we just want to get on the other side of the fence, mon!"

"When is the next meeting?" asked Wulfe, holding up a hand in an attempting to calm the Scot.

Jeffrey looked across at Ned: "Ned? Could you nip next door and ask the chaps, please?"

"Will do, Jeffrey," said Ned as he unlocked the door and disappeared. A moment later, he came back and nodded to Jeffrey.

"Well that's good news!" said Jeffery with a clap of his hands. "Your escape has been approved. Congratulations! Let's get to work."

"It is that easy, yes?" asked Wulfe.

"Of course," replied a bemused Jeffrey, "we don't get paid to have meetings, this isn't the public sector!"

"Oh," replied the Swede, "of course."

"Now," continued Jeffrey, "as everyone knows, successful escapes can only be accomplished with an extremely complicated and complex plan, which we shall come to in a moment, but first we must decide when…" he mused as he walked over to a wall planner and studied it. "The soonest we could possibly make an escape attempt would be sometime between International Transgender Day of Visibility on the 31st of March and Pansexual & Panromantic Awareness and Visibility Day on the 24th of May."

"What about Mayday?" suggested Ned helpfully.

"Of course! You're a genius, Ned."

Donald and Wulfe looked at one another quizzically as Jeffrey lifted the model to reveal a network of pipes beneath.

"Well now," continued Jeffrey, "as you may or may not know, myself and the chaps have been responsible for facilitating a number of escape attempts over the years, most of them successful, contrary to what the Commandant may say, and here is how." Jeffrey pointed proudly to the pipes. "This is a 1:200 scale model of the complex of underground service tunnels. We obtained the plans from our man on the inside, at great peril to everyone involved," he said gravely as he touched one of the pipes. "This particular tunnel, after a few twists and turns, eventually leads to the outside world. The gate is lightly guarded, two men maximum, and as long as you keep to the left, you should reach it with ease."

"What happens if you go right?" a curious Donald enquired.

"If you go right, you eventually find yourself underneath the generator room and if you continue, the Fundamentalists' complex. I would advise you to stay left," a granite-jawed Jeffrey said as he replaced the top half of the model. "Here," he pointed, "is the way in- a small manhole, or woman hole, I don't care. Simply lift the cover, climb down a small service ladder and you are into the main service tunnel."

RESET

"That manhole cover is in the middle of the parade ground, yes, yes it is," stated Wulfe sceptically. "How do we get to it without being seen?"

"Ah, good question," Jeffrey responded. "That's where myself and the chaps come in. As trustees, we are allowed certain, shall we say, privileges in return for promising not to escape. These include light weeding duties around the pathways as well as some flower and shrub maintenance."

"And how does weeding help us?" asked Donald.

"All will be revealed in due course," replied Jeffrey.

"Are they not concerned you may try to escape?" asked Wulfe.

"No, they've given up, they know they will never change us and we have nothing to run for so they allow us a certain slack. They even allow us into the woods at certain times of the year- Beltane, Spring Equinox, that type of thing- in order to gather the necessaries to perform our rituals and rights such as flowers, holly, hazel etcetera."

"And how exactly does that helps us get down the manhole?" asked Donald impatiently.

"Patience, my friend, all will be revealed," replied Jeffrey calmly. "We are also allowed to practise our dance...on the parade ground."

Donald's eyebrows raised at the implication.

"In a few weeks from today, we shall celebrate the coming of the May Queen, the culmination of our year- Mother Nature's rebirth, one might say," enthused Jeffrey eagerly. "This, we celebrate by going into the woods, cutting down an ash tree, bringing it back into the camp, tying ribbons and dancing around it. The guards and re-educators pretty much leave us to it. Unfortunately for them, they have lost their connection with nature unless of course, it involves hurtling through it on a piece of expensive sporting equipment. However, I digress...as well as dancing around the maypole, we also perform other dances-the Curly-haired Plough Boy and the South Oxhey Handkerchief Dance to name but two."

"But how does that help us?" asked a bemused Donald.

"Elementary, my dear friend. We teach you the dances, supply you with the outfits and you will join with us in the dance."

"Aren't the guards going to get a wee bit suspicious when you turn up with an extra nine dancers?" observed an incredulous Donald.

"Ah, as you may know, we lost three of our original troop sadly. But as a result, the authorities allow us to co-opt three fellow prisoners to join us for the duration of the dances, fill in the numbers you might say."

"I will tell you about this," stated Wulfe, "there are nine of us."

"Nine?" quizzed Ian, doing some quick mental arithmetic.

"Aye, nine. You're coming too!" said Donald.

"I am?"

"You are, yes" confirmed Wulfe.

"Oh. Alright," replied a confounded Ian, "carry on, Jeffrey," he said as he slowly pulled the bridge of his glasses over the bridge of his nose with a thumb and forefinger.

"Yes, of course," replied Jeffrey. "Here's where it gets interesting...during our Mayday dance celebrations, we get two breaks in order to drink beer and revitalise ourselves, our 'beeriods' as we call them. This means we can smuggle three sets of three people to the manhole at a time. The first set can escape down the hole while we provide the dance cover and once they are successfully away, the remaining six of us have our 'beer o'clock' break with the next three joining us before commencement of the next dance etcetera."

"But won't someone notice?" asked Ian as he fiddled nervously with his specs.

"No, nobody is interested, not the Commandant, staff or guards, they just think we're strange and leave us to our own devices," finished Jeffrey triumphantly.

Ian looked expectantly from Donald to Wulfe and back again. "Well, what do you fink?"

Donald's rugged face contorted into what some may consider a grin. "That's pure dead brilliant!" he said enthusiastically.

Wulfe didn't look so convinced. "It seems extremely…complicated, yes complicated."

"You heard the man," replied Donald, "all the best escape plans are complicated."

"There is one problem, however," advised Jeffrey.

"And what's that, pal?"

"We only have a few weeks until Mayday."

"Well that's impossible!" said Ian. "We'll never learn all those complicated dance steps in time."

"You will have to," said Jeffrey seriously.

RESET

"We will," said the Scot with a determined set to his jaw, "we will."

CHAPTER TWENTY-SEVEN

During the witch hunts of the 16th and 17th century, the ducking stool or cucking stool was a useful device for determining a suspect's innocence or guilt. The accused witch, usually a woman, would be tied to a chair and lowered into a river or village pond to establish whether or not they were indeed a witch and after a set amount of time, the unfortunate would be hauled out. If they survived this trial by water, obviously they were a witch and taken away to be burned at the stake. However, if they drowned, they were presumed innocent and given a Christian burial.

Stalin used the same principal during the Soviet Union's show trials, condemning millions of people to death. Chairman Mao used a similar tactic during China's cultural revolution and again, millions paid the ultimate cost of being on the wrong side of an argument which is impossible to win. Critical Race Theory works on the same principle; the catch is, if you criticise Critical Race Theory, you must be a racist. The genius of this argument is that you can accuse anyone of racism and they have to defend themselves from the charge. Most right-thinking people would be appalled to be accused of being a racist and they may become angry or defensive at such an accusation. Critical Race Theory interprets these protestations as an attempt by the accused to deny their complicity in the system of racism that they benefit from: 'White fragility'. You're damned if you do and you're damned if you don't.

The next day found the group of friends sitting in the lecture theatre. This particular seminar had come at an inconvenient time for the group as they each had a long list of preparations to get through for the escape. They had become accustomed to less frequent re-education classes and lectures over the past few weeks, almost forgetting that this was the primary reason they were here, but the Centre's authorities had seen fit for all the inmates at various times during the week to attend this Power Point presentation entitled: 'White Privilege is Original Sin.'

The lecture was being given by an eloquent, rotund woman of about fifty years, with short blue hair, yellow Doc Martin boots and ubiquitous black lycra uniform. Critical Race Theory was Dr Di Ablo's bag, for she was a scientist- not a scientist as defined in any dictionary, the sort whose hypothesis would stand or fall by experiment- but a critical theory social scientist whose hypothesis could easily be proved to be correct by manipulating the statistics and data. Her theories were Maoist in nature, a Kafka Trap or an unproveable double bind built on 'Straw Men.' Scientific inquiry was not her strongest asset but her ability to punt her ludicrous notions based on scant misleading evidence was her greatest gift. Like a snake oil salesman of yesteryear, she could peddle her pseudo-scientific wares to corporations, politicians, the media and the middle classes through books, courses and personal appearances and her consumers were all too happy to lap it up, all wanting to be seen to be doing the right thing or having the right attitude regardless of reason or logic. This is what earned her a handsome living. Di Ablo was a self-proclaimed guru, piggy-backing on the ridiculous proposition that all White people are inherently racist and taking it further into the realms of absurdity. Unfortunately, any dissenting voices were immediately accused of racism- Di Ablo used any denial by the accused to serve as evidence of guilt and very few people wanting to keep their job would argue against her theories, therefore her notions could carry on unchallenged, undebated and unscrutinised. She was literally getting away with murder, as many people had already died as a direct or indirect consequence of her preposterous theory. But Di Ablo didn't care, 'Show me the money' was her mantra. The irony being, the biggest racist in the room was in fact Di Ablo herself- she was her own source material and case study, she had built her reputation on the realisation and interpretation of her own bigotries, prejudices and racism, which she actually believed everybody else shared with her. Unfortunately, the simple-minded and board members of money-hungry corporations went along with her narrative, desperate to be seen to be doing the right thing…even if it was ridiculous. But most ordinary people saw her for exactly what she was, a hypocrite.

This morning, it was the turn of the captive audience at the Re-education Centre to endure Di Ablo's lecture. Today's unproven and unprovable hypothesis went thus:

Before White babies are born, they are racists. This, she classed as 'pre-conscious racist bias,' thus the child would be born with inherent flaws, an internalised sense of superiority and entitlement which had been acquired in the womb. In addition to this, they perceived any challenge to their racial world view as an affront to their identities as good moral babies. This, she called 'White baby fragility' and it would materialise as 'race-based baby stress.' As newborn babies cannot talk, this makes it extremely difficult to discuss with them how their attitudes and beliefs make them complicit in the perpetration of institutional racism.

Only by signing up to one of her franchised courses or reading her books, could middle class virtue signalling parents cure their fascist babies, which they did in droves. Part of the course was to encourage your baby's first words to be 'Defund the Police.' This, you would achieve by saying it repeatedly to your baby like a mantra with the exclusion of anything else being said in front of the child. Another was to encourage it to 'take the knee' before it stood up on its own for the first time. This would be accomplished by binding one of its legs and removing any furniture which may aid the baby in its quest to stand up. The results could then be recorded and downloaded onto various social media platforms as proof that your baby wasn't a racist, as well as earning virtue points for the parents.

The substance of today's lecture on White Privilege boiled down to Di Ablo's assertion that White people, especially straight men, were responsible for all the evil in the world. Nain and Jessie were getting agitated, they both liked straight White men and felt duty-bound to defend them against this ridiculous onslaught.

"-slavery," concluded Dr Di Ablo, "cultural appropriation, exploitation, colonialism, rampant capitalism- all these have one thing in common," she womansplained gravely, "the fingerprints of White straight men. Now you know," she concluded, "you need to show you can do the work to understand your own racism, you need to go away and educate yourselves. Thank you," she said, giving a small bow and waiting expectantly for applause. It never came.

"The lady doth protest too much, methinks," muttered Donald.

"So, any questions?" Dr Di Ablo asked, without the slightest embarrassment from the absence of whoops and hollas she had become accustomed to.

Jessie raised her hand. "Slavery wasn't invented by straight white men, it's been happening since time began and still continues today," she stated defiantly, "and you seem to have missed out all the positive contributions White men have made to mankind or womankind- I really don't care. Things like the abolition of slavery for instance, which had been a blight on the human race since the earliest civilisations and before. The rule of law, parliament, human rights, democracy, let alone the fact that they pretty much invented our modern world during the Industrial Revolution. Almost every technical innovation can be traced back to a White male, or if not a man, a woman or person of another race living in the free society created as a result of Western civilisation. You're pretty selective with your facts but you can't dispute the truth."

"So," replied the lecturer, "you need to do some privilege checking- these things were only possible through the exploitation of women and other races."

"No," Jessie persisted, "these things were possible as the result of the Enlightenment, I think you'll find, when the state removed itself from the oppression of the church and White Western society began to flourish. This could have happened anywhere on the globe, but it didn't because other cultures were under the yoke of their own oppressive hierarchs. Had it done so, do you honestly believe that any other race would behave differently? Do you think that straight Black men or straight Asian men have some kind of inherent goodness, or women for that matter? Especially women, they may not be as violent as men but they can sure as hell be as greedy, selfish, scheming, exploitive and self-serving. It doesn't matter what sex you are or the colour of your skin, we all have one thing that unites us- it's called human nature, get used to it. The fact that we have the freedom of speech, human rights, equality and self-determination is a direct result of straight White men and women and gays. What we have may not be perfect and people were exploited on the way, but the West has been trying to make up for it ever since, that's undeniable. Western society is constantly evolving for the betterment of all, that's irrefutable, and the West is a lot better than anywhere else- we have freedom and equality in the West. You're a Marxist masquerading as a scientist but even Karl Marx was a racist, and a straight White man. It's people like you that are trying to turn the clock back with your puritanical intolerance- you're the racist."

"So" replied the lecturer coolly, "obviously you're the victim of a White patriarchal society, low information and White-washing. I would even go as far as to say you may be suffering from Stockholm Syndrome."

No, I don't think so," replied Jessie unflinchingly, "you're the one with the problem, you're a victim of White middle class guilt, and you and your intolerant ilk want to pull Western civilisation apart by taking away all the freedoms we enjoy and replacing them with oppression."

"Yet another fatality of straight White male privilege, you appear to be exhibiting White fragility."

"Hold on just one minute!" fumed Nain, pulling away from Pauli who was gently trying to restrain the indignant Welsh woman. "You're spouting this rubbish as if it were as accepted truth, as if it were obvious that straight White men have some inherent evil gene and have some great privilege over everyone else. I don't think my Gwilym would agree with that, he spent most of his adult life working down a coal mine until they closed the pit and threw him and his workmates on the scrapheap. I don't think there's much privilege amongst the working classes, whatever the colour of your skin, but you conveniently forget about that."

"Fossil fuels contribute to the death of the planet, so that was probably a good thing they closed the mine," retorted the faux scientist smugly.

"I haven't finished yet," continued a furious Nain, "and you're missing the point anyway, you seem to do a lot of that around here, you don't seem to like the inconvenient truth. What about the beggars on the streets? There are plenty of White faces there, have they got White privilege? No, the real problem in society is between those who have and those who have not, the same as it ever was or ever will be. Self-righteous people like you are trying to turn the rest of us against one another, trying to disguise your own privilege with your pathetic virtue signalling, hoping that by doing so no one will notice that it's you and your kind who are privileged and that's what you fear- you fear that you'll be found out. I bet you don't live in a working class community."

Nain took a deep breath before launching another tirade at the stunned woman. "Divide and conquer, that's what you're up to, it's the oldest trick in the book. It doesn't matter where in the world you go, you will always find a minority elite lording it over the rest of us, whether it's a political elite, religious elite or wealthy educated elite like you. Now if you've quite finished, I've got more important things to do than listen to your drivel!"

Nain made her way to the exit at the back of the lecture theatre, two guards blocked her way.

"Get out of my way!" she bristled.

Jessie and the rest of the militant group from hut 1688 followed her.

"You should probably do as she says," said Jessie to the guards.

The guards moved aside and allowed the small group of friends to pass.

Over in the rustic quarter, the rain was pouring hard on the tin roof. Fairport Convention was playing gently in the background as Bob attended another session of the Morris Men's Purple Pill De-feminisation Program, or PPP for short, with his mentor Fred. They sat opposite one another at the rear of the hut 1689, Jeffrey with a J was listening in as he prepared the potatoes Ian had furnished for the hooch the Morris Men supplied the camp with, when circumstances allowed.

"You can take the blue pill," said Fred with a slow West Country drawl, "and the story ends: you wake up and remain blissfully ignorant. You can believe what you want to believe, that women are incapable of lying for instance, and should be believed at all times without question, especially with regard to uncorroborated accusations of sexual harassment and assault, without even the slightest necessity for evidence."

Bob sat transfixed.

"You can take the red pill, stay in wonderland and see how deep the masculine toxic techno culture of the manosphere goes. Believing that men are victims and not permitted to complain about a world run by women, but instead having to conform for the benefit of women.

You can vent your hatred of female independence and generally have an unhealthy view of women."

"Or," Fred continued, "you can take the purple pill and not play with fire in the first place by leaving women out of the equation all together, giving them a wide berth. Steering well clear of the internet and embracing more wholesome activities in the company of other like-minded fellows- fishing, carpentry or long rambles for instance. Unfortunately, this is not the easiest pill to swallow- some self-discipline and organisation is required, like tidying your room, shining your shoes and standing tall with your chest out and your shoulders back, generally being responsible for yourself and your own actions, that sort of thing. So which pill will you choose?"

Bob thought for a moment. "The purple one," he replied.

"Good man, good man" replied Fred cheerily, "the pills are just a metaphor by the way, I don't actually have any pills."

"Oh," said Bob.

"Right," said Fred, "let's start today's session with pornography. Pornography is as old as time and there for a reason," he continued, "consensual, of course, all above-board. Obviously we're men and we have our urges, of course we do, and sometimes a cold shower is just not enough to quell them. Pornography can be one of the many harmless ways to relieve those urges. But too much pornography is not so good, it can become addictive or even a bad habit, a bit like picking your nose-"

As Fred was getting into his 'nose picking pornography' analogy, the cardboard door suddenly flew open and Ian's face appeared.

"Oi, oi!" he blurted, "hut inspection!" before winking at Bob and disappearing again.

RESET

"We'd better call it a day then," said Fred. "Same time tomorrow?"

"Ok mate," replied Bob enthusiastically.

The Commandant's electric buggy drove her through the mud and around the huts. She was flanked by two senior guards on mobility scooters either side. A further four of the compound's guards followed two abreast on Segways as the convoy made its way toward hut 1688, the body armour and full-face helmets glistening in the rain. They pulled up outside the building as one of the guards dismounted and waddled through the door.

"Sand eye or eds!" came the muffled order from the guard.

The inhabitants did as they were bid and stood at the foot of their beds.

The rest of the detachment double-timed their way clumsily in through the door and formed a line against the wall. Eventually the Commandant marched in, followed by her two senior aids, and disdainfully reviewed her honour guard as she swept by. She stopped and began to scrutinise the hut and its residents. Slowly she began walking from one bed to the next, saying nothing but looking into the eyes of each detainee. She reached Jessie who defiantly looked back, as did Nain. Pauli smiled, but looked defiant on account of his facial tattoos. Gradually she made her way over to Brad, looking defiant despite the fact he was wearing Nain's traditional Welsh top hat, the box of electronics still plugged into his head beneath. She moved on to Bob, standing with his shoulders back and his chest out at the foot of his immaculately made-up bed- he gazed confidently back at her. Donald regarded everyone with defiance and suspicion and the Commandant was no exception. She stood in front of him for a while then turned and left just as swiftly as she arrived, followed in quick succession by the rumble of waddling boots and squeaking leather as the corpulent guards attempted to vacate the hut, two abreast through the door.

Once outside, the Commandant turned to one of her senior aids.

"Something's going on," she said "and I vant you to get to ze bottom of it!"

The Commandant climbed into her electric buggy.. "Welcome aboard, Commandant," said the perky buggy. "Please make yourself comfortable and don't hesitate to let me know if there is anything I can do for you to make this journey a positive life affirm-"

"Just shut up and take me to Admin City," replied the Commandant curtly.

Commandant

CHAPTER TWENTY-EIGHT

The following evening, the group of potential escapees waited patiently in hut 1688 for the self-flagellations to commence- a demonstration of solidarity with minority cultures of mixed race.

Self-flagellation Wednesday was the brainchild of '#Mixed Race Lives Matter,' a Marxist-Anarchist movement which commemorated the lives of anybody of mixed race (White race excluded) killed by police whilst committing a crime in another part of the world. This particular event was a great prospect for any White middle-class narcissist in the virtue signalling or performative protest game, to be seen publicly grieving and distraught. An opportunity for uber-sexual hipsters and snowflake influencers to appear visibly anguished and mentally distressed on behalf of people they don't know, thousands of miles away.

In the camp, Self-flagellation Wednesday was only taken up by the re-education staff, but the guards would be fully occupied recording them flailing about on the floor, tearing at their hair and weeping bitterly, salving their collective guilt at White colonial history. The results were to be uploaded on social media for the edification of like-minded social justice warriors around the Anglosphere and the amusement of the Black community worldwide.

The event had occurred on the previous two Wednesday evenings and it was a good bet that it would play out over the next couple of Wednesdays too, five weeks being the average for such demonstrations of White middle-class social outrage, or until the participants' enthusiasm waned and they moved on to the next exciting global outrage or catastrophe. However, Self-flagellation Wednesday was an ideal opportunity for the inmates to move freely around the camp during curfew, and so, at eight o'clock on the dot, the wailing began and Nain led the group to the hut next door, where upon arrival, Ian ushered them in quickly. The French had vacated the space to visit their country men and women over in hut 1789 and the Morris Men had cleared an area for the commencement of rehearsals.

Jeffrey popped his head around the cardboard door as the rehearsals rolled into their second hour.

"No, no, no!" yelled Jed at Donald. "You have to raise the pig bladder above your head!"

"It's no a pig bladder, it's a condom on a stick!"

"We call it a pig bladder, it's all we've got. They confiscated our pig bladders a long time ago, the Commandant tried to humiliate us by replacing them with novelty balloons, but we keep our pride by using condoms. She left us alone after that."

"We need a break," complained Pauli.

RESET

"No breaks until you can dance the Buttered Pea Hornpipe!"

Jeffrey came in.

"How is it going, Jed?" he asked.

"Not good, Jeffrey, if I'm honest."

Jeffrey led Jed away from the group.

"What goes? Level with me, Jed," asked a concerned Jeffrey.

"They keep resorting to their native dances, they just don't seem to get it, muscle memory or something."

"What do you mean?"

"Right Mr J, here is the situation:

That one keeps going into the Dashing White Sergeant after the first few bars.

That one dances in circles.

That one jumps up and down.

That one just stands there.

That one just sits there.

That one does the Lambeth Walk.

And that one just gyrates her bottom everywhere.

It's hopeless, Jeffrey!"

Jeffrey shook his head gravely. "It's never hopeless, Jed," he said.

"But Jeffrey," interrupted Jed, "we've only got two weeks left!"

RESET

"We can do it. We will do it and we must do it," Jeffrey said. "Go hard on them, Jed, I trust in you. You're my right-hand man." Jeffrey placed both hands on Jed's shoulders.

"Will do, Mr J, will do," said a grim Jed.

"Well done, Jed. Stiff upper lip, we've been here before."

"Of course, you're right as always. I'm just a bit tired, that's all."

"Yes, we all are, Jed, but when this one is over, we'll open the cask of Firkin Maiden. I promise you that, Jed."

"You're on, Mr J," said Jed with a happier tone. "How are the lads?"

"Everything is going to plan and we should have our Maypole soon."

"Very good, Mr J. I'll get back to it."

"Well done, keep your chin up and remember what I said: drive them hard."

"Right-o," said Jed before making for the group.

"Oh, Jed?" called Jeffrey, "Are you keeping them well lubricated?"

"Indeed I am, got them running at a steady two pints of Rider's Brew per hour."

"Good, good. Remember what I said, toodle-pip!"

Jed returned to the group.

"Ok, finish your pints then we'll go straight into 'Weasel's Revenge' and follow it up with the 'Rochdale Coconut Dance.'"

RESET

In 213 BC, history tells of Emperor Qin Shi Huang of the Qin Dynasty who had all the books in his kingdom burned, in order to control how history would remember his reign. This atrocity to history and literature was followed a year later by a human atrocity, when the Emperor ordered four hundred and sixty scholars to be buried alive for the same reason. Ironically, history best remembers Emperor Qin Shi Huang's reign for burying four hundred and sixty scholars alive and burning all the books in his kingdom.

A similar erasure of history was taking place in the Re-education Centre with the annual Cancel Culture Book Burning event. The whole camp was gathered on the drill square to witness the proceedings. The lucky re-educators, who had risen to the rank of victim, had the honour of casting socially taboo books onto the pyre.

No author of sound mind would be brave enough or ignorant enough to contradict the progressive neo-Marxist social justice narrative of these days and therefore, no new books capable of causing anyone anywhere any offence, anxiety or upsetting a deeply infantilised society had been published for a number of years. As a result, the organisers of tonight's event were forced to rely on the classics to vent their groupthink outrage and ire upon. Unfortunately, due to the popularity of Book Burning Day over the years, no classics existed anymore and so in the weeks leading up to the event, the classics had to be reprinted in order to be hurled into the flames once more during this long night of offence archaeology. The classics had become a dark phoenix of literature.

Bob, who had never read a book in his life, was mildly upset to see books thrown into the fire, for reasons that he could not altogether understand. However, the event affected Nain profoundly, being a keen collector and reader of books.

"How can we go on living in such a world?" she said to Pauli, who was standing next to her with a comforting arm around her shoulders.

"We'll be away from here soon," he replied with a smile.

Nain looked to the heavens as the cinders and smoke rose into the night air, mixing with the aroma of self-satisfaction from the re-educators, knowing they were on the safe groupthink side of history.

"Forgive them," sighed Nain, "for they know not what they do."

Self-flagellation Wednesday had come around again and while the staff were earnestly engaged in an orgy of self-accusation, self-abasement and confessions of sinfulness and minor infringes against progressive thought, the escapees were diligently rehearsing their steps. Jeffrey entered the rehearsal room.

"Well, how are they doing, Jed?" asked Jeffrey.

"It's touch-and-go, Jeffrey, it really is," replied Jed.

"Are they mastering the complexities of the Maypole?"

"They're tying themselves in knots, Jeffrey, and as for her..." Jed pointed to Jessie who was performing gymnastics on the Maypole.

"We're behind schedule," said Jeffrey, "they have to master the Maypole and start working on their Handkerchief Dance. We're running out-"

"-of time, I know Mr J, but I can only work with what I've got."

"It is imperative Jed, up the dose to three pints an hour."

"But that could take them right over the limit!"

"Remember the big chap is Scottish. Just do it, Jed."

"If you say so, Jeffrey."

"I do, Jed, I do."

"But what if we push them too far?"

"We've only got one shot at this."

"But Jeffrey- "

Jeffrey cut him off.

"Just do it Jed, just do it!"

"Ok Mr J, you know best."

Jed got up and clapped his hands:

"Ok, unravel yourselves and start again. Let's take it from the top: Harper's Frolic- go!"

Over at Admin City in the Geldof Human Resources building, a select group of self-important 'experts' were gathered around the twenty-metre long mahogany table in the meeting room, engaged in an orgy of thought showers, having had a tremendously positive response (by themselves) from a recent feasibility study. It only remained to make the final preparations for the integration of the fundamentalists of X Facility and the inmates of the Re-education Centre. Having all overwhelmingly agreed on how clever they were, the group had only to wait for the final results of the computer modelling department.

RESET

Professor Niall O'Ferguson, head of Computer Modelling, was summing up his latest algorithmic data. To the progressive members of the gathering, he was a hero capable of interpreting computer models in order to arrive at the desired result. However, to the many millions of victims worldwide who had been directly affected by his erroneous modelling techniques in the past, he was something else altogether. Professor O'Ferguson had a long history of incompetence: during his career, he had advised the UN, the WHO, a number of governments, corporations and industry with his implausible models and moronic advice, telling them whatever they wanted to hear and leaving a trail of destruction wherever he went. Many people the world over had been adversely affected by his computer models and believed him to be a spunk worm or even a wank stain, whilst others thought of him as a peanut-brained jizz monkey. Some thought him more of a clunge puppet, a braindead tick dick or crap wizard and in Australia, he was known as the ginger shit biscuit. Meanwhile in the unemployed farming communities of the West, he was referred to as a knob turnip or a pickled horse penis; to bankrupt hairdressers worldwide, a blue rinse fuck muppet. European industrial towns bereft of work due to his inept modelling knew him as a steam fanny or a blast kunt furnace. In India, where his inaccurate data was directly responsible for thousands of deaths due to famine, he was known as a very silly man whereas in the rust belt of the USA, he was often referred to as a shit-kicking son of a whore, retarded ball sack or crap bandit. Some people in the Independent European English State of Germany knew him as a swivel-eyed dick brain, a fuck weevil, a spunk trumpet, a window licking turd burger, a twat axle, a purveyor of wank, or a shit goblin but most working class people just referred to him as an egotistical brainless cunt or just the cunt whose flawed data was responsible for one of the biggest recessions the world had ever known.

RESET

"So," he concluded, "according to the computer models, the integration of both facilities would appear to be an excellent course of action with no negative impact for either group."

The Commandant smiled. "Very vell zen, ve shall proceed vith ze plan. We instigate tomorrow, dismissed," she said, before directing her gaze at the Head of Security. "Not you, I have some matters to discuss vith you," she said ominously.

The last night of rehearsals was going apace, the air of confidence was tangible, as Jeffrey entered the room.

"Well Jed?" asked Jeffrey, "How's it going?"

Jed held up a hand to silence Jeffrey.

"No no no NO! Again, again, the Maid and the Palmer again from the top. Pick up those handkerchiefs, and do it like you mean it!" roared Jed, he turned to Jeffrey. "Come back in an hour."

"I'll leave you to it," Jeffrey said gingerly as he sloped out of the door.

"Who hasn't finished their pint?" he heard as the door closed behind him.

Later that same evening, as the distant sound of thunder rumbled and the air became electrified, two of the Centre's guards manoeuvred themselves into the shadows of hut 1688 as all the occupants rehearsed next door.

Jeffrey stood expectantly. Jed's granite features began to soften.

"Watch this, Mr J," he said with a half grin. "Ok, drink up!" he barked at the group. "Hurry up, we ain't got all day! Now, square off."

When Jed was satisfied that he had everybody's attention, he addressed them directly:

"I've taught you all I can, it's up to you now," he said. Turning to Fred on the melodeon, "South Oxhey Handkerchief Dance, from the top maestro!"

Jeffrey looked on in awe and wonder as the group danced the South Oxhey Handkerchief Dance perfectly. He clapped his hands together with glee.

"You've done it, Jed! You've done it, you've achieved the impossible!" He took Jed by the hand and shook vigorously whilst simultaneously patting the exhausted Morris dancer on the shoulder.

"Well done, well done. You really are the master!"

A bashful Jed looked down at the floor.

"Ah well, it was nothing really, Mr J," the big man said as the dancers waved their handkerchiefs with expert timing and intricate footwork, the sound of clogs echoed around the hut. Jeffrey stood open-mouthed at the whirl of colour and the jingle of bells.

Jed grinned at Jeffrey conspiratorially.

"It gets better," he said.

"How could it possibly be better?" Jeffrey thought for a moment. "Unless you've taught them…"

"…the South Oxhey Stick Dance," finished Jed with a nod.

RESET

The Commandant stood on the glass floor, high up on the observation deck of the Tony Blair Institute for Global Change Tower, the Big C Tower for short, and scanned the flat arable landscape that seemed to stretch out infinitely all around. The full moon illuminated the scene in a cold clear light until the distant thunder clouds finally obscured the moon and the pastoral panorama from beyond the perimeter gradually darkened as if with black ink, leaving Admin City and the collection of satellite buildings as the only source of illumination for miles around once again. The Commandant flinched imperceptibly as the first heavy sheets of rain lashed the glass panel which shielded her. She turned her attention to the direction of the Re-education Centre and smiled malevolently.

The torrent of rainwater began to drum a staccato beat on the tin roof. If everything went to plan, this would be the last night the detainees would have to spend in hut 1688. The mood was nervous yet upbeat as the thunder rumbled and the group of friends made the final preparations for the escape attempt the following day. The professionalism, discipline and comradery of the Northwood and South Oxhey Morris Men had instilled confidence amongst the group of former strangers who, after everything they had endured together, were now firm friends and all about to engage in a risky venture. Pauli's nerves had been calmed and resolve hardened by spending the afternoon with Nain as she told him more tales of Wales, in her gentle Welsh lilt, and how he was to stay with her, Gwilym and Tinkle until he could be re-united with his people or not, whatever the case may be. She had told him all about Dot, her best and most trusted friend, whom she had first met when they were both schoolchildren.

RESET

According to Nain, the pair had first laid eyes upon one another during an argument over which one of them was going to be asked out on a date to the school dance with the handsome young fifth former named Gwilym. Nain had won the argument, but this hadn't prevented the young girls becoming firm friends throughout all the hardships and good times of adult life, right up until the present day. Unfortunately, Dot had lost her husband Mostyn over ten years ago, she was very lonely nowadays and having a new friend next door in the shape of Pauli was sure to cheer her up no end. She did have plenty of room and maybe Pauli could stay over with her on occasion. Pauli was thrilled at the thought of living in Pwllheli with Nain, especially as she lived just a couple of miles down the road from the source of his beloved Portmerion Pottery.

Nain had nipped out into the rain on a quick errand for Ian, leaving Pauli knitting and day-dreaming with a broad smile as he watched Wulfe and Donald sparring together, practicing their fighting skills in preparation for tomorrow because they, along with the Maasai who sat watching silently, were to be the first down the manhole. They knew for certain they would have to take out the two guards at the entrance of the tunnel complex, but judging by the physical condition of the majority of Centre's guards, they did not expect too much opposition. Brad had decided not to escape via the manhole- but instead he was going to make a break for it through the main gate, having done 'the science,' he was confident that his machine had the necessary power and speed to 'bust' open the gates creating a diversion for the others at the same time. Snow Dragon was taking his place amongst the dance troop escapees and she worked feverishly on Brad's head in an attempt to de-commission his neuro-link. Jessie held his hand as he tried to invent new profanities to distract himself. A re-invigorated and successfully de-feminised and re-masculated Bob was busy packing his things on a perfectly made bed. Since first arriving, he had acquired an enviable wardrobe thanks to the efforts of Nain and her cohorts and his biggest problem now was which waistcoat to leave and which to take. Ian was sitting at the table merrily singing "*I'm Henry the Eighth, I am. Henery the Eighth I am, I am,*" as he made sandwiches for the journey ahead. Nain had nipped out to get some tomatoes for him from the allotment, but was taking her time about it.

"Blimey," Ian suddenly said impatiently, "where's she getting them tomatoes from, Italy?"

"I'll go and help her," Jessie said, getting up, wrapping a black sheet of plastic around herself and heading out the door. A moment later, the calm atmosphere in the hut was shattered by hysterical screaming. Pauli immediately ran for the door with incredible speed and when he got outside, he saw two of the guards disappearing into the shadowy distance, one of whom Pauli recognised immediately. He looked towards the sound of frantic sobbing and found Jessie covered in blood, kneeling in the mud and cradling Nain's body.

Nain looked up and smiled at her. "Look after them," she said as she tried to catch her breath. "Yr Arglwydd yw fy mugail..." she whispered slowly as she closed her eyes.

Nain

PART FOUR

"Gradually it was disclosed to me that the line separating good and evil

passes not through states,

nor between classes,

nor between political parties either-

but right through every human heart-

and through all human hearts"

Aleksandr Solzhenitsyn

CHAPTER TWENTY-NINE

A cloying early morning fog from the East rolled inland from the sea, coating all in its path with a heavy dew, relentlessly smothering hill and dale as it gradually drove toward the hamlet of Lower Chipping. The call to prayer echoed around the narrow streets of the village, slashing through the haze like an audible rapier, the sonic boom rattling the boarded-up windows of the local pub and thundering in the ears of the village sheeple as they cowered fretfully under their sheets. The relentless tanoy blare alarmed the ducks and the solitary black swan on the sleepy parish pond and cut through the stained-glass windows of the seemingly-empty rural church, invading and occupying the empty spaces where once the faithful would sing in praise of their own God. This invasive noise permeated all around like a shockwave veiled in the mist, washing up into the hills and over the heads of the anxious sheep, giving them something new to worry about.

The vicar looked up momentarily as she pushed open the heavy oak doors of St John's Church. She entered her domain and made her way between the empty pews; this would undoubtably be her last visit. The Church leaders had betrayed her and abandoned her to her fate, the flock had forsaken their church, their God, their faith and her. The faith of the congregation had been tested and found wanting, overcome with fear and doubt.

From the very beginning of this manmade crisis, the doors to the church had never been locked and yet in all this time, not one parishioner had dared to enter, more fearful of incurring a petty fine from the police than the disappointment of their God, conforming to the state's dictate banning congregation and worship without so much as a whimper of protest. A rare moment in time to stand fast by their beliefs had been squandered on fear. For her, action had always spoken louder than words and her parishioners' actions, or lack of them, spoke volumes.

And where were her flock? Cowering at home, religiously obeying the words of the authorities rather than the word of God. It couldn't be more obvious, not one of them had asked: 'What would Jesus do?' or if they had, they had certainly not acted on the inevitable answer.

For the vicar of St John's, this state of mind was inconceivable. "Where is your faith?" she whispered under her breath as she sat down. Surely God's authority was higher than any authority of man, but a ban on communal worship had been imposed, as well as many other basic civil liberties which she had always taken for granted. Just taken away, overnight, on some spurious justification and a kind of medical marshal law had now been imposed. The streets were unsafe, especially after the midday curfew, with squads of police roaming feral, paedophile gangs, people traffickers, drugs smugglers and gangs of self-righteous 'mask' vigilantes, ready to pounce on 'non-conformers' and hand them over to the authorities in exchange for virtue credits.

RESET

She slumped into one of the pews and regarded the large wooden cross.

"Oh, faithless generation," she recited, "how long will I be with you? How long will I endure you?"

"Not much longer!" a deep voice answered from the cloisters. "Come on, Preacher, we gotta go."

She turned around to see the old Rastafarian standing in the doorway. She smiled sadly and made her way to the door, quoting to him from the bible as she went. "Jesus answered them: 'Do you now believe? Behold, an hour is coming, and has already come, for you to be to be scattered, each to his own home, and to leave me alone; and yet I am not alone, because the Father is with Me."

The pair made their way down ancient stone steps which descended down towards a small oak door, the vicar produced a rusty iron key and began to unlock the door. The Rasta kept watch, peeping over the top of the uppermost stone stair.

All eight calculating eyes of the black spider watched the pair, as it waited patiently for the venom to take effect. The brightly-coloured wings of the butterfly flapped pathetically in the web in its bid for freedom, the silky threads binding the creature tighter with every beat of its death throws, the venom working its magic, the spider biding its time.

The same early morning sunlight that illuminated the dazzling colours of the butterfly and the silvery threads of the web, slowly began to burn through the mist and washed in through the small skylight window that lit the cellar of the church.

RESET

Once inside, the young vicar closed and locked the door. The old Rasta sat down on a rickety wooden chair and both man and chair groaned simultaneously. "You can come out now," he said.

A small child's head popped up from a cardboard box, then another from behind an old moth-eaten sofa. Before very long, a small group of children of all ages had appeared and gathered around the old Rastaman. They all sat down in silence and waited for him to speak.

"Well," he started, "we are all gonna be going on a long journey soon, dis will be de last time I can read to you for a while." He pulled a folded sheet of paper out from his shirt pocket.

Disappointed groans came from the children.

"But," he said, "I wrote dis las' night, well I copy most of it, but it a good story."

The children sat up excitedly and became more animated.

"Shhh," he said as the children gathered around him and they quietened down, hushing one another and gazed up in silent anticipation and wonder.

"*No one in de Anglosphere,*" he began, with a deep captivating voice, "*would 'ave believe in de last years of de twentieth century dat Western affairs were being watched keenly and closely by intelligences infinitely less progressive dan ours.*

Dat as de Justice Warriors busied demselves about their vacuous concerns, dey were being scrutinised, as a vegan studies dem ingredients of a vegetarian sausage roll.

Few people even considered de plight of life in oder countries, and yet across de gulf of da Mediterranean, minds immeasurably more intolerant dan

RESET

ours regarded de West with envious eyes and slowly and surely, dey drew deir plans against I… Babylon…"

The Vicar aka 'The Preacher'

CHAPTER THIRTY

Apparently, no one in Admin City considered the fact that minds over in X Facility were infinitely less progressive either. And in the office of the Re-education Centre's administration building in the heart of the micro-city, the Commandant busied herself with the final preparations for the merger of Facility X and the Re-education Centre, in her relentless battle for inclusion and diversity.

The road to hell is paved with good intentions. The Commandant had had good intentions once; like most socialists, she wanted to make the world a better place and build a socialist utopia for all, mainly to salve the guilt she felt, having been born into a wealthy German family, but also in a bid to look virtuous to others in order to disguise her sociopathic tendencies. Her meteoric rise to power had started in a local Frankfurtian charity shop where as a teenager, she spent her days fiddling the till and blaming the octogenarian volunteers or bullying the customers, climbing the ladder to reach shop manager status.

RESET

One day, whilst she was arranging and categorising books on the shelves, she caught sight of a small book, tucked in behind a German translation of celebrity chef, Ainsley Harriot's book, 'Can Cook, Will Cook.' On retrieving the hidden book, she discovered the Communist Manifesto by Karl Marx, which the young Commandant took home and becoming an instant convert. This was the start of her deep passion for such ideas as collectivism, outlawing private land ownership and state control over all areas of a citizen's life, in the name of equality and a fairer, greener society. She never did learn to cook.

At the age of eighteen, whilst still working in the charity shop, she uncovered 'An Idiot's Guide to the Frankfurt School,' effectively sealing her fate. She locked herself in the changing room and didn't come out until she understood Critical Theory and all of its devilry. She emerged from that changing room a changed woman; she immediately handed in her name badge and pricing gun, left the charity shop sector and enrolled on a Critical Theory course at university.

Upon graduating three years later with a third-class honour's degree in the 'History of Inherently Racist and Misogynistic Cro-Magnon Cave Art from a Neo-feminist Critical Racial Perspective,' she almost instantaneously got a job in the prison service. In her new role, with her instinctive understanding of society and how it should be run, she organised a number of rehabilitation programmes, including courses on basic thinking skills, victim awareness and why BAME prisoners were the victims of an oppressive White patriarchal society. One of the Commandant's proudest achievements had been building healthy relationships between paedophiles, with her 'Paedophile Prisoner Pen Pal Programme.' Her 'Risk Reduction' initiative which involved 24-hour lockdowns, had won awards and it wasn't long before she was head-hunted to run the HR department of a major corporation. Like most major international corporations, this particular company pleaded allegiance to 'Black Lives Matter' whilst simultaneously using forced child labour to manufacture sports shoes, in countries where Black lives don't appear to matter as much.

At this point in her career, the Commandant had become part of a trans-global elite with no interest in country, community or family and so when she was offered the chance to run the Re-education Centre in Norfolk, the opportunity to re-educate people for their own good and tell them what to think was more than she could have hoped for and she took the job immediately.

The Commandant had high aspirations, however, she had long outgrown Norfolk and now she had her eye on the political playing field. She had been educated into imbecility, had no practical skills or common sense, yet had managed to convince herself that she was somehow more intelligent than most other people, had better informed opinions and could thus make better judgements. Coupled with her high levels of compliance and low levels of competence, this made her a natural candidate for the Applied Behavioural Psychology Insight Team in the Cabinet Office, at the very heart of a totalitarian Government on the fringes of a Deep State. If Agenda 21 was actually happening, she was going to have her finger on the 'RESET' button: to destroy...and then 'Build Back Better.'

The Commandant waved a hand across the intercom. "Jones, get me ze acting head of Facility X on ze line," she snapped to her assistant.

"Right away," came the reply.

RESET

The Commandant reclined in her executive leather chair, rested her feet on the desk and waited.

"Doctor Jullybut here," came the voice.

"Jullybut, are you ready to implement ze necessary changes?" inquired the Commandant.

"Yes, we are ready to release them, but I have some reservations."

"Reservations? Like vat?"

"Are you absolutely sure this is the right thing to do...?"

The Commandant stoically managed to hold in her fury. "Are you questioning ze experts and my authority, Acting Head Jullybut?"

"No..." came a hesitant reply, "but you do realise we have some of the most dangerous and deranged extremists on the face of the planet contained within these walls, including child rapists and mass murderers?"

"Jullybut?" said the Commandant. "Do you not believe in rehabilitation?"

"Of course I do," pressed the Doctor tactfully, knowing his career lay in the balance, "but some of these people are religious zealots, so radical they may be incapable of being integrated successfully. Would it not be...prudent to initially trial some of the less...extreme elements of X Facility The faith paedophiles for instance, maybe start with them to see how they assimilate with the detainees of the Re-education Centre and then consider the progress of their rehabilitation...? They should be harmless without any children around."

"Vy single out ze faith paedophiles? Are you a paedophobe? Call yourself a doctor, Jullybut? You must know zat paedophilia is a mental condition and zerefore, a protected characteristic, are you victimising people with mental health issues and stigmatising a whole religion vith your 'faith-based' bias? Zat could be considered a hate crime, you know."

"Of course not, but these people-"

"These people?" exclaimed the Commandant indignantly. "Are you a racist, Jullybut? Our institutions seem to be crawling vith bigoted racists and Zionists zeese days."

"No-no, I'm not a racist," stammered the Doctor, knowing full well that an accusation of racism, whether true or false, was one of the most heinous allegations one could have levelled upon oneself in the public sector. Even a humiliating public apology was not guaranteed to get you off the hook and save your career from the witch-hunters.

"Zeese people as you say, are victims of the ignorance and prejudice of a bigoted White society, surely you must know zat. It's obvious zey really only crave inclusion," said the Commandant knowingly. "You may be a doctor, Jullybut, but you're not a critical social scientist, are you? Maybe you should have stayed in the lab with your cadavers and your rats, Jullybut."

"No, I'm not a critical social scientist but I was just thinking that maybe the Jihadi extremists-"

I zink you'll find the term 'faith-claimed fundamentalists abusing religious motivations' vill suffice, Jullybut, or even 'Irhabi', or maybe you like to use offensive vords because you have a phobia."

"Of course not, but I was thinking-"

"Shouldn't you leave ze sinking up to the humanities experts? I've often vondered how progressive you really are, Jullybut," she said menacingly. "Maybe I should take zis up vith my good friend, ze Minister."

"Oh no, that won't be necessary," replied the Doctor, sensitive to the cost of his children's education.

"Good, zen make it so," she said.

"Yes, right away, Commandant."

"Oh, and Jullybut? I shall be holding a small velcoming reception at midday in meeting room 179 of ze Big C Tower, for ze spiritual leaders of ze X Facility inmates. Please make sure you accompany zem over, I think ve may need to take zis conversation further."

CHAPTER THIRTY-ONE

The Mayday sun evaporated the last remnants of mist and hung in the clear blue sky like a golden coin as Ian and Jeffrey made their way solemnly to the hut next door.

"I'm afraid it's now or never, Ian," said a concerned Jeffrey. "Something's afoot, the guards have been decanting huts 1099 to 1244 all week. I hear the authorities are planning on housing a couple of thousand new arrivals here, which could result in tighter security." Jeffrey stopped, awkwardly trying to find the suitable words. "The chaps and I feel terrible about what happened to Nain, please accept our deepest condolences, I know she was a friend of yours," he said as he gave Ian a manly pat on the shoulder.

"Thank you, Jeffrey," replied Ian, just as awkwardly as he absently fiddled with his glasses.

"We shall, of course, take care of all the necessary arrangements, and please rest assured we will get to the bottom of it."

"Thank you very much, Jeffrey."

"A mere bagatelle, my friend," said Jeffrey, as they continued their walk.

"Did you find out 'ow she died?" asked Ian pensively.

Jeffrey paused for a moment. "Hmmm," he mused, "well that would depend on how willing you are to suspend disbelief, my friend."

"Come again?"

"According to our man on the inside," Jeffrey went on unconvinced, "the death certificate states she died of a virulent virus named C -19.84...apparently."

"A virus?" replied an astounded Ian as he squinted at Jeffrey. "But she was covered in blood, 'ow's that work out?"

Jeffrey thought for a moment in order to choose his words. "As you well know, Ian, this whole facility has been locked down for a number of months, with no explanation being given."

Ian nodded.

"According to our man on the inside, the outside is in a state of lockdown too."

"Wot, Norfolk?"

"No... not just Norfolk," said Jeffrey gravely, "the rest of the whole wide world."

Ian's jaw dropped. "The world," he mouthed silently.

"Yes, the world," continued Jeffrey. "It would appear that for the first time in the history of mankind, or womankind, if one chooses to be pedantic, an outbreak of influenza has bought the entire world to a complete halt."

"The entire world? But how…?"

"It would seem, from what the 'experts' say, and according to 'the science,' this C- 19.84 is the most contagious and dangerous virus ever to attack humanity. It's a pandemic of seismic proportions…allegedly."

"What's that got to do with Nain?"

"It would appear from our source, that anyone who has had the misfortune to die of anything over the past few months, the world over, has in fact had their death attributed to this virus, including such a demise as heart attack, cancer, motorcycle crash, being run over by a bus or eaten by a shark. Cause of death…C-19.84. This would include our dear friend Nain," he looked Ian directly in the eye. "I fear this could be the prelude to what we have long dreaded, my friend," he said solemnly.

Ian nodded sadly. "Not good," he said grimly.

"No indeed," said Jeffrey. "It gets worse, of course," he continued, "it has also emerged from our sources that a number of human rights are being abused under the guise of emergency procedures to contain this alleged pandemic, not only in this country but around the world."

"Which human rights?"

"Most of them," he went on. "It appears there are restrictions on movement and economic activity worldwide for instance, the right to education, the right to liberty, the right to private and family lives, freedom of religious beliefs and expression, the freedom of assembly and association. Under the guise of public health, interestingly enough, long held and hard-earned freedoms are being swept away on a global scale simultaneously."

"You said 'alleged pandemic.'"

"Yes," reflected Jeffrey, "apparently the numbers just don't seem to add up." He paused for a moment. "I have been hearing alarming reports from a number of reliable sources, just rumours at present, that this virus emergency could all possibly be one great big ruse, a 'plandemic' or 'scamdemic' if you like, in order to herald sweeping changes as to how the world runs. An end to meritocracy, entrepreneurialism and free markets and the ushering-in of worldwide socialism under the title of the 'Great Reset.' It would appear to have the backing of the elites, royals and world leaders and it would seem that they want to push humanity toward greater government control and less freedom, the end of the individual and the birth of worldwide collectivism, in the name of saving the planet allegedly."

"The Great Reset?" spluttered Ian. "Blimey, sounds a bit like Mao's Great Leap Forward or Stalin's Great Terror." He sighed. "Even idiots know socialism don't ever work, except for the ones at the top of the pyramid, of course, 'uman nature innit, always gets in the way. These socialist eutopias always end in oppression, execution, famine or bloodshed."

"Quite," said Jeffrey, "unfortunately nobody ever seems to learn from history. Yes, we'll get a Great Reset alright, it will be radical, catastrophic and put ninety-nine percent of the world's population into subjugation and slavery most likely, regardless of race, sex, or religion."

"True equality of outcome."

"Indeed," agreed Jeffrey. "Sorry to press you, old chap," he continued, deftly changing the subject, "especially at a time like this, but have you decided whether or not to abort the escape attempt? It would be completely understandable under the circumstances if you opted for a no-go, especially after what I've just told you about the outside world, but we have to know one way or another soon. Our window of opportunity is closing, a matter of hours, in fact."

"Yes, I've decided," replied Ian, "but I'll wait until we get to the rest of 'em, if it's all the same to you."

"Of course, old chap," said Jeffrey, "not a problem at all. I shall of course, leave it up to you as to how much of what we have just discussed you wish to divulge to the rest of the group."

Ian thought for a moment. "Fanks, I fink," he replied.

They walked on in silence for a while.

"I must admit," Jeffrey said suddenly, "I have grave reservations about our new arrivals. We should have had some idea of who they might be by now, we usually do, but this operation has been very cloak-and-dagger and what with everything that's going on outside, something's not right. I smell a rat."

"French?"

"French?" quizzed Jeffrey.

"The new inmates," Ian went on, eager to change the subject. "Yeah French, could they be making room for more French protesters?"

"From what I hear, the French authorities have pretty much crushed the yellow vests. No, this level of accommodation requirement points to a much larger group, but I really have no idea who. That's the problem, it's all very hush-hush."

"Could they have rounded up more geezers 'oo fink a woman with a penis is really a man?"

"No," replied a reflective Jeffrey. "I think the authorities have managed to get most of the population to suspend disbelief on that particular issue."

"What about a coupla fousand White people who fink White lives matter?"

"No, I believe that the White population generally understand that sort of language could get you locked up. I haven't come across any radicals with views like that for a long time."

"How about 'Me Retrospectively Too' sex offenders perhaps?"

"Not so many of those these days since they started putting sexual consent contracts into condom packets. No, this is bigger, much bigger."

"Climate change deny-ers?"

"Unfortunately not so many of those left either since the care home holocaust, remember?"

"Yeah, the geriatric genocide, who could forget?"

"Or forgive" mused Jeffrey. "This is quite a conundrum, I just can't seem to get to the bottom of it and nor can our man on the inside."

"I've got it, I've got it, I've got it," said Ian, clicking his fingers. "Refugees."

RESET

"You mean, economic migrants?" corrected Jeffrey. "Surely that's what our four star hotels are for?"

"Oh yeah," said a crestfallen Ian. "Jews?"

"Not unless they've invaded Israel," replied Jeffrey. "There's not many Jews left in Europe these days, certainly not enough to fill two and a half thousand beds."

"T.V Licence?"

"Does anyone watch the Bias Brainwashing Corporation anymore? I thought they had been defunded anyway."

"No, I fink it's still running, running on fumes but still running. It's really only the sort of people who bake sourdough bread and appreciate progressive echo chambers that watch it nowadays. Bit niche," said Ian.

"Oh."

"Care 'ome survivors watch it, of course," Ian mused, "...poor sods." Ian thought for a moment. "What about smokers?"

"No, the progressives have been going easy on the working classes lately, ever since they realised that they actually needed them. Who else is going to unblock the nation's toilets? And they can't call on the services of illegal immigrants anymore, not since the subsidies."

"Greeks," said Ian, having a lightbulb moment. "All those wandering Greeks, they 'aven't got anywhere to go since the Bundesbank repossessed their country. Stands to reason, their countrywide eviction notice should be up about now. Got to be the Greeks, innit?"

Jeffrey paused for a moment. "Hmmm, you may just be right. I'm sure every nation will have to take its quota of Greeks and with re-education camps up and down the country, there would be enough room to accommodate them-"

"On second thoughts," interrupted Ian, "the Greeks would probably all want to stick together and move en-masse, resettle in Eastern Europe or somewhere like that, plenty of room and close to 'ome. Well, former 'ome anyway."

"Ordinarily maybe, but we live in extraordinary times and Eastern Europe is full to the rafters with White South African refugees." He scratched his head. "No, I think you're probably right...Greeks. I shall have to make preparations to welcome our descendance of King Nebuchadnezzar, how jolly! But I shall endeavour to keep an ear to the ground, just in case."

Ian had wanted to make a joke about trojan horses and Greeks bearing gifts, but the Nebuchadnezzar comment had thrown him so he raised his eyebrows and allowed the thought to continue its journey, unmolested to the back of his mind.

They reached the door of hut 1688. Ian knocked. "Let's 'ope they 'ave an answer," said the Londoner.

"Well, I'm sure we'll find out soon enough," said the Northwoodian. "Shall we go in and find out what the decision is?" He opened the door and waved Ian through. "After you."

"This shit just got real," Brad was reflecting sadly as he shook his head slowly whilst Ian and Jeffrey quietly entered the hut.

"You've been saying that all night, cobba," said Bob.

"Och, it's your good selves," said Donald looking up at the sound of the pair entering the hut. "Come in."

"Hello chaps," said Jeffrey as he regarded the dejected-looking group of friends assembled around the table, positioned exactly where he had left them the evening before. "Still no sign of Pauli then?" he asked as he noticed the empty chair, empty bed and empty teapot.

"No," replied a gloomy Donald.

"He'll turn up," said Ian, trying to lighten the mood, "he always does. I'll put the kettle on, won't suit me though," he muttered automatically as he made his way to the sink.

Jeffrey sat down in the vacant chair awkwardly. "We'll do the necessaries for Nain."

"Thanks, cobba."

"Aye, thanks man."

Wulfe nodded his silent gratitude.

Jessie sat with her head on the table, nestled onto her folded arms. As she looked up, her eyes were reddened and puffy from a long night of grieving. "Thanks Jeffrey," she said and smiled sweetly.

Brad and Snowy nodded sadly, as did the Maasai with a broken-hearted expression. Jeffrey regarded him for a while and raised an eyebrow.

"'Ave you decided?" asked Ian cautiously.

"We're going," mumbled Jessie.

"Excellent," said a surprised Morris Man, "you still want to go?"

"Of course we still want tae go, ya numpty," said Donald with passion, standing up abruptly. "It's what she would have wanted."

Jeffrey looked about the table, they were all nodding.

"Well, in that case," said Jeffrey gathering himself, "let's synchronise watches."

"You will try your best, won't you, Jeffrey?" came Jessie's frail voice again. "I mean, to get us out of here."

"You have the word of an Englishman," said Jeffrey proudly.

"Och yer arse!" said Donald impulsively with instinctive disdain.

"The word of an Englishman may not mean much to anyone else these days," stated an indignant Jeffrey, "but it means a lot to me."

Donald was impressed with the steely look in Jeffrey's eyes. "Aye," said the Scot nodding, "och aye mon, I cannae help it. I'm Scottish you know, sorry mon." He sat down abruptly, his mind desperately trying to make sense of what his mouth had just uttered.

"Indeed," said Jeffrey as he marched over to the window and looked out. "According to the sundial, it is ten a.m. and that gives us two hours until the lunch guards come on duty." He looked back towards the group. "My hut…one hour…for immediate evac," he said with a confident nod of the head before heading towards the door. On reaching it, he paused and turned to address the group one last time before zero hour.

"I knelt me down and sat there weeping," he said solemnly, "and over the sides of my cheeks the tears did flow." And then he departed.

RESET

The two breathless guards stumbled frantically and fatally, straight into a dead end, amongst the collection of low buildings that constituted the Re-education Centre. They slowly turned around simultaneously, only to find the large frame of their pursuer barring any hope of escape. The figure closed in slowly, a knitting needle clutched tightly in each fist.

CHAPTER THIRTY-TWO

The air of nervous tension was palpable as Jeffrey-with-a-J Jefferson stood by the board of no colour and began to explain his elaborate escape plan, with the aid of various colours of erasable felt-tipped pens, to the nine potential escapees who were gathered around the table. Jed, Ned and Ed of the Morris Men were also present in the small hidden room whilst Ted and Fred guarded the door from the outside. The French Gilet Jaunes provided a distraction around the hut outside by practising songs. Ted and Fred listened intently for the first strains of 'Le Mans' or 'Joe Le Taxi' which would signal the approach of any guards.

"Group A will comprise of Wulfe, Donald and our friend from Africa. Once suitably attired, they will join the rest of us Morris Men as we proceed to the square. Once there, we will form up and go straight into the 'Curly-haired Plough Boy.' Once we form a circle at the mid-point of the tune, Ed here-" Jeffrey pointed to Ed who gave a quick nod, "-will lift the manhole, or indeed woman-hole cover, I really don't care," he continued. "Now listen up carefully. We have only thirty seconds to get all three of you down the hole before we switch to 'Molly from the Wold.' It is imperative that Ed has the cover back in place before the first handkerchief crossover. Then once the dance is finished, the Morris Men will return to the hut for heavy refreshments before heading back out to the square with the Maypole and the next three escapees in group B. Meanwhile, group A will be en-route to the Guard House, having first relieved themselves of their outfits which group B will be changing into during the 'beeriod' period.

Once group B have been deposited down the hole during the finale of the Maypole dance, the Morris Men will return to the hut for more refreshments, allowing group C to change clothes."

"There won't be a group C," said Jessie, "I'm taking my chances with Brad."

"But what about the 'Cumbrian Weasel Clog Dance?'"

"You'll have to do it without us."

"I quite understand," said Jeffrey, "we shall push on regardless. As I was saying, -by which time group A should have reached the Guard House, overpowered the guards and await their comrades. If the balloon goes up, it's every man- or woman- for themselves. Jed has taught you the stick dance but let's hope that you won't need to use it.

This has to go like clockwork and I can't emphasise enough how dangerous this operation will be, but just remember your training.

Good luck everyone. I think Jed would like to say a few words."

Jed stood up and took his hat off.

RESET

"I'm sorry for your loss," he said awkwardly, "she was a fine woman and an inspiration to us all and although I didn't know her quite as well as all of you, I think I knew her well enough to believe that this is what she would have wanted, her friends to escape to freedom. I've taught you all I can, it's up to you now. Remember your steps and keep it tight. Good luck. You know this, you can do this and I'll see you on the other side." Jed finished, wiping a tear from the corner of his eye.

Jeffrey stood up and looked around the group.

"Thank you, Jed," said Jeffrey glancing at his watch and smiled confidently. "Ok everyone, this is it. To your posts, and good luck!"

In Admin City, the Commandant looked at her watch and smirked menacingly.

"Ok people, zis is it, make it happen and remember your annual review," she said through gritted teeth.

CHAPTER THIRTY-THREE

The trio, consisting of Donald, Wulfe and the Maasai, disrobed from their Morris dancing attire and cautiously made their way down the service tunnel that led to the outside world and freedom. The regular soft slapping of the Maasai's sandalled feet was the only sound. The bore of the tunnel was about twenty feet in diameter and constructed of concrete sections with support rings equally spaced along the full length of the structure. Illumination was provided by low level LED strip lighting secreted into the walls, which shone a bright incandescent light upwards. The tunnel began to curve to the right, gradually at first but as they progressed further, the curve became tighter until eventually, they couldn't see far ahead. The three stopped instantly when they began to hear voices just around the bend.

Donald held up a hand and gestured his head towards the source of the utterances. "I'll go take swatch," he whispered to Wulfe.

Wulfe looked confused.

"A look, mon. Ye ken?"

Wulfe kenned and he nodded before Donald disappeared off into the distance. A few moments later, the Scot came trotting stealthily back.

"There's a squad of guards coming, we'll have to take them by surprise, we're outnumbered," whispered Donald, "and they're heading oor way, ye ken?"

"I thought we were only likely to come across two guards, yes? How many were there?" Wulfe asked in hushed tones.

"At least eight."

"A trap?"

"Aye, could be," reflected Donald, "should have listened to my mammy, never trust an Englishman."

"Are they heading this way?"

"Aye," replied the Scot, "on foot. They seem to be in a bit of a hurry and they're moving at quite a trot, especially for fat folk."

"We don't have any choice," reflected Wulfe, "we're going to have to take them out. yah"

"Aye, now you're talking," said Donald with relish, a gleeful look in his eyes as a menacing grimace crossed his lips. "How?"

"An ambush," confirmed the Swede. "We need to lay an ambush and drive them into it."

Donald's eyes lit up.

"An ambush! I like yer thinking, big yin," he said.

"We need to set a trap" said Wulfe thoughtfully. "We need to get someone behind them, panic them and then drive them into the teeth of the trap. Snap! Yah."

"Brilliant mon," said Donald eagerly, "but who's gonnae go round them up and who's gonnae be waiting for them?"

"Hmm," mused the Swede, "it will need to be a skilled and fearless hunter. I will go and drive them towards you two, then CRACK! The jaws of the trap will snap shut," said Wulfe, punching his fists together with a grimace.

"Woah woah woah, big yin, whoever gets behind them has the most dangerous job, ye ken? I'll go, rounding up furry animals is one thing but getting a group of dangerous individuals to panic is quite another."

"Do you have experience?" asked Wulfe earnestly.

"Aye, Sauchiehall Street on a Friday night, mon" said a passionate Donald. "I should be the one."

Wulfe didn't quite understand what the Scot had just said but judging by the manic gleam in his eyes, it must have been profound and maybe indeed, Donald should be the one to go.

"You may be right," agreed Wulfe, never one to let his ego stifle his common sense. "Yes, stay here, hide behind this support and get behind them unseen, before charging them. Hopefully you will have the element of surprise on your side and can panic them into a stampede and drive them towards us." He paused. "Wait a minute, we have the ultimate hunter amongst us."

They both looked at the Maasai.

"Of course, pure dead brilliant!" said Donald in a moment of clarity. "His people hunt lions, for fuck's sake, I saw it on a documentary. The wee mon should stay here."

The Swede nodded sagely. "Yes, it has been selfish of us to leave him out of the debate. He would not thank us."

"No, he wouldnae," conceded Donald. He turned to the Maasai, "Sorry pal, I wasnae thinking."

"It would be wrong of us to deprive the greatest hunter here of his sport, yes," said a serious Swede, slapping the Maasai on the back manfully. Donald did the same as they manoeuvred the Maasai into the shadows of a concrete support ring, gesticulating at him wildly for a moment.

"Wire in, wee mon," were Donald's parting words as he and the Swede retreated back the way they had come, to lie in wait.

The Maasai watched as the pair disappeared out of sight, with eyes wide open.

CHAPTER THIRTY-FOUR

Further down, the Scot and the Swede found cover in the shadows either side of the tunnel and waited in silence, breathing imperceptibly and gazing intensely into each other's cold blue eyes, anticipating the battle to come.

Wulfe squinted as he thought he heard something in the distance, Donald picked up his cue and listened intently. Somewhere from around the curve of the large tunnel, he thought he could make out a faint echoey sound, a kind of slapping noise and a low panicky voice. The Scot listened as the sounds got louder and echoed around the tunnel. He strained to hear hysterical breathing. Suddenly, both men could clearly make out the words: "I don't want to die!"

Donald grinned wickedly and moved deeper into the shadows. The Swede tensed, ready to strike. The heavy panicked breathing was almost upon them when suddenly, an alarm sounded and all the lights turned red. Without hesitation, Wulfe thrust out a muscular arm and a figure ran neck first into it, swinging high into the air before crashing down hard on the ground, where it lay groaning.

RESET

Donald was impressed and involuntarily raised his eyebrows, but on noticing a pair of sandals that he recognised, the brows automatically re-constituted themselves, into the default frown.

The Maasai lay squirming on the floor, clutching his neck and struggling for breath in the flashing red light as the guards approached.

"How the hell did he find himself running ahead of them?" a confused Donald asked an equally baffled Wulfe. "Do you think that's how they do it in Africa?"

Wulfe looked up and saw large shadows nearing. Donald listened closely as the Maasai attempted to speak.

"Run!" shrieked the Maasai in a strangled voice.

The two big men exchanged puzzled looks.

"He must be delirious," said Wulfe.

Donald nodded in agreement and hauled the Maasai to his feet.

"Wait a minute, he spoke ENGLISH!" exclaimed Donald.

"That's because I AM English!" yelped the Maasai.

Donald immediately dropped him as if the scarlet robes of the Maasai were red hot. Wulfe tensed as he began to make out large, dark figures waddling with speed and intent towards them.

"He's English," repeated the Scot, completely bamboozled. Donald's eyebrows knitted together as he dragged the petrified Maasai once more to his feet and invaded his personal 'safe' space.

"I should have known," he spat with contempt before shoving the English Maasai warrior into the Swede's open arms and leaping into the crowd of oncoming guards, all suffering from the highly contagious disease of morbid obesity.

The giant Swede turned his captive around and looked down angrily. "Now you can speak," he said with menace. "Start talking…"

…The one-man Highland charge plunged his shoulder deep into the first guard, flipping him like a sack of potatoes over his back and sending him crashing to the floor…

"…Well?" demanded Wulfe.

The petrified Maasai looked up with wide eyes.

"My name's Terry," he mumbled faintly, "I live in London…and I work in IT…"

…Donald charged at two guards with glee, lifting them both by the throat and smashing their helmeted heads together like ripe melons before ripping their helmets off in frustration and giving them both a Glasgow Kiss apiece…

"…What did you say?" Wulfe growled.

"My name's Terry, I live in London and I work in IT," repeated Terry. "I'm not supposed to be here."

"Keep talking," said the Swede…

…Donald swung a guard by his feet into two more, then leapt mercilessly upon them like a wild haggis during the rut. As they toppled backwards, he rained down a barrage of blows on all three before hurtling himself onto another pair of guards attempting to escape the tartan fury…

RESET

"…I- I was on holiday when they picked me up," stammered Terry. "I- I couldn't say anything to them because I'm supposed to be on the sick."

Wulfe's suspicious eyes narrowed. "Yes?" he said

"I'm a civil servant…I was on sick leave…due to stress," Terry explained. "It got a bit boring after the first six months, so I thought I'd take a holiday." Terry took a deep breath, then continued. "I'd been tracing my ancestry, you know, with one of those DNA kits."

Wulfe nodded, he had knowledge of such things, as grunts of pain echoed around the tunnel.

"When I got the results," Terry continued, "they indicated I was distantly related to the Maasai of East Africa. As I said, I was bored, so I zipped up my boots and went back to my roots…on a safari holiday. I wasn't supposed to, of course, being on the sick. If my work found out I could get seriously disciplined…"

…Donald lifted a guard off the ground and flipped him around like a cheerleader's baton, before launching him headfirst towards the ground, crashing him down on his own head…

…Wulfe regarded the man of distant Maasai heritage warily. "So why do you wear these clothes?"

"I borrowed them," Terry said shamefully. "I was having my photo taken with a travelling Maasai dance troupe, and that's when the Relocation and Preservation Squad came and rounded me up. The rest of the troupe ran into the bush, leaving me standing there. I couldn't tell the Ree-Pee squad who I was, I could be disciplined like I said, so I played along with it, especially when I overheard them say I would be taken to England for preservation. All I had to do was get back to Britain, walk out of the relocation camp, jump on the train and

I could be back in my flat before the next sick note was due." Terry sighed. "But they sent me here by mistake."

"You have deceived us all!" raged the Swede.

"I- I know, but I was in too deep by then. I didn't want to deceive my friends but what could I do?" Terry implored.

"You deceived Nain!" roared Wulfe.

"I know and believe me, I feel terrible." Terry looked earnestly up at Wulfe and his body slumped. "If- if you want to beat my brains out, I'll understand...I deserve it." He closed his eyes as the giant Swede gripped him tightly around the throat with one hand and slowly lifted a hammer-like fist into the air high above the public sector worker's trembling head...

...Guards flew through the air as the Scot scythed through them with a mighty haymaker. Donald ducked, as a heavy wooden baton whooshed just inches from his head, then springing to his feet, he grabbed his assailant's arm and twisted it up behind his back, forcing him to release his grip of the weapon. Donald grabbed it and knocked the guard to the ground with one mighty blow...

...Time passed slowly for Terry, the civil servant with Maasai bloodline. He kept his eyes tightly shut and bravely waited to be reunited with his African ancestors. When the vice around his neck began to slacken, he opened one eye only to find the Swede looking mournfully down at the floor in the red emergency lighting. He looked up at Terry momentarily before dropping to his knees. The big man's fur-covered shoulders slumped and started to quake. He began to cry bitter tears, much to the astonishment of Terry.

"I cannot judge you, no" wailed Wulfe, "when I have deceived my friends too!"

RESET

"How?" asked a tentative Terry.

"You see, I'm really a woman…" came the mournful reply…

…Donald snatched another baton from an unconscious guard, sending bodies flying in all directions like skittles, smashing against the walls…

…Terry's faculties suddenly returned. "What?" he exclaimed in disbelief.

The giant Swede sobbed uncontrollably. "I am really a woman," repeated Wulfe, as a guard slid along the floor between them, en-route to the wall.

"You see, I was a tomboy when I was a little girl," Wulfe explained through the tears. "My parents even encouraged it with their 'affirmation only' approach to parenting. I think they really always wanted a boy, yes, they would dress me up in boy's clothes and I didn't complain. I liked playing football and climbing trees so boy's clothes were more practical, yah, but even the bad haircuts were not enough to quell my parents' insatiable desire to turn me into a boy, no. It was a fashionable thing to do, yes, in the gated communities of Stockholm. It is quite common for the upper middle-classes to want to change the sex of their children, fashion, some might call castration and female genital mutilation child abuse, but they call it gender dysphoria, which does actually exist, but only in a tiny proportion of the population."

Terry stood open-mouthed and completely dumbfounded at Wulfe's confession, as Donald repeatedly smashed his fist into one of the guard's visors like an epileptic jack hammer.

"I was just a non-conforming and confused child, yes," Wulfe explained bitterly," but they gave me gender realignment surgery."

RESET

The bemused and stunned Terry nodded along absently in agreement. "Errr..." he began.

"And so," lamented the Swede sadly, "my gender journey began at the age of eleven with 'off label' puberty-blocking drugs at first, but then my parents called on the services of a Trans-gender advocating charity called Little Mermen, who advertised on children's gaming platforms. My mother noticed their ad one day when I was playing a game called 'Brainskill,' yes..."

...Donald's brain and skill were on full display as he punched and kicked with perfect timing, sending his enemies flying in all directions like tenpins...

"...Little Mermen pushed an extreme ideological agenda," continued Wulfe, "promoting an unscientific 'wrong body' narrative. They tested me by holding up a chart with a picture of Barbie at one end and a number of coloured stick men and women, leading to a G.I. Joe at the other. They then asked me to choose where on the spectrum I thought my identity might be. I pointed to the purple stick man, purple is my favourite colour," said the Swede wistfully, as the Scot sent a guard spinning into the wall like a spinning top. The newly-verbal Terry was speechless as he listened in disbelief to this tale of woe.

"Little Mermen told my parents that this test confirmed I had gender dysmorphia, meaning I had a boy brain in a girl body and was likely to kill myself if I didn't get medical help, yes, and so I embarked on a medical pathway, a journey that once you are on, you can never get off, no. The hormone blockers affected my moods, of course, as well as my bone density. They even made me feel suicidal which Little Mermen took to mean I needed surgery immediately or else I could die, yes, but before embarking on invasive surgery, I had years of untested treatments and regular assessments by psychologists and psychiatrists. Little Mermen coached me on all the 'right things' to say thus bypassing a proper assessment. I was confused and went along with it, yes, and so for my sixteenth birthday my parents took me to Thailand for gender re-assignment surgery, and I became a man, yes...no..."

...Donald drummed out a beat on a guard's head with two batons, before sending him hurtling through the air majestically and coming down to earth with a thud...

"...When the full gravitas of what had happened hit me, I became depressed and suicidal, yes. I was infertile and facing a future of potential health problems as a result of invasive surgery and synthetic hormones, yes. Little Mermen told my parents I had mental health issues due to living in a prejudiced world and it would be best for me if I were locked up in one of their clinics, which they have across the country, in order that I could be helped on my gender journey. My parents readily agreed, yes, always willing to trust the 'science' and the 'experts' and especially after being promised that Little Mermen's methods and goals were based on good intentions for outcome, yes, as opposed to good evidence for outcome. I tried to escape but they always caught me, they told me it would be bad for the community if I left and complained and that thousands of vulnerable young trans-curious children could die as a result. In the end I gave in, yes." Wulfe broke down and began to wail pitifully. "They wanted to make a penis out of a piece of my forearm, for God's sake! That's why I ran, yes."

Terry stood ashen and aghast. "Aaaah..." he croaked.

"I spent years in that institution," wept the Swede, "until a militant de-transitioning advocacy network rescued me, yes, and eventually after a number of stays in safe houses, introduced me to a travelling Viking re-enactment group, and with them I stayed, happy and safe, yes, until we were disbanded by the Swedish Culture Police, and I was forced to flee and live a life on the run and alone in the woods. The saddest thing is I would probably have resolved my feelings naturally by the end of puberty if they had all just left me alone, yes."

Terry stood silently for a moment, before patting the Swede gingerly on the shoulder. As the last guard dropped to the floor, Donald stopped to take a deep breath. He held it and strained to hear, as a strange noise echoed from further down the tunnel. He raised an eyebrow.

"Oh," replied Terry cautiously, "err…ummm…yeah…so, the reason I came running back was to warn you that the guards were being chased by a bunch of geezers with beards and swords, shouting 'Ali Ba Ba' or something like that… they didn't look too happy, I think we need to get out of here pronto."

CHAPTER THIRTY-FIVE

Bob grinned to himself as he stepped off the ladder that led down from the manhole and into the emergency red illumination of the tunnel. As soon as both feet touched terra firma, he heard the familiar sound of skin on thong echoing all around him. He peered down the tunnel and saw three distant figures making their way toward him at speed.

"Get. back. up. the. ladder!" echoed Wulfe's roar.

"Go blow up my bladder?" Bob shouted back in confusion.

"Nooo…" boomed Donald's voice, "Get back up the ladder, ya deef wee dobber!"

"Will do, cobba," replied a confused but compliant Bob.

He turned to mount the ladder when suddenly, a black leather-clad hand of chubby proportions clasped his shoulder. Bob whirled around in a flash, fists raised, no stranger to sudden Dingo attack.

"Don't hurt me!" cried the guard frantically. "They're coming!"

Bob was momentarily taken aback. How could a twenty stone leather-clad man have waddled up behind him and taken him by surprise? "Must be losing it..." he muttered aloud but before he could take his musings further, the Swede was upon the guard and pinning him to the ground.

"Who is coming?" Wulfe demanded with menace, as Terry and Donald caught up with the Viking.

"The fundamentalists," wheezed the frantic guard, "they've been let out!"

"Let out?"

"Yeah, they've cut the power and they're coming!"

"They've cut the power?" a highly agitated Terry interjected. "What do you mean, they've cut the power? How can they cut the power? They're prisoners!"

Bob turned to Donald. "He speaks English?"

"Aye," said a still confused Scot, "you cannae shut him up."

"Strewth, he's a quick learner," mumbled Bob to himself as he scrambled up the ladder.

"Where are they exactly?" interrogated Wulfe, her muscular hands tightening around the guard's throat.

"Everywhere," squeaked the guard, "they've taken the generator room and the gate house, they're in the city. I only just got away, they're using the service tunnels, they haven't reached the re-ed centre yet but it's only a matter of time. They'll be here any minute, let me go!"

RESET

"They're coming out of the service tunnels…" a panicky Terry repeated anxiously, rubbing his hands together with a horrified expression on his face. "They're coming out of the freaking service tunnels!" he cried as he stumbled over to the ladder and scrambled up after Bob. Donald and Wulfe were hot on his heels.

"Wait for me!" cried the guard, struggling to his feet like a beached narwhale.

Snowy watched anxiously as Ned and Fred lifted the womanhole cover ready to deposit Ian, when suddenly Bob's head popped up. "Change of plan, mate," he said, as he pulled himself out.

Fred scratched his head. "Now, what's all these shenanigans?" he politely demanded as Terry's head emerged.

"That's it, bro," jabbered the frantic civil servant. "They're coming out of the walls, it's game over, bro, it's game over!"

"He speaks English!" said Ian in surprise, Bob nodded. "Blimey, he's a quick learner," mused the Londoner.

Just then, Donald appeared.

"What are you doing back?" asked a startled Ned.

"No time to explain, pal," replied the Scot hurriedly as he scrambled out of the hole. Ned helped him out to the tune of 'Molly in the Wold" which Jed was playing enthusiastically on the harmonium in the background.

Wulfe appeared next and flopped onto the tarmac. "Cover up the womanhole, quickly!" she ordered.

RESET

Ned and Fred were about the seal the hole when they heard the sound of the guard below.

"Wait!" implored the guard.

The two Morris Men waited, as the desperate guard's head appeared at the entrance of the hole.

"Help me," the guard wheezed with outstretched arms.

All the assembled Morris Men took a hold of the man and pulled, but the pie-curious guard was far too crippled by the disease of obesity to fit through the aperture.

"Help me, pull me out!" he cried out desperately.

Soon everyone gathered around the hole, without the slightest hint of appearance-based discrimination, grabbed what they could of the man and pulled furiously but he would not budge. Worse still, there appeared to be a counter-force pulling the poor wretch back down the hole. Try as they might, they could not pull the hapless guard free. Eventually the counter-force soon became overwhelming and the guard was dragged screaming, back down into the red glow of the hole and his inevitable fate.

With a jingle of bells, Ned and Fred quickly sealed the hole with the heavy iron cover, as the rest of the gathering watched on in horror.

"Well I'm blowed," said Fred. "That was a bit of a to-do, so what's all this kerfuffle about then?"

"Fundamentalists, fanatical members of a religion of peace" replied Jeffrey-with-a-J as he marched over to the group. "Just got valuable intel from our man on the inside, the fundamentalists have escaped from the de-radicalisation facility, whether by accident or design we know not, but there it is." He turned to Ian. "Mystery solved, no Greeks it would appear," he said.

"Sheiks airing tiffs," Ian mumbled, slightly embarrassed with the quality of his own joke.

"No good will come of this, I shouldn't think," said Fred shaking his head philosophically. "So, what's the plan, Mr J?"

"We have to evacuate everyone immediately," said Jeffrey, "especially the women, with or without cervixes." He reflected for a moment. "Thank God we haven't any children here."

"Just hold on one minute," Snowy said defiantly. "Why especially the women? I can take care of myself."

"I'm sorry, Snowy," replied Jeffrey, "I didn't mean to be sexist, but the fundamentalists like to indulge in a thing they call Taharrush Jama'a."

"What's that?" asked a curious Snowy.

"You don't want to know," Jeffrey stated, with a sage-like shake of the head. "I understand it's very popular in certain regions of the world and it would appear it's becoming ever more popular in Northern Europe."

"Oh, I won't ask," replied Snowy thoughtfully. "I'm gone."

"Best."

She turned to leave but paused momentarily. "I need a plan."

"Well you've come to the right place," said a cheery Fred. "Ain't that right, Mr J?"

RESET

"Indeed, Fred," replied Jeffrey to his cohort. "Now, the fundamentalists have control of the tunnel network and underground exit, it would seem, so we really only have but one option: the main gate."

"The main gate?" repeated Snowy.

"The main gate," Jeffrey confirmed, "and out onto the ring road that encircles Admin City. From there, it's only a matter of taking the second left and heading straight out of the main entrance to the whole complex." He paused for a brief moment, finding the words. "The only trouble is, however, some of us will have to stay behind to defend the fence that separates us from X Facility," he paused again. "It would appear that they are gathering for a frontal assault and now that the power is out, I'm afraid to say that the electrified fence will no longer acts as a deterrent. Through sheer weight of numbers, they shall be over it and amongst us in moments. Some of us will have to stay behind, of course, and act as a defensive rear guard in order for as many people to escape as possible before we get overrun."

There was a moment of tense silence, mercifully broken by Fred.

"Cummus 'zon," he said to his fellow Morris Men, "we best be off, times a-wastin'."

The band of Morris brothers formed up and marched off, double-time, towards the fence.

"We shall see ye all d'reckly!" shouted Fred over his shoulder, as the small contingent disappeared into the distance.

Jeffrey addressed the rest of the group: "You had better warn everyone in the camp," he said with authority, "then head over to the compound gates and make your escape. The boys and I can hold them off for a while, but you have to make your escape NOW!."

"But what about the bleedin' guards?" exclaimed Ian.

Jeffrey pointed to the main exit. All the guards were heading towards it, like rats gliding off a sinking ship.

"I don't think you will have any trouble walking out of the front door," he said as he turned to join the rest of his troop. "But you'd best hurry- we can't hold them off forever, good luck chaps!" And then he disappeared.

The six friends stood in a small circle in silence; alone and disorientated, lost in the wide expanse of the drill square as the world they had come to know came crumbling down around them. A slight breeze gently rattled the wire lines of the flagpoles and the sound transported Donald back to the cold wet autumn night of his arrival. He unconsciously clenched his fists: this time, he would be in control of his own destiny.

Donald came out of his reverie with a jolt of realisation, noticing that every member of the group was looking at him, as if awaiting their next instruction. This was Donald's moment.

"Wit yooz lookin' at me fur?"

PART 5

"The only thing necessary for the triumph of evil

Is for good men to do nothing"

Edmund Burke

CHAPTER THIRTY-SIX

A dark avaricious soul, combined with an insatiable lust for power, an ego bereft of conscience and a blackened heart wanting of humanity, are a combination fortunately few possess. However, some do and on occasion, unconcerned as to whether or not their actions lead to dire consequences, these purveyors of evil ascend into offices of power, indifferent to the trail of death and destruction left in the wake of their meddling and the legacy of bloodshed rippling far out into the future, claiming the lives of the souls yet unborn.

In the Tony Blair Institute for Global Change Tower, located in the heart of Admin City in meeting room 179, the Commandant had assembled a small gathering of the great and the good from various progressive institutions across the City. The Commandant was throwing a party to celebrate her Multicultural De-radicalising and Re-education, Inclusion and Diversity Initiative, and a small delegation was assembled here to welcome the leaders of the fundamentalists. The group, exemplifying the crème-de-la-crème of the City's illiberal liberal thinkers. Abundant amongst their numbers were the overeducated imbeciles, grievance mongers and morality Olympians, essential for the smooth running of the City. Representatives from the mainstream left-wing media were present, as well as the usual self-serving heads of NGOs, experts from integration and diversity thinktanks, money-spinning charities and a couple of left-wing politicians, prostituting themselves to whichever ideology was currently fashionable. These people all had one thing in common: they had all been through the progressive neo-Marxist indoctrination factory, formally known as University, where young minds had been taught what to think and how.

A handful of re-educators from the Re-education Centre were also present, on hand to answer any questions. These included Myles who was enthusiastically handing out promotional goodie bags, whilst Farquhar was offering head coverings to the ignorant or less progressive females amongst the gathering who had failed to get the memo. Ms Dubois was hurriedly putting the finishing touches to the culinary spread, with some creations of their own baking. The Commandant scanned the room proudly as she drew her speech to a close.

"Ven people look back on zis time and look back on zis amalgamation, I honestly believe zey vill see zis as one of ze defining moments in our Re-education Centre's history, as ve together take one more small experimental step on ze Autobahn from conceptualising a just and inclusive society and making it a utopian reality. The forward sinking and hard vork of the steering group in helping us reach zis day cannot be underestimated," the Commandant said as she turned towards Shea and the other members of the steering group, giving them a small nod of appreciation and a rare smile. "Our esteemed guests should be here at any moment now," she continued, "so it only remains for me to thank you all for coming here today and I'm confident ve shall all have an enlightening and life-affirming afternoon. Danke."

The Commandant took a moment to savour the ripple of applause, self-assured and quietly confident that her mini-managerial coup and cost-cutting exercises would get noticed by the all the right people.

The buzz of the intercom cut through the murmurs of admiration, as Jones at reception announced that the elevator containing their honoured guests was on the way up. The room was silent with expectant anticipation as the ding of the elevator rang and a chirpy voice sounded from beyond the doors.

"Thank you for choosing to ride in this elevator. I hope you enjoyed your journey, I am aware that you could have chosen to use the stairs. Please call again and have a nice day."

A muffled thump followed, before the large oak doors burst open and a large group of bearded and fearsome-looking men strode in, dark of eye and humourless of disposition.

The silence was broken as the Commandant instigated a round of applause for the new arrivals.

"Velcome," she said as she approached the head man. "Is Dr Jullybut vith you?"

The head man produced a recycled jute shopping bag and dumped it on the table next to the cous-cous. Reaching inside, with a twisted grin, he produced the severed head of Dr K.G. Jullybut M.D. Governor of X Facility.

The Commandant began to shake at the realisation of the situation, suffering a major identity quake "Jullybut," she mouthed with horrified eyes, her world view built on the weak foundations of feelings over facts and virtue signals over common sense, now turned on its head and rendered incomprehensible. "But...but... Jullybut..." she stammered.

"Shut up, bitch!" roared the man, as he slapped the Commandant across the face and sent her sprawling to the floor. "Take the women to our 'special' cells," he ordered his underlings, as they eagerly coerced the women out of the room at knife point.

"But I'm not a racist!" the Commandant could be heard pleading as she was dragged by the hair unceremoniously from the room, wretchedly unable to comprehend why these BAME men should be 'enacting Whiteness.' The Commandant was confused, her virtuous critical thinking abilities abandoning her in the current situation. Not wishing to be accused of White fragility, her brain had become impervious to reasoned and rational thought after years of practice and neglect. She went into meltdown, woefully unable to compute that some people just don't care about such things as Social Justice or Human Rights. Unfortunately for the Commandant, each of the fundamentalists carried an instruction manual, enlightening them as to exactly what to do with her.

As Shea was brusquely bundled out of the room, she thanked God that she had had the foresight to get the boob job, it just may well save her life.

Ms Dubois' attempt to leave with the other women was halted by the tip of a bloody sabre, which had been lovingly constructed during the de-radicalisation facility's 'ornamental metal work' classes.

"Take this one to the roof," said the head man.

RESET

"But I self-identify as a womxn," remonstrated Dubois, reeling from a reality shock. "I should go with them, I made you falafel," she pleaded to her assailant as the chirpy voice of the elevator welcomed them onboard.

"Rooftop viewing platform," said the perky lift. "Going up!"

The gravity of the situation wasn't lost on Myles as the fundamentalists closed in on the remaining party-goers. After countless hours and copious amounts of money spent at the gym, Myles's body was toned to perfection, his shaven calves glistening in the artificial light. The years spent practicing Mixed Martial Arts and Pilates were about to pay-off as his razor-sharp reflexes and athletic ability bought him supplicating down upon one knee in less than a second. Head down, he sobbed as he awaited his fate.

Josh Farquhar's instantaneous and miraculous conversion to Christianity was something to behold as he knelt beside Myles and prayed furiously to the deity that, up to this moment of his life, he had so vehemently dismissed. Displaying a complete lack of Mindfulness, he recited the Lord's prayer frantically, beseeching God with all sincerity to save his soul. Unluckily for the green evangelist, it was the wrong God.

As the last cervix-having woman was dragged out by her culturally-appropriated straight hair, the large oak doors were shut and locked.

CHAPTER THIRTY-SEVEN

Jeffrey lined up alongside his five comrades and gazed up the hill towards X Facility where he could see figures milling about and organising themselves for a full-frontal attack. Hanging by the neck from the lampposts that illuminated the facility's courtyard, were the guards. The lampposts bowed under the weight, having been manufactured using cheap Chinese steel, leaving the corpses to swing in the breeze like giant black fish on the end of a rod.

"There must be at least two hundred of them," said Jeffrey.

"Two hundred and forty-three, to be precise, Mr J," remarked Ned absently.

"I fear we won't be able to hold them off for long." Jeffrey turned and looked at his comrades.

"No," replied Ned, "but we can give 'em a bloody nose."

"That's the spirit, Ned, but if only there were more of us, we could give them a jolly good kick up the arse!"

"But you are not alone," came rich Russian baritone from behind.

The Morris Men whirled around to find Ivan, the head of the Cossack dance team, having marched over silently, leading his men, in his soft leather fur-topped boots.

"How did you know?" asked Jeffrey, full of admiration for his former foe.

"Russian intelligence," replied the intelligent Russian.

Ivan pointed to his left and Jeffrey could see the members of the Harlesden Calypso band approaching, followed by the South London Bhangra dance troupe and the sound of clogs, heralded the arrival of the Irish- travelling Riverdance tribute dancers. Jeffrey was speechless as he turned his head to the opposite shoulder, observing the breakdance crew arrive in high spirits, chanting 'U.S.A.' at the top of their voices, as Americans are fond of doing, followed in turn by a group of misplaced Zulus and a hi-vis army. Suddenly, a handful of Polynesian dancers appeared, led by…Pauli! The Maori and the Morris Man smiled at each other sadly, just as a loud spine-chilling chant began to emanate from the compound on the other side of the fence.

Jeffrey snapped to attention. "Northwood and South Oxhey Morris Men…square up!" he cried.

"Mother-frackers!" yelled Brad, as the last of the guards drove off in the perky electric buggy, which had personally assured them of a pleasant journey, leaving the heavy compound gates shut, and the inhabitants to their fate.

RESET

"So, what now?" asked Jessie as the buggy disappeared merrily off into the distance.

"Open the trunk," replied Brad with a steely look in his eye. "I need my lid."

Jessie did as she was bid and produced Brad's matt-black helmet, just as Donald and Ian reached them.

"What are you planning to do?" she asked.

"Have I ever let you down, Jugs?" he replied, fastening the strap of his helmet.

"No," replied Jessie honestly, "but I've never asked you for anyth-"

"And I ain't gonna start now." He cut her off as he focused his full attention on the gate. Donald and Ian watched on in silence as Steven Hawkin impersonator and minor celebrity, Brad Blanchett flipped a switch on the steering column of his 'whip' and disengaged the speed limiter. "My homies," he grinned with an air of satisfaction.

A crowd of internees had begun to gather as Brad backed up the Silverado and unhurriedly selected a tune on his device. Many eyes watched with baited breath as the American pressed play.

"One foot on the metal and one foot in the grave!" he roared as the torque-infused machine began to wheelspin wildly, chewing dust to the opening strains of the Prodigy's 'Smack My Bitch Up.'

"Yee ha!" Brad whooped, turning to Jessie. "Pick you up at eight," he said before launching himself at the heavy gates.

Donald and Ian looked on open-mouthed.

RESET

Over at the fence line, the defenders stood in silence as up on the hill of the X Facility, the fundamentalists were gathering ready to charge. The chanting was growing gradually louder and louder, slowly building to a crescendo.

From where Jeffrey was standing, his adversaries didn't look very much fun, but they did look like mentalists.

"Surely we can do better than that?" he said through gritted teeth. "Does anyone know the words to 'Men of Harlech?'" he called out hopefully, remembering Nain's spirit in the face of adversity.

Nobody did.

"Anyone know any rousing tunes?" bellowed Fred.

"Vat about 'Disco Inferno?'" came a Germanic reply from the lederhosen-clad traditional Alpine dancers from further down the line.

Before Fred could reply, the Maori had launched himself at the fence and clambered over. He landed on the other side with a thud, raised himself up to his full height and began to perform the Hakka.

Fred looked quizzically at Jeffrey.

"Well, we can't leave him on his own," said Jeffrey.

"He's quite right, you know," said Ned, "we need to take the fight to them."

"Well, we best get to it then," reflected Jed.

Jeffrey grabbed the fence and began to climb, the Morris Men hot on his heels and closely followed by every defender up and down the line. Before long, the entire fence was covered in climbing bodies wearing traditional attire.

"Good luck, Mr J!" said Fred as they climbed.

"And the same to you, my friend," replied Jeffrey as he jumped down into the compound.

The fundamentalists charged.

Jessie and Donald pulled Brad from the wreck, as hundreds of former 'wrong thinking' prisoners filed by. Brad was out cold; Ian and Snowy came over with a stretcher from the guard house and the four of them loaded the unconscious Brad onto it. Snowy regarded the mangled wreck of the gate, the blood and the mobility vehicle, she shook her head slowly. "He didn't need to do that," she said.

"Ya," replied Jessie as she unbuckled the strap under Brads chin. "that was pretty brave."

"No," said Snowy, "I mean, the guards didn't lock these gates."

The group all looked knowingly at one another before each in turn taking a handle, lifting Brad and joining the throng of refugees.

Wulfe shepherded the last of the evacuees out of the gateway, took one last look behind and joined the long line of people, as they silently snaked their way towards the ring road, and freedom.

The sound of a perfectly-pitched, baritone scream in speedy descent, emanating from the direction of Admin City, went largely unheeded by the crowds of people. They had something more immediate to concern themselves with.

RESET

"What's the hold-up?" grumbled the Scot as they stopped near the junction that led to the main gate. "I'd better go up and see what's going on," he said as they lowered Brad to the ground. Donald pushed his way to the front and was stunned by what he saw there.

The buggy used by the gate-keeping guards for their escape, lay on its side, engulfed in flame with smoke billowing up high into the air.

"You, 'the user,' have failed to comply with our terms and conditions," the not-so-perky buggy was saying authoritatively, "and all applicable laws. Therefore, you 'the user' have invalidated our hire contract under section 9.3:

a) failure to pay due regard to our tutorial- 'tips for safer driving'

b) failure to abide by the highway code

c) failure to observe all traffic signs and signals

d) failure to use the vehicle reasonably, considerately and responsibly

e) failure to take reasonable care of the vehicle

You must contact our Contact Centre immediately, otherwise you will incur additional charges and/ or legal action."

The buggy droned on, quite unaware of its own imminent demise.

Oblivious to the threats of legal action, the decapitated bodies of the three former occupants lay alongside the mangled buggy. Three helmets sat neatly lined up in a row with flashing amber lights attached to each. The ultimate act of cancel culture.

RESET

The Scot presumed the heads were still inside as he regarded what lay before him. More mutilated guards were strewn across the road and a group of fundamentalists stood, grinning, in front of the gated entrance with bloody swords in hand, barring any means of escape.

"Damn it," Donald muttered to himself. He felt the hesitancy of the crowd and instinctively knew that hesitation would lead to failure. There was no going back.

He charged.

As the razor-sharp blade cut into his right arm and sent him sprawling to the ground with the force of the blow, Donald wondered if he might have made a fatal mistake. He hit the kerb with a crack and lay dazed and confused as the bearded mentalists closed in on him. The Scot wiped blood from his face and spat, blinking, desperate for his eyes to focus.

When they finally did, he wished they hadn't. A man with emotionless, shark-like eyes leered over Donald, grinning menacingly and raising a sabre high above his head. Donald met the evil sneer with cold contempt, he turned his head and spat blood.

"Cheerio tae fuck, ya wee fanny baws," he said as his executioner bought down the blade.

CHAPTER THIRTY-EIGHT

Suddenly, a streak of grey fur swept the man aside- it was Wulfe. The Swede raised a Segway into the air and bought it crashing down onto the man's head like a mighty Thor hammer. The grey streak laid into the next sabre-wielding assailant like a werewolf on acid, forcing him to swallow his own sword. The furry fury then unsheathed the sword from its owner's throat and bought it to bear on the next attacker, whom, moments later, found himself holding his own head with a puzzled expression across his bearded face. Wulfe dispatched the next two assailants in a similar fashion. Donald watched with wonder as Wulfe skilfully skewered another fundamentalist to the door of the guardhouse, his feet just high enough from the floor so that the door was still fully functional. The furious Swede dispatched her final foe by posting him, head first into a storm drain.

Donald passed out.

☺

RESET

Pain.

Darkness.

Voices.

Flying.

Black.

The long march.

As Donald regained consciousness, he could hear voices, a familiar Swedish voice was speaking above his head.

"The reason that human beings are able to exist on earth is because they are part of a larger system, yes, encompassing the atmosphere, weather, plants and animals. Mankind can have influence on all these factors, of course, either positively, but mostly negatively. Human beings have forgotten that they are part of a whole, yah, of a wider chain of circumstances. The chances of these circumstances occurring in such favourable conditions was so minute in the first place, yes, it's crazy, humans breaking their links with their environment has caused existential repercussions throughout the globe, of course. They have become fixated on the minutiae and are missing their bigger picture, yes. They used to feel their connection through their very survival, yah, working with the environment to ensure the survival of their species, yah. When they were able to learn from and control their environment to ensure survival, without hardship, they looked to a belief in gods to understand their special place in the universe, yes, now that religion has been replaced by contraction of their world into smaller, more easily controlled systems and distractions by unimportant issues, severing that final link with the miracle that is life on earth, yah, that is what I believe...I must go on point now."

"Yeah, thanks for that...catch you later. So, as I was saying, the countryside is definitely racist..."

"No it ain't, you're talking bollocks! What manor you from?"

"Camberwell."

"Well there you go mate, you're a city boy! It don't matter what colour you are, people in the country just don't like city dwellers. Country folk don't really like anyone they aven't known all their lives, it's the country, they do fings different there."

"S'pose you've got a point."

"Stands to reason, don't it? Anyway, what part of Camberwell you from?"

The Scot drifted in and out of consciousness, feeling the warm breeze against his face and hearing snippets of conversation as he was lifted and carried along by his comrades, half-sleeping, half-dreaming, semi-aware but unable to open his eyes or communicate his thoughts, spinning in a churning kaleidoscope of colour, sound, smell, touch and darkness.

"No way!" came the voice. "Well stone the crows, me ole muver lived at number sixty-two, three doors down from the Saracen's 'ead!"

"You're shitting me!"

"No, straight up! She lived there for about fifty years, 'til she went in the sheltered."

"I'm number forty-seven, across the road."

"Forty-seven, that's where Bikini Jesus used to live."

"Bikini Jesus?"

RESET

"Yeah, he was this geezer 'oo used to like to ride round town in a blue bikini on a woman's bike."

"What?"

"Yeah, straight up".

"Why Jesus?"

"On account of his long hair and sandals."

"Weird."

"No, not really, you just got used to it. He never bovered anyone, live and let live...he was very good at bike repairs, as I remember. Broken chain? Straight round to Bikini Jesus."

The temperate sun shone warmly on Donald's face. Above the muffled sound of hundreds of feet dragging on tarmac, he could hear the buzzing of the occasional bee diligently working close by and the smells of familiar wild flowers and plants. The cool breeze rustled the young green leaves of spring high above, like the friendly voice of an old and intimate friend.

"So, are the gasworks still there?"

"Yeah, the gasworks are still there, but the pub got taken over by a chain. It's called the Prosthetic Arms now."

The sounds of many conversations raising and falling like waves, gently washed over Donald in the mild balmy air.

"No, I couldn't afford to own it, not on my wages. I rent the upstairs, you know, properties around that area are fetching well over a million these days."

"Leave it out!"

"No, straight up."

"That Brutalistic social housing dump? Your 'avin' a giraffe!"

"Not anymore. It's been gentrified, mate."

"Blimey."

Donald felt the warmth of familiar hand on his forehead as his mind drifted and his thoughts swam.

"- anxiety."

"Blimey, and you can get off work for six months with it?"

"Yeah, well in the Civil Service you can. It all started with this critical race bullshit and the racism it causes."

"Oh yeah?"

"Yeah, I went to a school with all races, where we were taught that we were all equal and race didn't matter. You know what working class kids are like, they don't judge you on the colour of your skin, just how good you can kick a football, yeah?"

"Yeah."

"I'm not saying there wasn't some racism but kids pick on you for anything- bad skin, wrong shoes, ginger hair, smelly, goofy, swatty, batty…"

"- fatty, speccy twat."

"Yes, that as well. If your family's poor or not, what part of town you're from, what team you support- that's kids, they're evil, It's not nice but it happens, it's part of growing up, but on the whole I enjoyed school and did well, ya know?"

"Yeah."

"Left school, went to college, worked hard, studied, got into IT, got a job in the Civil Service, cushty. Didn't encounter many problems, played five-aside with my workmates, golf, dinner parties, theatre, ballet, yeah…"

"You're losing me."

"Well my life was ok, I lived in a multi-ethnic country with laws against discrimination equal rights laws and equality laws. A country so welcoming that the rest of the world wants to come here. I honestly thought the racism fight had been fought and won a long time ago and although things weren't perfect, on the whole things were getting better not worse, and certainly better than most places in the world, yeah? In fact, in the whole history of humanity, now is the best time to be alive- life expectancy, infant mortality, access to education, penicillin, water purification, eradication of disease, even more so in the West, yeah?"

"Yeah."

"My life was sweet, I had a good life, until they introduced compulsory Critical Race Theory training classes at my work. So, this race missionary or ethnicity adviser turns up to give us 'Racism Awareness Training.' She was White, of course."

"Of course."

"Charging a fortune, of course."

"Of course, racism is a booming industry. As long as there are White people, they've got plenty of work."

"She gives us all an 'Implicit Association Test,' then she tells me I'm a victim of White oppression and tells my White work colleges that they're all racists, ya know?"

"Yeah, I've heard that somewhere before."

"So, my mate Ginger Balls get up and says: 'How dare you call me a racist!' She goes: 'You don't even recognise your own racism.' He says: 'How am I a racist then?' She says: 'Because you're complicit in a system of racism.' He goes: 'But the system isn't racist.' She says: 'No, but it results in racial inequality and therefore it's a racist system, and if you're not seeking the destruction of that system you're complicit in that racism, and therefore you're a racist.' He says: 'But all systems generate and perpetuate inequality.' And she says: 'By even saying that, you're demonstrating your White fragility, which means you're a racist.' He told her to fuck right off and got the sack for his troubles…I suspect she was the real racist. She kept acted weird around me, overcompensating, awkward, you know what I mean?"

"Yeah."

The uplifting sound of bird song gradually began to subside as the voices and laughter wheeled louder in Donald's head. His skull began to throb. He groaned.

"You just lay there, cobba, and relax," came the positive tone of a familiar voice.

Time passed.

He felt the comforting touch of the hand once more.

"- so we get split up into two groups, what she called 'affinity groups.' Whites in one group and people of colour in another. I was the only person of colour in my office apart from Indian Dave, but she accused him of being a 'Brown gatekeeper' so he had to go in the White affinity group. Then our groups had to go off into two separate rooms and think- my workmates had to think about, how racist and privileged they were for being White, and I had to sit on my own and think about being an oppressed victim, because I'm Black. This went on for weeks and needless-to-say, it caused division in my workplace, people I had known for years began treating me differently, some of them going out of their way to be nice to me. I kinda know how Brad must feel, you know, being in the chair, different and all that, people overcompensating and virtue-signal constantly. For instance, I would go to a dinner party and a White kid would run up and say something like 'I want you to know that I don't think I'm better than you' or 'I'm sorry you have to live in a country where White people are superior' or sometimes they wouldn't say anything, just go down on one knee and cry...it was weird. I also noticed at dinner parties, ethnic food started appearing and the hosts would look at me expectantly. I don't like coconut. And then there were the colleagues that started getting resentful, if I got a pay rise or promotion, they always put it down to positive discrimination. Some, after weeks of fruitlessly pleading their racist innocence to this woman, eventually gave in and became racists, just for a quiet life. The worst were the ones that became 'White saviour zealots' as a result- once they found out I voted Conservative, they accused me of not being Black or not being the right kind of Black. They viewed such things as politeness, punctuality, good timekeeping and management, hard work, objectives and rational thinking, justice, science, individuality, delayed gratification, all problematic outgrowths of an evil system and onerous tasks for people of colour. I don't, I believe in hard work, ambition and enterprise, that's how I achieved the lifestyle I have. Or had..."

"Yeah, quite agree with you mate, you only live once and you gotta make the most of it. You can't be a victim all your life."

RESET

"But then Critical Race Theory started affecting my work, people dropping down on their knee left, right and centre or accusing me of being an Uncle Tom, constant virtue-signalling or being accused of being a racist or being accused of receiving preferential treatment. It all got too much and I had to go off on the sick with stress…and now I'm here, wherever here is, but at least we're out. I've just got to get home now, what about you?"

"I don't know, I hadn't thought that far ahead. I can't go home, maybe you've got room in your flat for me and a few hundred friends?"

Donald blinked and the light flooded in. At first, he shielded his eyes but as his retinas adjusted to the light, he lay motionless, marvelling at the majesty of the clouds as they drifted gracefully by, ever-changing shapes across the sky. He gradually began to collect his thoughts.

He wondered where his journey would lead him to next, not back to Scotland since the country was being governed by a Puritan feminazi dictatorship, whose figurehead had openly admitted that she cried if she saw young people drinking and having fun.

"Scotland, no more," he thought morosely to himself. He couldn't go home even if he wanted to, he was on the run, along with everybody else. With the exception of Terry, the civil servant, apparently.

"I suspect all this Critical Theory is designed to divide people."

"Blimey, where you been for the last few years, mate? Of course it's designed to divide people, all this identity bollotics originated from the Frankfurt school, in order to dismantle and destroy every healthy aspect of society. It's Marxism in action, sunshine, or a form of it. This version divides people into groups and sets 'em on each other, they 'ate the idea of the individual, you see, and the notion of judging by a person's character and not their colour. You can't argue wiv 'em, they just close down the debate. Cancel culture provides a defence against criticism, scrutiny, reason, logic, analysis. Debate to them is like garlic to a vampire, to be honest they really don't care if they're hypocrites or if what they say is nonsense, they just don't care, it's all about the ideology for them. Why do you fink they hate the word colour-blind? It doesn't fit the narrative, they want to tear us apart not bring us together. The good news is, their arguments are built on shaky foundations so anyone with a bit of common-sense can see right froo 'em. Eventually the lizard will eat its own tail as they fall out with one another, inevitable really, the journey from left to right is like fantasy to reality. The pendulum will swing back, it always does as young idealistic people grow older, 'ave kids and get tied into a steady job to pay for the mortgage and the motor. You know the saying: 'If you're not a socialist in your twenties, you have no heart...'"

"And if you're not a conservative in your forties, you have no brain."

"Yeah you got it, but the bad news is, I think we may have got bigger problems than political correctness ahead of us."

"Blimey Ian, you know a lot of stuff".

"Never judge a book, mate".

Donald blinked again and turned his head to one side, he saw a stretcher being carried parallel to him. It was borne by four people, they were all blurs except for the nearest who was Jessie- she smiled over at him. The occupant was Brad, who lay motionless, a fixed grin on his face like a Cheshire Cat staring upwards from his horizontal vantage point, hypnotised by the regular pendulous motions of Jessie's bosoms as she helped carry him.

The Scot sat up and could make out the familiar shapes of Ian and the Maasai, or Terry as he was now known, carrying him at the head of the stretcher and chatting like a pair of old ladies at the bingo. Beyond them, strode Wulfe with purpose, two sabres sheathed in her leather belt.

"Bigger problems?"

"Yeah, much bigger."

"Multiculturalism?"

"Bigger."

"Will yooz two shut the fuck up!" Donald yelled.

The pair turned their heads and grinned toothy grins.

"Oi, oi!" said Ian "Sleeping Beauty's back from the land of nod."

"Aye," mumbled the Scot, as he examined his bandaged arm. He nodded his approval.

"Learnt first aid on the purple pill program, cobba," came Bob's voice from behind.

"Aye, very good. Ye did a fine job," replied an impressed Donald as he looked up and noticed Wulfe again. He smiled and held up a hand. "Thanks for the ride, but I think I'll walk for a while. It's a bonny afternoon, after all" With that, he hopped deftly off of the stretcher and joined Wulfe at the head of this mass exodus.

The pair walked together in awkward silence but after much agonising, Donald decided it was time to talk.

RESET

"So, you're a lassie then?"

After an excruciatingly long time, Wulfe finally broke her silence.

"Yes, I was born a girl," she said softly.

"Oh," said Donald sagely, "do you want to be a man then?"

"I thought I did, when I was eleven."

"Oh."

Wulfe turned to look at Donald.

"I'm sorry if I deceived you."

"You didnae deceive me, it's none of my business, ye ken?"

"But friends need to be honest with each other. That's what Nain would say."

"Aye," said Donald thoughtfully, "I suppose, but under the circumstances, it's understandable, hen."

"So, you don't hate me?"

"No, to be honest I'm relieved. It was getting weird, I thought I was on the turn, ya know?"

"Yes...but look at me."

"I've never been a man to judge folk by the way they look, the colour of their skin, or their sexual orientation for that matter. I just judge folk by whether they are a fanny baws or not...and the sad truth is, in my experience of life, most people are fanny baws. Regardless of the colour of their skin: black, white, brown, straight, gay, trans- I tend to treat most folk with equal contempt. It's easier that way, it saves a lot of time, ya know? Getting to know someone, investing that time and effort, only to find out they're not the person you thought they were."

"But it's the same with me, is it not?"

"No, you're trying to find yourself. You're real, you have honesty, authenticity and integrity, you're still the same person, man or woman. Most folk are trying to be someone else, their whole lives are a deceit, an elaborate disguise and they hide behind masks so you can never really know them. They won't let you, so I don't bother."

"It must be a lonely life."

"Aye, but you just have to keep the faith, real people do exist. I know, I've met them- very rare but worth keeping one eye open for. It's tricky, they come in all shapes and all sizes, all colours, all sexes, all ages and all faiths, and they are the ones worth holding out for...and I believe you are one of those individuals."

"But...I'm hideous."

Donald turned to look at her.

"I know you have the body of a strong and virile man, but you have the heart of a lioness, lassie."

"I like the way you say 'lassie,'" giggled Wulfe.

"So, how ye doing, hen?"

She looked at Donald and smiled. "You know, for the first time in my life, I feel truly free."

The Scot smiled warmly "Aye blossom, you're no a victim. Free your mind and the rest will follow, ye ken?"

Wulfe kenned.

"So, what can be worse for a society than multiculturalism?" asked Terry "Two separate groups occupying the same space but not mixing? Recipe for disaster, if you ask me."

"Oh believe me, I'm all for integration" Ian answered "but what's coming is going to render race and religious difference pointless, or any other difference for that matter. We're all going to be the same."

"That's good, isn't it?"

"Better ask a North Korean. That's if you can find one who's allowed to come out and play…"

"What are you saying, Ian?"

Up ahead, Donald and Wulfe came to a halt and signalled the human train to a stop. Further down the line, hushed tones washed over the crowd like gentle waves lapping on a pebbled beach.

Donald and Wulfe exchanged the briefest of glances as they watched two adult figures approaching, followed cautiously by at least twenty children of all ages, sizes, shapes, colours and skin complaints. The children paused warily as the two adults walked up to the curious Nordic and Scotian pair.

An old Rastafarian held out a friendly hand. "I is da Teacher" he said with a warm grin. Donald clasped the hand instantly and shook it manfully, subconsciously grinning as he did so, instinctively sensing one of his own kind.

"Donald MacDonald, clan MacDonald, at your service. And this bonny wee lassie is Wulfe," he said proudly.

RESET

Wulfe blushed momentarily, half covering her face with a giant hand and bashfully gave a reserved nod.

The Rasta's eyebrows knitted for a split second before he grinned an even broader grin.

"Pleased to meet you, Wulfe," he said as he turned to his travelling companion. "An' dis is da Preacher," he pointed to the children "and deese are I and I's responsibility," he said.

Winston aka 'The Teacher'

CHAPTER THIRTY-NINE

The human caravan had made camp in a small woodland at the side of the road. It provided the only reasonably sized cover in an otherwise flat and open landscape, uniform and unexciting, with the exception of a small grassy hill which stood alone some distance away.

"Good lookout post," Donald had thought to himself when he had first spotted the hill.

The sparks rose into the starry abyss, spiralling upwards high above the canopy of the woodlands from the fire burning heartly in the small clearing below.

The children were being put to bed and being made as comfortable as possible, under the circumstances, by the Rasta and a small army of volunteers from the camp, many of them thankful for the distraction from tomorrow, in the short term at least. Amongst their number was Terry, busily distracting himself by telling stories or singing songs to the exhausted children. The majority of the escapees were gathering around the fire, eager to hear the Preacher tell of events in the outside world.

"Where to begin?" she said. "I'm the vicar of St John's in the village of Lower Chipping and the gentleman I'm travelling with is Winston, or 'the Teacher' as the children like to call him. He is, or was before the lockdown, the caretaker of our local school and he also ran the after school extra curriculum gardening club. That's how we know one another, I help out on Tuesday afternoons." She paused. "I'm sorry to hear of your incarceration, of course we knew of the Re-education Centre, but the whole area was out of bounds and it sounded so harmless, 'Re-education Camp'...I always thought it sounded quite fun really, like team-building exercises or something."

Brad and Jessie looked at one another with raised eyebrows.

"I'm sorry," continued the vicar, "I understand now, of course. But while you've been locked up on the inside...the rest of the world's population has been locked up on the outside."

In a small quiet coppiced part of the woods, Ian unpacked his small emergency pack and began to arrange the tea things on a large tree stump, having first pitched a small green tent, arranged a couple of logs for seating and lit a small gas stove which the kettle sat merrily whistling on. He turned off the gas and poured the boiling water into the teapot, he added two teabags and stirred.

"Just wind 'em up," he mumbled to himself before replacing the teapot lid and tuning in his radio. The set whistled as he tried to tune it in with one hand whilst polishing his glasses with the other. The faint sound of hip hop came wafting over the air waves momentarily before it was drowned out by a high-pitched alarm. Ian turned the volume down. "Ice Cube?" he asked himself.

CHAPTER FORTY

"We will starve them all into the New World Order,

Take away the food and they will accept anything."

Henry Kissinger

They want a one world religion," said the vicar as she settled down to tell her story. "Places of worship have been shut for the first time since the general Papal Indict was placed on King John in twelve hundred and eight: this is the biggest abrogation of responsibility in history! Places of worship must be used as places of refuge in such times, the bishops should hang their heads in shame. My church was kept secretly open but every other closed, that was until one of my parishioners informed on us to the authorities."

"Where did the children come from?" asked Jessie.

"They kept turning up at the school," the vicar explained. "The virus marshals and police began to lock people in their own homes and many people starved to death. Some of the children escaped and made their way to the school, I suppose they went there for safety.

Luckily, Winston was staying in the empty school so he could keep an eye on his plants and so, once the children started to appear, he bought them to me and we sheltered them in the church. The streets are full of paedophile gangs, it's not safe for anyone on the streets, especially children. The police just turn a blind eye."

"And your church leaders did nothing?" asked Jessie in surprise.

"No, they abandoned us in our hour of spiritual need and disappeared".

"Maybe those creepy mutherfuckers are the ones be in the gangs," suggested Brad helpfully.

"Church leaders of all colours have become supine," replied the vicar sadly, "and committed to a new global religion called 'Chrislam.' The Christian leaders have betrayed us: we had to run, any dissenting voices are silenced or are hiding away. The Vatican has made a deal with China, just like they did with Nazi Germany and Fascist Italy, the Chinese want to regulate Christianity. This is the same regime that locks up Muslims." She paused for breath. "You see, the global elites are creating a New World Order, they want a one world government, they are crashing the world economies in order to create a global bank with a digital currency and control every area of our lives. They are setting up mayoral dictatorships and city states. This is the insanity we are dealing with today- it's across all borders, all barriers, all religions and beliefs, every divide that there might be. They want to turn us all into digital slaves."

"Mutherfuckers!" Brad exclaimed freely from his stretcher bed. "What's happening in the rest of the mutherfucking world, dawg?"

The Preacher produced a large leather-clad book and turned back the cover.

RESET

"I have this book," she said. "These are the last communications from around the world that I managed to print before the internet went down and the lights went out. I wish I had started sooner, I had misgivings about how the world was moving, but who could have predicted the speed of events? I took these words from the comments pages of news outlets around the world, those outlets that were independent and free and had an uncensored comments page. I bound them as a book, I wanted to keep a physical record and document the last days before the inevitable darkness came to estrange all humanity and cut us off from one another. Although my worst fears have come to be, it helps me to know that I'm not alone, my brothers and sisters are out there somewhere, fighting the same fight for freedom... I bound this book with love, love for all humanity, with hope, the hope that we shall overcome with faith, my faith that God watches over us all." The vicar paused for a moment, letting her words sink in. "Shall I read?" she asked.

The group gathered around the fire were quiet and motionless, anxious, in the true meaning of the word, to hear any news from the outside world, having been denied such luxuries for so long. She had their full attention.

"Please, any news from South Africa?" came a voice from the shadows.

The Preacher produced a small torch from her pocket and switched it on, a red glow illuminated her tired young face as she flicked through the leaves of the book.

"Yes, here we are, the last messages. They began to dwindle around two months ago," she said. "Here are some of the last few:

'Aktivnyye mery – Active measures

RESET

1) Demoralization
2) Destabilization
3) Crisis – virus
4) Normalisation (new normal) criminalisation of social life / individual
5) Communism subversion 101

We must unite before it's too late!

Support from Serbia !! show them that you are not afraid !! only together we can fight and win this psychological warfare!! Good Luck South Africa

We are all grown ups. We all value live. Our country is heading for a different pandemic named hunger.

Why the fuck am I getting these vidios? I'm not south African.'

I'm sorry," said the Preacher before continuing, "I have no idea how that one got in..." She continued:

"'The lies, today install an app, tomorrow a forced vaccine for travel, work and food. Woe to the wicked.

Support and love from Holland, keep fighting South Africa.

Good afternoon from South Africa. People, all the stores, business, everything are closed, but remember heaven is open, talk to God, he is in control, lets all talk to him always.

This is the last message I managed to copy down," said the Preacher.

"'Truly anti Christ is here now.'"

No one spoke as the firewood crackled and burned, keeping the cold of the night at bay, at least for the moment.

RESET

"Any news from Oz?" Bob enquired quietly.

The Preacher smiled sadly and turned the pages of the book.

"Here are a few of the last comments from Australia:

'The Victoria police is the most corrupt police force to ever grace this country since modern recorded history. They have arrested a pregnant woman in her home in front of her children. They smashed down the front door of a veteran who wanted a safe, socially distanced protest. They stomped on a mentally ill man's head and put him in a coma. They harassed two elderly women sitting on a park bench and even stole the phone of one of them trying to film it. They harassed a thirty-eight-week pregnant woman who was resting on a park bench because she was puffed from exercise and walking. We have police check points all around Melbourne, manned by police and ADF twenty-four seven and if you don't have the required permit or reason to pass it, you are fined and arrested. They have unparalleled power and they revel in it because no one dares to stand up to them, intimidation and fear tactics. Our courts are strangely silent and our stupid lame duck Governor refuses to condemn or dismiss the Victorian Labour Government, as is her right, under constitution, but she was appointed by a dictator so she won't dismiss her friend. All the goodwill and trust the police have earned over the decades has been lost and to many they will never get it back. I myself run a risk of being targeted or having my house raided because I dare to criticise them online. Many people have had their houses raided for online posts under the guise of 'health orders'. As for the ADF, what a low act for the Australian Défense Force to patrol alongside a corrupt police force, their forebears who served bravely in many wars must be so ashamed, these 'solders' now are enforcing state border checkpoints as well as enforcing illegal 'arrest' and 'fines'. I will never help the police ever again, next time witness something, I will never report it. Oh, and the police in their effort to cause fear amongst those of us brave enough to speak up, their modus operandi will be to level false serious disturbing charges to discredit those who dare to criticise them.

Signed a scared, frightened Victorian living in a police state under martial law, as the new world order take control.

It's us against them, make a decision, the fate of humanity is in the balance.

Support from New Zealand, they will not win

We need to wake up the sleeping sheep! Talk about this! Share it! Be the resistance! We must stand up to them, are there any real men in Australia? prove me wrong.... please!

The police are out of control, stasi-esk in brutality and disregard for human rights. We are not allowed to leave Australia, our state, our city, our town, our homes. We are imprisoned in a ring of steel

People are rising up, Melbourne, Victoria, Sydney, Byron Bay. Before we become slaves, we have to stand fast, have faith and know you fight for the light and the future of humanity, we have to pushback, we have no choice.

When they came for my neighbour, I said nothing, then they came for me

We must fight them to the death, we cannot run, we cannot hide, plead, beg, apologise.

We can only fight.'"

The Preacher looked up at Bob. "That was the last message I managed to receive from Australia, I've heard no news since, it's been six weeks now."

"Oh" said Bob grimly, "thanks...better get off now, it's my turn to keep watch."

He stood up and walked slowly into the woods.

Terry helped the young boy string his hammock between two trees. They stretched a tarp a little higher up and tied it off.

"That should keep you dry if it rains," he said to the boy.

"Thank you," said the boy quietly as he unrolled his sleeping bag.

"No problem, laters," Terry said as he picked up the small sketch pad and pencils that Nain had given him and slid them into the hidden pocket in his robes. He headed toward the centre of the small community of hammocks strung from the trees, noticing how well disciplined the children were, not to mention well equipped.

The old Rastafarian was sitting on a blanket next to the small fire he had made, reading a story to the children. Terry thought it sounded a bit like 'Treasure Island' as he sat down on the blanket next to the old man.

"*Da sharp voice,*" the Teacher read from a large notebook, "*O' Captian Flint still ringin' in me ear; Freedom not Gates! Freedom not Gates!* Da end …time for to put dem light out," he said.

Young voices called out from the trees, wishing the old man goodnight.

"Goodnight, children."

"Nice story," said Terry as the Teacher closed his book.

"Tank you," replied the old man, "me wrote it meself, well, most of it, me have to teach dem how it is, so me use old story and bring it up to date." His expression became grave. "Da world have change, dey gotta survive, dey gotta fight, we all gotta fight."

The small fire crackled.

"I've never really been much of a fighter," Terry confessed to the Rasta.

"Everybody a fighter, you just have to 'ave sometin' wort fighting for."

The pair sat in silence as the heat warmed their faces.

What are you fighting for?" asked Terry eventually.

"I?" replied the old man as he gazed at the fire. "I gotta deliver a letter, me make a promise."

"A letter?"

"A letter..."

"Canada?" asked Jessie.

"Canada," repeated the vicar of St John's church as she leafed through the book. She placed a finger on one of the pages and began to read:

'Canada has never been in such a DISASTEROUS state of affairs......all thanks to that evil lunatic by the name of Justin2face.... True Dope for Treason

We're fed up! They seem to think that we're still willing to jump when they say jump. We're tired and we're done with the 'good, obedient citizen' that used to be our proud Canadian claim to fame.

RESET

March to unmask

Support from France, you are not alone Canada

Talk of East/ West civil war

The best way to keep a prisoner from escaping is to make sure he never knows he's in prison- *Fyodor Dostoevsky*

Support from Amsterdam, Good luck and let's hope we can say goodbye to our corrupt governments quickly

Look for the dirt, love from South Africa

We have to make a stand, it's now or never, we have to pushback.... not only for ourselves but for the ones who put their trust in us as their guardians, we have to defend our culture, our humanity, our history, our individuality, our spirit and our souls.

We are sovereign and divine, no man rules over us.'"

The Preacher looked up. "That was the last contact, two months ago." She waited expectantly for the next request.

"How about Uncle Sam?" came Brad's hesitant voice.

"Let me see," she said, scanning the book's pages before starting to read aloud:

"'This is the end, the final sealing of the doors of centuries of human liberty, and the transformation of one of the freest countries on earth into a Marxist, conformist society, under constant surveillance, in which a subservient people scurry about beneath the stern gaze and constant control of the Techno-elites USA.

We the people have to fight; we have no choice!!

People are being disappeared in Houston, Atlanta and Georgia

RESET

Step up and Stand by

This is it; they've turned out the lights, time to roll, remember the Alamo!'"

"No more," said Brad, "that's enough from the USSA."

The Preacher nodded her understanding.

"A letter," replied the Teacher, "a little girl ask I to deliver dis to de prime minister, she wrote it jus' before 'er parent 'elp her escape, she give it I to deliver and den she run back 'ome. Me try an' stop 'er, but me too old." The Rasta passed the letter to Terry. "…she never make it," he nodded that Terry should read it aloud:

"Dear Prime Minister,

I am writing to you because I want you to end the lockdown. Here are my reasons why:

1) *we need friends to be happy, lockdown stops us seeing our friends. If we are happy we have happy minds.*
2) *I really miss school, I am bored with being at home all the time and I miss my class friends.*
3) *We cant keep the shops running from home, they'll run out of money.*
4) *we're ready to come out of lockdown, we know how to keep safe with hand washing and masks, please let us go outside.*

Thank you for reading my letter.

Emily, age seven"

The old man took back the letter when Terry had finished. "I gonna deliver it by 'and," he said.

"En France?" asked Severine.

The Preacher read aloud in a surprisingly accurate French intonation:

"'Beau travail mes amis francais, continuez a lasser votre voix se faire entendre. Ne les laissez pas prendre tout vos droits et libertes!! J'anticipe beaucoup plus de protestations a l'echell modiale dans les prochains mois/ annee et je crois que nous allons voir du changement eventuellement. Gardez le moral haut et battez vous pour nos libertes si precieuses!! Vive la Revolution, Vive la France.'"

"Espana, por favor?" called a voice from the trees.

The Preacher turned the page gently and continued to read:

"'This is the moment, freedom will take back that bloody and often mistreated country called Spain, Viva Espana!, Viva la Liberta!!'"

Terry had a troubled mind as he made his way cautiously through the darkness. The leaves and twigs scratched at his face as he walked awkwardly along the dark path, occasionally catching a twig or other forest floor detritus in his sandals, stumbling he navigated towards the light of the fire in the clearing. He was lamenting the fact that he had not been honest with his friends, especially Nain, and his heart hung heavy in his chest. He couldn't lie to himself anymore, deep down he was a coward and he hated himself for it. On reaching the bounds of the trees, he waited in the shadows for a moment. Terry scanned the anxious faces of the gathered assembly, trying to locate a familiar face. Amongst the crowd, there was an all-prevailing spirit of friendship, solidarity and cooperation which had become infectious during this long day but the Londoner, reserved by nature, still sought the company of his tribe: his friends and members of hut 1688. Eventually, his tired eyes made out the features of Brad and Jessie illuminated in the firelight and he made his way towards them, skirting cautiously around the back of the crowd as the Preacher read historical commentary from around the 'old' world, with empathy and compassion.

"Any news of the Swiss, please?" came a voice.

"Of course," said the Preacher. "Here we go:

'Bravo les Suisse revolution et resistance.

Well done Zurich, Berlin, London, Serbia, Thailand, Poland, Dublin and whoever else is waking up! Defend human rights, fight the lies, expose the truth and make the accountable pay!!

Mi unisco a voi popolo della Svizzera'"

"What about dear old Blighty?" Ian asked

The woman turned to a page toward the back of the book, took a deep breath and continued to read:

"'This is a Marxist take over, the majority of the political class in the UK have completely lost it. They're going to take us all to hell with this and we won't be coming back. Week by week I fear the only way we will be able to change this is to get out on the streets in massive groups to rebel. I'm scared, I wish this wasn't the case but surely it become inevitable! A just man will do what is right, not what is easy, good luck.

'and the load doesn't weigh me down at all, he ain't heavy, he's my brother'. It's time to decide who's side you're on!

CHOOSE YOUR SIDE! CHOOSE YOUR SIDE! CHOOSE YOUR SIDE! CHOOSE YOUR SIDE!

Unite for freedom

Circuit breaker or people breaker, mind breaker, soul breaker, resistance breaker, hope breaker, lets call it what it is…spirit breaker.

No to deathmask

We need to strengthen our bonds and celebrate our differences, all lives matter for we were created by God and Divine, we are all unique and we are all special. These people want to amputate our gods and beliefs, our culture, our communities, our friends, our family, our true selves

God doesn't want monks right now he wants warriors

Poverty, despair, murder, suicide, bankruptcy throughout the planet.

Stay strong UK, love Russia

The Government has betrayed us, the church has abandoned us, the monarchy has failed to defend us, they have failed to uphold our common law rights, as is required by oath

We're going down like BHS!"

"'Sake…" muttered Donald under his breath. "Have you no word from Scotland?" he called out.

"Yes," came the reply. "One moment, here:

It's us against them now. Race colour creed religion is unimportant. We must all unite! From the Bravefart, Dundee resistance movement.'"

"'Sake…" muttered the Scot for a second time, before standing up, picking his way through the people and striding into the woods.

The Preacher looked up and noticed the troubled expression on the Maasai's face. She smiled at him compassionately before searching through the book and reading to the man as best she could.

"Kenya, three months ago," she said to him. "'Hiyo kweli kabisa maonevu mbona tangu lockdown hauhaona watu kupatikana na virus hizo area wana yao hawa.'"

Brad turned to Terry and grinned impishly, his teeth catching the light like wet marble flagstones. The Preacher read on earnestly:

"'It's very true that Kenya police kills. Protest and expose the brutality even children. Stop this Brutality help the people instead. Love your neighbour, Help the people get the medicines and supplies they need. It is not a crime to have the virus, the people are afraid, with good reason please do not hurt them.

I am with you, my dear Kenyans! I bless you! Respect from Kazakhstan! No justice! No peace! We will win Good will conquer Evil

Kenyans should get out and protest this Government is jarring every day wake,
Keep up the good work, from your friends in Iceland

RESET

This one time I must rebuke you all, you have been programmed with ignorance, and therefore should sit at the Heels of the elders to learn as was expected of our ancestors. How arrogant we are.'"

The Preacher looked at Terry with a sad understanding smile. Terry nodded awkwardly and cast his gaze toward the fire.

CHAPTER FORTY-ONE

As Donald made his way stealthily through the wood, he could hear the Preacher's voice receding into the distance.

"'...an unjust law is no law at all- *Saint Augustine*

All Nations must look to their people's guidance and trust in them

Support from Argentina, you are not alone in the darkness.'"

The Scot strode on until eventually he was alone in the silence and darkness of his own thoughts, he had a lot of thinking to do. He slowed his pace as the calming effect of the trees cast their spell on him, and a slight breeze caught and rustled the leaves above his head. An owl called from the depths of the wood, the familiar and comforting sound, a welcome distraction to Donald's ears from the dismal news of the outside world.

He made his way through the wood, the darkness proving no obstacle, as he navigated easily towards a small hillock silhouetted against a clear starry sky, which he could just make out through the gaps in the trees. Eventually, Donald emerged from the woods out into a vast area of grassy flatlands from which the hill rose, exposed and alone like an island. The moonlight shone down on the grassy plains, creating the illusion of a vast silvery sea as it rippled gently in the warm breeze of a balmy night. Donald paused and regarded the hill before him bathed in moonlight, his eyes made out the start of the track that spiralled its way to the flattened summit. He noticed that the mound was strangely uniform in shape, manmade yet grafted to the landscape and blended with the environment. The Scot concluded it must be ancient- an old bronze age fortress, or a monument to some king or queen of this land's long forgotten past. Having spent much of his life wandering the remotest parts of Scotland, Donald was used to happening across primordial structures in the middle of nowhere; defensive ditches, burial barrows and standing stones, edifices which were created for reasons important to the ancient ones but now lost in the mists of time.

The owl called once more and Donald snapped out of his musings and strode on towards the hill. He began his ascent, gradually spiralling upwards and soon reached the plateau, which was crowned with a small stone circle. Sitting in the centre of this ancient monument was Bob, naked except for a grubby-looking loin cloth. Donald's bushy eyebrows rose in astonishment.

Bob was sitting cross-legged on a fallen stone monolith, looking out across the flatlands. His sinewy naked torso was bathed in a translucent sheen of moonlight, glistening like a much-handled ebony idol and he was encased in an aura of other-worldliness. It was clear that there was something different about Bob; something deep, something profound, something ancient as he gazed out into the depths of an infinite heavens. Donald could sense the change in his antipodean friend. "A wee bit akin to a garden gnome ...fishing," he thought before trudging over to the silent Bob and plonking himself down on the rock beside him.

The two sat silently together for a long while, just breathing in the still night air and staring out into the glorious panorama of a clear star-filled cosmos. The owl called.

After some time had elapsed, Donald turned to his friend. The 'wee mon' appeared revitalised, invigorated and re-animated, his chiselled features of stone-like resolution, his eyes set and intense as if all the knowledge and wisdom of the universe were revealed before them. Donald scratched his crotch thoughtfully before breaking the silence.

"I dunny know what to dae, mon, I'm at a loss," lamented the Scot. "Folk keep coming up to me and asking: 'what are we doing next, Donald?' as if am in charge, as if am some kinda leader. Am no leader, I can barely lead masel', ye ken, once we were out of the gates it was every man for himself, or woman, I dinnae care. But I didnae sign up to lead anyone, am a loner. I don't even know what am gonnae dae next, where's my next meal coming from? I dinnae ken, how am I supposed to feed all these people? I don't make plans, that's what Jeffrey did, I couldnae plan my way out of a paper bag. I always mess things up, that's how I got in this situation in the first place, ye ken? And where would we go? Where would I lead them to? All roads lead to shite! There's nowhere to go, this thing is worldwide, there's nowhere to hide, nowhere is safe. The Preacher told me everywhere is controlled, drones patrol the skies, the stasi patrol the streets, neighbours turn each other in for money or spite." Donald spat. "Scum that they are, where do you hide hundreds of people from all the curtain-twitching bawbags? This is beyond my abilities, am a simple mon, I travel light, I travel alone, how can hundreds of people march across the countryside undetected, foraging for sustenance and stealing for survival like members of some thieving multi-ethnic travelling community? They would hunt us doon and pick us off like they did with the American Indians, the native indigenous ones, I mean, ye ken? Sitting Bull, the Sioux Nation, all that bollocks." He shook his head. "They will hunt us doon like wild animals. How long could a mass of people like us live on the run? Not long, that's for sure…" He shook his head slowly. "No, we should split up and take oor chances, maybe some of us will find refuge but the rest…" Donald mused for a moment. "The rest will be re-captured, re-programmed and released back into the collective, lobotomised, obedient slaves, de-humanised, watched, monitored, assessed and collated by psychopathic elite overlords. That's the future, they are just too powerful, they've won." He put his head in his hands and gave a mournful cry. "Oh, this is the end, I didnae ever think I would live to see such dark days!"

Bob reached out an arm and placed a hand on the Scot's back.

"They want us to believe we are small," he said in a distant voice, his gaze fixed on the stars. "But we are as infinite as the universe. As human beings, we are a unique expression of all that is, all that has been and all that ever can be. The human family across the world need to awaken to who they really are and it is not small. Remember, remember who you really are, we are of one consciousness. There is no death, it is all a dream, we are the imagination of ourselves. The world is but a dream and we are all dreamers, the dream is the dreamer and the dreamer is the dream…we have to take our dreams back. The choice is dark or light, fear or love…and love cries freedom."

"Aye," whispered the bewildered Scot, "aye, freedom…" Donald stood up, turned and thoughtfully made his way back, winding his

RESET

way down the hill towards the darkness of the wood, his encounter with Bob leaving him even more confused.

Bob blinked his eyes and scratched his arse.

"Who said that?" he puzzled to himself.

CHAPTER FORTY-TWO

As Donald ambled his way through the wood, buried deep in his own thoughts, he suddenly stopped as the deep tuneful sound of a lone voice came drifting through the trees. Donald changed direction and headed toward the melodious noise until he came to the area where the children were bedded down for the night. Through a gap in the trees, he spied the old Rasta walking amongst the children and singing them to sleep gently with a low rhythmical lullaby. The Scot moved closer and stopped by a towering oak, he leant his back against it and listened in the darkness to the Teacher's song.

"When dey kick at your front door

Ow ya gonna come?

Wid your hand on your head

Or on de trigger of your gun

When da law break in

How ya gonna go?

RESET

Shot down on da pavement

Or waiting in death -." The Rasta stopped and smiled when he noticed Donald.

"What kind of lullaby is that?" asked Donald.

"Da Clash" came the reply.

"A bit heavy for bedtime, is it no?"

"Dey gotta learn how to survive, dis is da 'new normal', dey gotta learn to wise up and protect demselves. Da streets are full of dem batty paedophiles, dem rape gang, dem people traffickers, dem drug runners 'n' gangs 'n' ting. Dem pig do nutin', dem choose dem side, babylon." His grey dreads swayed gently as he shook his head mournfully. "Da good people are all locked away and dem prisoners in dare own home, welded in, slowly starving to death, most of deese kids' parent amongst dem. No, deese kids gotta learn to survive, and quickly, dem gotta learn to fight for dare freedoms and not just give dem away like dare parent did."

The Scot thought for a moment. "I suppose you have a point, aye."

"I an' I have a point, that's why me is da teacha," said the old man proudly. "Me teach dem to fight."

"Aye."

"I an' I."

"Aye, my friend," said Donald profoundly, "but there is a time to fight and a time to dream. After all, your dreams are what you're fighting for, the way to change the world is to have a vision of the future and we need dreams for that, ye ken?"

RESET

The old man nodded his head in accord, he did ken. "Humm, da teacher must always be willin to learn, I suppose" he replied solemnly, before bursting into good-natured laughter.

Donald held out a hand and the two men shook. "Sleep well," he said, turning around and walking back in the direction he had come from, humming a melancholy tune and quietly launching into song:

"Oh the summer..."

The Teacher chuckled to himself as the Scot's voice faded tunelessly into the night.

The Preacher continued to relate the news of the outside world to a rapt audience of former detainees.

"Survival networks were set up across the world by those who knew something was wrong from the very start, celebrities started to complain and push against the authoritarian measures whilst the humanitarian organisations stayed strangely silent to the welfare of the citizens of this country and the draconian measures imposed upon us. As for the opposition parties, for them the measures weren't severe enough and it saddens me to say the church which I belonged to actively worked against their own parishioners, to their eternal damnation." She sighed. "As always, the church chooses the winning side, not necessarily the right one.

A handful of academics, scientists, judges, politicians, journalists and even stand-up comedians were sensitive to the encroachment of civil rights and freedoms, they tried to raise the alarm, but they were too few and easily silenced. They were no-platformed, cancelled, censored, criminalised, ridiculed or disappeared.

RESET

Musicians began to speak up against the oppression and began to lend their voices to the growing dissent...but by then it was too late. The trap, decades in the planning, had already been sprung and the jaws are about to snap shut, condemning ninety-nine percent of the world's population into digital slaves or worse. Humanity is on the edge of a precipice." The Preacher turned to the back page in the book. "These are the last printed words I have, it's almost a poem, I suppose," she said. "It may help you fill in the gaps, I'd like to read it to you:

It's Just

By Montana Creed

It's just three weeks

It's just to keep the hospitals from being overwhelmed

It's just until the number of cases reduce

It's just until Easter

It's just a few weeks

It's just non- essential businesses

It's just to flatten the curve

It's just until we get a vaccine

It's just until we lower the R number

It's just a mask

It's just six feet

It's just groups larger than six

It's just six months

RESET

It's just restaurants and bars

It's just after ten pm

It's just a temporary curfew

It's just Christmas

It's just an app for your phone

It's just fake news

It's just the far right

It's just conspiracy theories

It's just a little inflation

It's just a few job losses

It's just to let others know your safe to be around

It's just a ring of steel

It's just a swab

It's just a blood test

It's just a little micro chip

It's just so you can leave your home

It's just so you can go to the grocery store

It's just so you can travel

It's just so you can vote

It's just another six months

RESET

It's just our liberties being taken away from us, piece by piece, according to the plan, the agenda, the reset.

It's just our lives

Just Wake Up, PLEASE

...and then no more," said the Preacher. "We were cut off from the rest of the world and the rest of the world has been cut off from us."

The assembled crowd were silent.

A lone fox barked into the night.

Donald heard the faint noise of a radio being tuned and he followed the whine as a barely audible song came wafting over the airways and dissipating amongst the woods. He followed the music, as it led him to a small clearing of recently felled trees.

"Oi, oi," came Ian's perky voice. "Good, innit?"

Donald emerged from the darkness.

"It's Van Morrison, he's singing protest songs nowadays. Fings must be bad outside."

"Really?"

"Yeah," continued Ian, "he's not the only one eva, sounds like a few famous musicians are protesting: so far, I've 'eard, Oasis, Ian Brown and Right Said Fred, all protesting or singing free speech and anti-lockdown songs."

"Where'd you get a radio?" asked Donald as the tune faded.

"I've always had me tranny," replied Ian earnestly, "but it never worked in the camp, they must 'ave 'ad some blocking device. Don't work much better out 'ere, keeps fading in and out with this bloody government emergency broadcast, must be a pirate station."

"Stay tuned to this wavelength," said the voice, "this is an emergency broadcast by the BBC…normal programming has been suspended…the current threat level is critical…civilians are ordered to stay in their homes…all motorways and airports have been closed for military use…all non-essential – BEEEEEEP!"

"Och," complained Donald, "turn it doon."

"Come in, make yourself at home, why don't you?" replied Ian sarcastically.

"Och, sorry pal, it's been a strange day."

"Yeah, I know what you mean, mate."

"What's going on, Ian?" asked the tired Scot earnestly. "One day I'm a free man roaming the Highlands, next I'm being hunted doon halfway around the world, dragged kicking and screaming to that prison where they attempted to brainwash me into thinking a mon can turn into a woman on a molecular level just because he says he's a woman and that I'm a racist just because I'm White, amongst other nonsense, only to escape and find the population of the country is locked doon under hoose arrest. I mean, what the hell is going on, pal?"

"Free words, if you didn't already know," replied Ian. "New World Order."

"Och, I still find that hard to believe. It just sounds like one of your conspiracy theories."

"I wish it was, mate, but unfortunately it's actually 'appening and the citizens of the world appear to be letting it 'appen. It's like everyone has got Stockholm Syndrome, it's nuts."

"What do ye mean?"

"Well, it seems that apart from a few people, most people appear to accept this without complaint. People have been starving to death in their own 'omes and the population of Britain just accept it, bizarre! And it's not just Britain, this fing is 'appenin' all over the world, its eerie. 'Ard won human rights have just been abused and trampled into the dust, old people have died at the hand of governments worldwide and apart from Right Said Fred, no one seems to be complaining. I mean, I knew that our own government 'ad been using behavioural insight techniques on the population for decades, but I never would 'ave fought it could be so effective."

"Behavioural insight techniques?"

"Yeah, brainwashing and behavioural psychology, the government has 'ole departments dedicated to it, it's a sort of hypnosis, propaganda, fake news, censorship that type of fing. They work with big Tech, the main stream media, the army, the filf, the banks, social media, it's a transnational corporate cartel really, spreading misinformation to the public and swaying opinion in order to follow the government's narrative on anyfink from smoking in public to going to war. It all comes out of the cabinet office but from what I'm 'earing, it looks as if they've taken it further. I mean, they've locked the masses up, silenced 'em and appear to be gaslighting 'em." Ian scratched his head. "It seems that the objective is to absolutely depress everyone, compromise people's ability to put grub on the table, sinking people so low they can't defend 'emselves; they can't come together or work together. This is what's 'appenin', the people are being completely demoralised and segregated...it's no accident, it's by design."

Donald sat dumbfounded; his bushy eyebrows fully arched as the lyrics *"I'm too sexy for my cat"* ushered forth from the radio.

"Wot?" asked Ian, catching the Scot's expression.

"How do you know all of this?"

"I lived with the Morris Men."

"And how exactly are they privy to all of this information?"

"Well...they aren't really Morris Men...well they are, but it's not their day job."

"Oh aye? Do tell."

"The Morris Men errr..." Ian thought for a moment. "The Morris Men are actually an elite special forces unit who have gone rogue, patriots, now that the British Armed Forces have decided that their role is no longer to defend the citizens of the UK, but instead spy on 'em in the form of 77th Brigade, or gather data on 'em in the form of 13th Signals Regiment."

Donald sat flabbergasted, his bushy eyebrows fully arched.

"Yeah, on the cat walk, on the cat walk, yeah..."

"And so the Morris Men, or 'Rogue Version 0.2' allowed 'emselves to be captured and inserted into the Re-education Centre, in order to gather vital intel from Admin City, right next door. It's the UK's Eastern hub of the Deep State."

"Deep State?"

Yeah, Deep State, the real power behind government. They believe governance is no longer equal to government and our government is now but one player in the new global framework. Currently, we 'ave a government of occupation and a sock puppet for a prime minister…we are in deep dictatorship do-do, an authoritarian police state, a coup 'appened and everybody missed it. I blame the Fabiáns but the UN, are involved as well as the WHO, CDC, IMF, World Bank, Bilderberg Group, all the usual suspects."

"Is there nuthin' can we dae?"

"Nuffink really," mused Ian, "I did fink for a moment that we should head to the South coast, try and get a lift with the people smugglers since they're always empty on the return journey. We could get back across the channel, or even get a lift on that artist Wanksey's boat, he's good at trafficking illegal immigrants, and the lifeboats run a regular migrant taxi service too. But then I fought, what's the point? There's nowhere to go, it's the same the world over."

"…too sexy for my cat, what do you think about that?"

"Naw much," replied Donald absently. "Can ye no turn that radio off, mon? It's doing my nut in."

Ian obliged.

"There must be something we can do?"

"Hmmm, not really mate, the wheels were set in motion a long time ago. People have been warning about it for years but they were filed under conspiracy theorists, no platformed or just cancelled. Plenty of people warned about the United Nations Agendas 21 and 30, about the World Economic Forum's 'Great Reset' agenda, a return to Marxist principles, under the leadership of Dr Evil…. I mean, Klaus Schwab and no one wondered for a moment why leaders around the world seemed to be using the same phrases. 'Build Back Better,' for example."

"What's that mean?"

"In simple terms," replied Ian, "restructuring society post-plandemic plague. Next step, use the climate emergency as an excuse to keep abusing civil liberties until such time as they can nanochip and neuro-link every soul around the world and condemn humanity to digital slavery, based on the Chinese model and using Chinese Tech. Game over. It's the end, mate."

"The end?"

"Yeah, the end, the end of freedom, representative democracy and Western civilisation. You see, these dark powers 'ave the support of the gullible left-wing champagne socialist transglobal elites, who are setting out to dismantle the fruits of Western civilisation. They view European culture as a toxic patriarchy that systematically oppresses women, minorities and fringe groups, while upholding the values of White male privilege; to them, somefing that should be forgotten and replaced by a new version of history. Unfortunately for them, they will get the equality they desire once they achieve their goals. The equality of slaves."

"Surely we can stop this insanity?"

"Too late, mate. Sounds like they've already pressed the 'reset' button and set the ball rolling. Welcome to the Fourth Industrial Revolution."

"The Fourth Industrial Revolution?"

"They are going to change every single area of society; educationally, religiously, politically, economically...no more privacy. Throw in a bit of transhumanism, merging people with technology, and no more freedom. We're fucked, mate."

"Och, you're great company," said the Scot as he let out a deep sigh.

"Well, you did ask! Anyway, cheer up Jock, we may as well enjoy our last few hours of freedom before they send the drones out looking for us. Got any booze in that sporran?"

A disheartened Donald reached into his sporran and produced his flask, he passed it to his friend.

"Tell me, pal," Donald reflected. "If you knew all this, why did you decide to escape with us?"

"It's a day out, innit?" Ian replied, before taking a drink and passing the flask back to Donald.

Donald took a long reflective swig, the familiar flavour of the peaty single malt like an old friend, and as he swallowed, the burning sensation reached deep into the pit of his stomach. The Scot's eyebrows suddenly arched.

"No!"

"No, what?"

"No, I do not comply, I do not comply."

"You don't have much choice."

"Och I do, I can choose not to comply."

"Not comply?" puzzled Ian. "Shine a light, mate, I just explained our current situation…It's us against a New World Order, we're buggered."

"Och, wit ye talking aboot, mon? I'm Scottish, it's in my nature to be obstinate and contrary, I cannae comply. If I comply, I become a slave, slavery leads to tyranny, and tyranny equals death… non-compliance, on the other hon', equals revolution and revolution equals freedom. Freedom, mon, they canny take my freedom!"

Donald replaced the flask back in his sporran and stood up.

"So you want to fight 'em?" said Ian incredulously.

"Aye," confirmed the Scot, "aye or die, there's nothing to be gained from being a slave." And with those words, he strode off purposefully towards the trees.

He stopped at the edge of the circle of light cast by Ian's gas stove and called back over his shoulder.

"Well? Are ye coming or no, ya big English jessie?"

"Keep yer barnet on, Jock," came the reply. "I gotta put the tea fings away."

CHAPTER FORTY-THREE

Wulfe stood up awkwardly to speak, her large calloused hands fiddling dextrally with her pipe.

"This is what I think, I believe we were all brought together in captivity for a reason, yes, because we are different. We should be honest, we do not run with the herd, no, we can think for ourselves, yes, and that's why they imprisoned us. We are independent and free, yes.

I think all of you are angry, yes, I know you're angry, yeah, and you are sad and upset and you are frightened. But you are also brave and you want to fight, yes, fight for your culture, your future, your children, your grandchildren, their future, yes, you are very upset about what has been done to you, your families, your society and your country.

We know what we must do, yes, but this realisation makes us responsible, yes, for the others, yes, this is a positive thing. We have to do something for the others, yes, help them not to be fearful, spread the word, yes.

We must believe in ourselves, yes. You don't have to listen to me, I am only saying what I think. We can turn this around, yes, of course we have to survive, yes, this is important, but we do have a job to do, yes, we must help the others. We cannot let these bastards tell us how to live our lives! Yes, okay, good." Wulfe sat down to silence.

Although initially confused at Wulfe's Norse code, her intention was unmistakable and Jessie instinctively gave a small clap of encouragement for her former roommate. Soon a small, bewildered, ripple of applause echoed around the wood as the crowd joined in. Wulfe smiled bashfully.

Since no-one in the gathering had anything to add to the Swede's discourse, bodies began to huddle close together for warmth as the fire crackled and waned, timber turned to ash and the cold of the small hours encroached. Heads hung low in the silence of the night as uncertainty and fear descended upon the people and placed a heavy burden upon their shoulders; they had won their freedom only to find themselves enclosed in a larger prison. Reality was dawning and it was particularly dark before this dawn, even Wulfe's speech had done little to boost morale.

The silence was broken as the fox's call was answered from somewhere deep in the wood. The primal call jarred the air and a sense of tension flowed around this mass of humanity; they were fearful, vulnerable and the future was bleak.

Donald was in a lighter mood, humming the tune to the 'Bonny Bonny Banks of Loch Lomond,' as he made his way along the track that would lead him back to the campfire and his friends. Whisps of mist were beginning to condense, swirling through the young ferns and bringing a damp chill to the air causing Donald to momentarily shudder. He came to a stop and rummaged in his sporran for his trusty silver flask. Unscrewing the cap with a grin, he sat down on a fallen tree by the path and raised the vessel to his lips. As he took a gulp, a cold chill ran down his spine and he felt something, a change in the air. He was motionless apart from his eyes which slowly turned in the direction he had been heading, following the path until it disappeared into the mist. The moon came out from behind a cloud and momentarily illuminated the woods with incandescent light and as Donald focussed his eyes, a stag appeared from the mist and stood on the path observing the Scot. Resplendent in the dappled moonlight, it raised its head and drew breath, the whites of its eyes visible as it strained to observe Donald, its nostrils widened and twitched as it inhaled the Scot's scent. It exhaled with a grunt, then slowly began to walk along the path towards Donald. When it drew level with the Scot, it stopped and smelt the air and gazed into Donald's eyes, Donald met the stag's stare and they stood there, frozen in time and space. A cloud crossed the face of the moon, casting a shadow across the moment and the stag broke its gaze and shook its head, grunting once more and exhaling a mist of warm air, before moving on its way and disappearing into the mist. Donald took a large gulp followed by a deep breath. He replaced the flask and fastened his sporran.

"An omen," he whispered to himself, his eyes twinkled in the moonlight as a grin played across his lips. Just then, Ian came lumbering up the path.

"Blimey, you shot off!"

"Did ye see it?"

"See wot?"

"The stag, mon, the stag!"

"Wot stag?"

"Ye must have tripped right over it!"

"Wot, like a beetle?"

"Wit?"

"A stag beetle?"

"Naw, no like a beetle, ye bam pot, a stag! Och never mind, let's get back to the others, we have work to do."

The group of newly-created refugees of all races huddled around the fire, the air was pregnant with fear and wide-eyed glances were exchanged as they looked to one another as if waiting for someone to take charge. Suddenly, the tense silence was broken as a large Scotsman stepped out from the shadows and strode into their midst, heading straight for the warmth of the fire. Donald lifted his kilt slightly towards the flames, he closed his eyes and gave a rare grin, ignoring the expectant crowd around him. After a respectable period of time, the silence was broken once more with an awkward cough, causing Donald to raise a curious eyebrow and turning his back to the flames, he raised the rear of his kilt slightly.

The Scot regarded the crowd keenly, the gathered assembly waited expectantly for the Scot to speak.

"I hope yer no expecting me to make a stirring speech. If ye are, I'm afraid yer going to be disappointed. I cannae give you a rousing speech to lift yer spirits or words of hope to inspire ye to action. I cannae promise ye victory over adversity, in fact I cannae offer ye anything at all, yooz all understand the situation as well as I."

Donald paused for a moment, allowing his words time to be imbued by his friends.

"I'm no leader, I didnae get yooz oot the camp, ye did it for yerselves, ye decided that it wasnae a good idea to hang aroond. Ye dinnae need a leader, ye can lead yerselves, ye have to stop being fearful and start being strong. I cannae do that for yooz, yooz have to find the strength to stand up and say 'No more, enough is enough. Up with this I will not put!' Yer gonnae have to, cos I'm going back to the camp, and ye wouldnae want tae follow me there."

"Do what?" came Ian's voice as he stumbled into the clearing. "Do me a favour, we only just made it out of there!"

Donald turned to face Ian, the light from the fire illuminating his ginger hair and beard in a halo of flames.

"I ken, but it's ma hame, the only hame I've known for a long long time, and I'm going back. Besides, it's where my friends are, fighting so we could escape, I cannae leave them back there."

"Spose you're right," Ian conceded reluctantly, "we've got to go back. Besides, we 'aven't got anywhere else to go. But what about the Great Reset and the New World Order?"

"Och," replied Donald, "we'll deal with that the morra afternoon."

"Yo yo yo!" cried Brad in alarm, "destination fucked, dawg! Destination fucked!" Brad turned to Jessie. "Tell him, Jugs," he implored her.

Jessie thought for a moment. "I'm tired of running too," she said, "I want to go home." She kissed Brad gently on his bandaged head and got to her feet. "You'd better stay here and look after the kids until we get back." Jessie moved through the crowd to join the Anglo-Scottish alliance, collecting a sabre as she did so.

Brad was about to utter a word beginning with 'F' when he suddenly thought better of it. Instead, he looked Jessie in the eyes. "Good luck," he said.

Jessie smiled.

Terry turned to Brad. "You're just gonna let her go like that?" he asked.

"We only got two choices, dawg, freedom or slavery. You heard what's been going down, the times they are a-changing," Brad said winking at Jessie. "Bitch can kick ass."

Jessie blew him a kiss.

Wulfe strode across the clearing to join Donald, they smiled at one another before being joined by Snowy.

"We must cut the head off of the dragon!" exclaimed the young American.

"Aye, they'll never expect it," Donald agreed, not quite sure what she had meant but getting the general gist.

The Preacher joined them and spoke. "Our leaders have forsaken us, we have to fight for ourselves. The cavalry isn't coming so it's down to us to stop this madness, may our Gods be with us."

Soon everyone was on their feet and making their way towards Donald, as he stood stoically on the road. Terry eventually resigned himself to his fate and joined the group after long moments of soul-searching. Soon, only Brad and the old Rasta were left to bear witness as the group gathered.

Donald turned to face his friends. "None of us want tae be here, but we have no option than to stand up to the blow that fate has struck upon us. This is our clarion call from the future and we have to heed it, we have no other choice."

And with that, the fearless Scot turned eastward and took his first resolute step forward, towards a certain sunrise and an uncertain future.

EPILOGUE

The Cat

Mrs Doreen Evans peeked across the street from behind her red velvet curtain.

"Yes," she said to the operative at the other end of the phone. "He's still out there, he's sitting in a deckchair now. The virus marshals have been around twice and warned him but I have it all recorded so he won't be able to worm his way out of it this time. Now, I understand the Neighbour Watch Scheme is increasing the rewards for turning in rule-breakers, will this arrest be included?...Oh wonderful, now while I'm on the subject, I haven't received any reward payments for the window cleaner I informed you of last week...that's right...Mr Evans, the window cleaner...oh marvellous...well you shouldn't break the rules, should you? Oh here come the virus marshals now, I'd better go just in case they need me as a witness...ok...bye for now, bye." Mrs Evans hung up. "What a lovely young man!" she said over her shoulder.

She peered through the window as a black van pulled up. The back doors had a large round yellow smiley face decal stuck to them which burst open and six paramilitary marshals jumped out in full riot gear, batons raised to shoulder height, ready to strike. The old man seated in the gayly striped deckchair looked up from his paper, he frowned and began to stand up indignantly, resplendent in his salmon-pink shorts and matching polo-shirt, white panama hat, brown leather sandals and bright white socks. But before he could raise himself to his full height, the batons and pepper spray were upon him.

"Shame on you!" he yelled at the top of his voice, before being beaten and electrocuted into silence.

"He said as well as the cash, I'm eligible for five good citizen credits," continued Dot Evans, "there's lovely for you, that means we have enough for a two travel permits, which means we can go to Bangor for a day out. Won't that be nice? But you must try harder to wear the mask."

The man lay unconscious on his perfectly manicured and striped lawn whilst the Robocop-esque paramilitaries masked, cuffed and dragged him to the back of the van, throwing him unceremoniously into it. The law enforcement officers lined up before taking the knee to the muted applause of a few local residents from behind the safety of their windows. Returning to their feet, the black-clad enforcers clambered into the van and screeched off in a moment of burning rubber, smoke, sirens and blue lights. The yellow smiley face glinted momentarily in the sunshine and then they were gone. Silence once again descended upon Ffestiniog Way.

An emaciated cat peered out from the hedge and cautiously made its way to the front step of the house where it sat and continued its vigil.

"Well that's taken care of him, who does he think he is, sitting in the garden bold as brass during a lockdown? Not a thought for the old people, no mask on either, and he's one of the chapel elders. Always had a ticket on himself that one, not so smug now, is he? I don't care how big his daffodils are."

The short sixty-something woman with a copper-coloured tight perm turned away from the window with a self-satisfied grin on her long ferret-like face.

"What you looking at, Gwilym?" she demanded of the frail old man who stood with his back to her, across the tiny room, gazing at a photograph which sat on the old, tiled mantelpiece. He gave a small grunt. She squinted. "Oh yes, that's on my list. I've seen a lovely one on Amazon, mahogany, very expensive". She made her way across the room, an obstacle course consisting of an oversized luxury leather suite, marble coffee table and a Persian rug which was far too big for the room. Her rotund frame was silhouetted against the wall-sized television set as she ducked under the chandelier. Eventually, she reached the old man, far away and lost in his own thoughts.

"What you looking at then?" Dot asked again. She followed Gwilym's gaze to the photograph, it was an old picture of three young schoolchildren, two girls and a boy.

"Oh, that's us when we were younger, do you remember?" she asked.

Gwilym shook his head and gave a small whine.

"Her?" replied Dot. "We went to school with her, full of herself she was, loved herself she did, I think she had her eye on you." She put her arm through Gwilym's. "But I got you, didn't I? Yes, I got you. I wonder whatever happened to her?" she said absently as she turned around and made her way back across the room towards the window, picking up the binoculars from the occasional table as she went.

Gwilym stared at the picture and sighed, his eyebrows knitted. He turned his gaze to a dark corner of the room where, hidden beneath a large Welsh flag, sat a spinning wheel.

Wake up!

SOURCE MATERIAL

The Rubin Report – Dave Rubin https://rubinreport.com/

The Free Speech Union – Toby Young https://freespeechunion.org/

Sanity 4 Sweden – Stefan Tunedal
https://www.youtube.com/channel/UCFSx08Ew0iiWKyAz54Opdhw
(inspiration for Wulfe's speech, pg. 369-370)

Brees Media – Anna Brees
https://www.youtube.com/c/BreesMediaOpinions/

Dr Vernon Coleman https://brandnewtube.com/@DrVernonColeman

Liberty Talk Canada – Odessa Orlewicz + Norb
https://www.youtube.com/c/LibertyTalkCanada/

New Culture Forum, 'So What You're Saying Is…' – Peter Whittle
https://www.youtube.com/playlist?list=PLEszGtr8C8961kZ8ZnmZriS3pEPs
niHTI

Sky New Australia – Rowan Dean, Alan Jones, Paul Murray, Rita Panhill,
Ross Cameron, Peta Credlin https://www.skynews.com.au/ *'The Great
Reset': World leaders to harness COVID and pursue 'sinister' climate agenda*
https://www.youtube.com/watch?v=GeykREAIYSg

UK Column - Brian Gerrish, Patrick Henningsen, Mike Robinson, Alex
Thomson, David Ellis https://www.youtube.com/user/ukcolumn/

RESET

Spiked Magazine - Brendan O'Neill, Tom Slater, Tim Black, Joanna Williams, Ella Whelan, Mick Hume https://www.spiked-online.com/

Keep Britain Free – Simon Dolan https://www.keepbritainfree.com/

'Plandemic' – Dr Judy Mikovits *(if you can still find it online)*

'The War of the Worlds' – H.G. Wells *(the Teacher's story, pg. 260-261)*

'Treasure Island' – Robert Louis Stevenson *(the Teacher's story, pg. 342)*

Speech at Trafalgar Square, 27th September 2020 – David Icke *(inspiration for Bob's speech, pg. 354)*

Thames Valley Police Consent Campaign

'Planet of the Humans' – Michael Moore

Suggestions for further reading

1984 - George Orwell

BEHIND THE GREEN MASK: UN Agenda 21 – Rosa Koire

The Madness of Crowds: Gender, Race and Identity – Douglas Murray

12 Rules for Life: An Antidote to Chaos – Jordan B. Peterson

Old Man in a Chair – Vernon Coleman

Don't Burn This Book – Dave Rubin

RESET

ACKNOWLEDGMENTS

During the course of writing and researching this book, the world changed fundamentally.

When I began, the world was normal.

When I finished, the globe was in lockdown.

Censorship in the mainstream media has been rife and many dissenting voices to the Government's narrative during this period have been silenced, no platformed or cancelled. Individuals have lost their jobs, their reputations and their incomes, purely for a having a different opinion. Freedom of speech has never been in such peril. However, there are people who have bravely stood up against this tsunami of Authoritarianism and refused to be silenced, I may not agree with everything they say but I defend their right to say it.

Following is a list of individuals who have proved to be fearless beacons of light in a period of darkness.

12th December 2020

RESET

Andrew Doyle

Anna Brees

Brendan O'Neill

Dave Rubin

Desmond Swayne, MP

Douglas Murray

Jordan Peterson

Julia Hartley-Brewer

Katie Hopkins

Laurence Fox

Lionel Shriver

Lord John Sumption

Mike Graham

Neil Oliver

Odessa Orelwicz

Paul Coleman

Peter Hitchens

Posie Parker

Sir Charles Walker, MP

Toby Young

Trevor Phillips

Venice Allan

Dr Vernon Coleman

...and all the voices from around the world who have expressed their fears on the comments pages.